Another Dead Republican is a mystery of familial destruction set in a world of violent intrigue and deadly ambition. A ringing phone in the middle of the night set Tom Mason and his lover, baseball player, Scott Carpenter on the trail of a vicious killer in a suburban enclave. Tom's brother-in-law has been murdered. Tom rushes to be with his beloved sister. The dead man was the son of the vicious Republican county that runs a county. The ruling cabal will stop at nothing to destroy people and lives that get in their way of accumulating more useless wealth.

MLR Press Authors

Featuring a roll call of some of the best writers of gay erotica and mysteries today!

Derek Adams	Z. Allora	Maura Anderson
Simone Anderson	Victor J. Banis	Laura Baumbach
Helen Beattie	Ally Blue	J.P. Bowie
Barry Brennessel	Nowell Briscoe	Jade Buchanan
James Buchanan	TA Chase	Charlie Cochrane
Karenna Colcroft	Michael G. Cornelius	Jamie Craig
Ethan Day	Diana DeRicci	Vivien Dean
Taylor V. Donovan	Theo Fenraven	S.J. Frost
Kimberly Gardner	Michael Gouda	Kaje Harper
Alex Ironrod	AC Katt	Thomas Kearnes
Sasha Keegan	Kiernan Kelly	K-lee Klein
Geoffrey Knight	Christopher Koehler	Matthew Lang
J.L. Langley	Vincent Lardo	Cameron Lawton
Anna Lee	Elizabeth Lister	Clare London
William Maltese	Z.A. Maxfield	Timothy McGivney
Tere Michaels	AKM Miles	Robert Moore
Reiko Morgan	Jet Mykles	William Neale
N.J. Nielsen	Cherie Noel	Gregory L. Norris
Willa Okati	Erica Pike	Neil S. Plakcy
Rick R. Reed	A.M. Riley	AJ Rose
Rob Rosen	George Seaton	Riley Shane
Jardonn Smith	DH Starr	Richard Stevenson
Liz Strange	Marshall Thornton	Lex Valentine
Haley Walsh	Mia Watts	Missy Welsh
Ryal Woods	Stevie Woods	Lance Zarimba
Mark Zubro		

Check out titles, both available and forthcoming, at
www.mlrpress.com

Another Dead Republican

Mark Zubro

mlrpress
www.mlrpress.com

This book is a work of fiction. Names, characters, places, and incidents either are products of the author's imagination or are used fictitiously. Any resemblance to actual events or locales or persons, living or dead, is entirely coincidental.

Published by
MLR Press, LLC
3052 Gaines Waterport Rd.
Albion, NY 14411

Visit ManLoveRomance Press, LLC on the Internet:
www.mlrpress.com

Cover Art by Deana C. Jamroz
Editing by Neil S. Plakcy

Print format: ISBN# 978-1-60820-731-2
ebook format: ISBN# 978-1-60820-732-9

Issued 2012

For their kind help and assistance I wish to thank:
Jeanne Dams, Barb D'Amato, R.J. Jackson,
Scott Jorgenson, and Neil Plakcy

One

Wednesday 2:37 A.M.

The phone rang. The digital clock read two thirty-seven in the morning. Heart hammering, I grabbed for the receiver. Some family tragedy, mine or Scott's, awful news, that's the only kind of call one gets at that hour of the morning, or a wrong number.

I said, "Hello?"

Between sobs my sister Veronica's frantic voice screeched at me. I couldn't understand her. She was so loud, I was forced to hold the phone away from my ear.

Scott lifted himself on one elbow and looked at me.

Veronica gasped for breath.

I said, "Veronica?"

She said, "Edgar is dead."

Edgar was her husband.

I sat up and swung my legs over the side of the bed.

She sobbed. I let her. What else was there to do?

Veronica and I were close. We talked frequently, and of all of us kids, she was the one closest to mom. She and Edgar had three kids; six, ten, and thirteen years old.

Her crying eased, and she gulped several breaths. She spoke between heaving gasps. "Tom. He. Was. Murdered." She wept some more.

"What is it?" Scott murmured.

I put my hand over the receiver. "Veronica. She says Edgar has been murdered."

Scott edged over to me and rested on his elbow, his other arm around me, his chin nuzzling my shoulder, and his breath on my neck.

I hated Edgar.

Two

Wednesday 2:39 A.M.

The first and only time my brother-in-law, Edgar, used the n-word in my presence was at the dinner table Christmas fifteen years ago. At the time he was Veronica's boy friend. It was my home, my turn to host the holiday dinner. The whole family had gathered as was traditional. It was Edgar's first time at a family event.

When he dropped the n-bomb, all conversation ceased. A dreadful silence fell, the kind that falls after the ignorant perpetrate an offense on the decent.

While the silence built, Edgar glared at everyone. Finally, he said, "I have a First Amendment right to say what I want."

I said, "No one has suggested that we get Congress to pass a law forbidding you to make a despicably ignorant statement at my dinner table in my home."

"See," he said.

I said, "What I am saying is that I find the use of that word offensive. I am saying that I will not have it at my dinner table. I will not have it in my home. You can exercise what you misunderstand to be a First Amendment right, but not in my home."

"The First Amendment says," he began.

I cut him off. "I know precisely what the First Amendment says." I quoted it to him verbatim. "You don't get to redefine what it means. You don't get to use it as an excuse to trumpet bigotry and prejudice, not in my home. Don't do it again."

I used my nastiest teacher glare on him. For years, it had stopped hordes of rampaging teenagers at Grover Cleveland High School where I taught. If looks could maim, he'd have left on a hospital gurney.

My sister said, "Now, Tom."

I gave her the same icy look and said, "This is my home. Other people can have whatever rules they want in their homes." I couldn't believe she would even remotely begin the slightest attempt to defend him. We'd discussed prejudice in my family often, frowned upon it, and condemned it long before I came out as gay and added another dimension to the dynamic of tolerance.

However, I had just violated one of the cardinal rules in my mom's family tradition. My mom always taught that the guest was king in our home.

Mom's holiday rules were weird like that. For example, start with the candy dish or nuts or hors d'oeuvres set out on an end table for guests on a holiday. My mother's rule was that in our home, we, the kids, were never to eat those treats because they were for the guests, but if we were the guests in someone else's home, we were still not to eat them because they were there for decoration or not to be eaten because it would ruin our dinner. Home or away, we never got the goodies.

Same with conversation: the rule was to swallow your feelings, your sensibilities, and your manners if the guest was in your home. The major goal was to have the guest be comfortable. Or if you were a guest in someone else's home, you were to remain silent because it was their home, and we were to follow their rules.

No possible way for us to eat or enjoy the good stuff or say what we thought or felt.

Yeah, well, I love my mom, but as far as I could see, her holiday rules were full of shit. The candy or nuts or hors d'oeuvres would never be eaten by anyone.

The rules of politeness extend both ways. In my home, there were limits, and Edgar had reached his.

The first time I met him, I'd taken an instant dislike to him. The first sentence he spoke included a racist comment.

Edgar and his family were involved in Republican party politics up to their well-filled martini glasses.

At that holiday dinner, after glaring Veronica to silence, I turned my steely gaze back to her eventual husband. He finally lowered his eyes and mumbled, "Okay."

My mother jumped in and began a conversation with my oldest brother, Lionel, about one of his son's hockey games and talk drifted off.

Edgar was just such a shit. My brother-in-law never let up in a real way.

Over the years our actual attendance at events in Edgar's home were rare. Contact with him was severely limited. Most often, visits with my sister happened when Edgar was at work.

Years later, after I'd met Scott, and he was attending all family functions, he and Edgar finally encountered each other. On first meeting, Edgar made the most obnoxious baseball fan appear to be a drowsy puppy. Edgar brought up games that Scott had lost, pitches batters hit for home runs off him, costly walks. Edgar ranted about what could have been done, should have been done, and how it could have been done. He was worse than a drunk at a ballpark sitting behind you bellowing with his beer breath. At least at a game, they'd paid to get in, and you could move, or tell an usher, or be obnoxious for your own team.

Edgar prattled and fumed about baseball then moved on to an idiot rant and tirade. It started with Edgar's view on how to throw curveballs to .250 hitters.

Even more odd, Edgar wasn't a particular fan of Scott's team, but that didn't matter to Edgar, and I learned from Veronica that he'd been a portly child, and except for one stint on the freshman football team in high school, had never even tried out for a sport.

Doesn't mean you have to play a game to be an expert, but to elevate an opinion to expertise, just because the opinion is uttered, is best left to the talk show morons on Fox.

At the dinner in question, Edgar waved his arms spasmodically in the air bringing himself to a dramatic finish and asked, "Do you realize what you did wrong?"

Scott is incredibly patient with fans, and he has a low boiling point. I've rarely seen him angry or lose control. I wanted to leap up and throttle Edgar.

Veronica's face had gone white. She looked as wives have looked for millennia who are powerless to stop their husbands who don't know when to shut up. My mom tried to change the subject. Edgar's voice overrode her, demanding, "Don't you agree with me?"

Look up calm in the dictionary, they have a picture of Scott, intense but calm.

Scott caught Edgar's eyes and held them.

"Well," Edgar demanded. "Why aren't you saying something? Why aren't you reacting?"

Everyone seemed to have stopped eating. Even my mother with her usual quick diversions sat with mouth agape.

Into this abyss of silence, Scott's deep voice rumbled. "I am." And the silence resumed, and he held Edgar's glare, and my husband's eyes didn't waver.

Edgar broke first. To be fair, many a fearsome batter in the Majors had broken long before he did. Edgar looked down and said, "I was just sayin'." He looked up for an instant into Scott's eyes, immediately looked away. "It's just my opinion."

I said, "Precisely."

Scott smiled at me. We gave each other a quick kiss.

Edgar did not puke at this, worse luck.

Recovered, Mom rushed in to talk about window treatments, blinds, and drapes in my younger brother, Darryl's, new home. Kind of a motif in our family. We can count on mom to try and switch topics if things get heated.

Three

Wednesday 2:41 A.M.

Veronica was pretty out of control. Who could blame her? When she had calmed her tears, I asked, "Where are the kids?"

"Still asleep."

Good as far as it went.

I asked, "What happened to Edgar?"

"He was shot." Her voice reached an even higher ear-shattering decibel level. Again, I moved the phone away from my ear. "The police were just here. A couple of them are still sitting in a car outside the house. You were the first person I could think of to call. You must come. You must get here as quick as you can."

"Of course," I said. It happened to be the Tuesday, now, Wednesday morning, before spring break. I would have taken the day anyway. Family tragedy trumps everything.

She said, "I have to go with the police. To identify…" She gasped, finally resumed, "Azure Grum is here. You remember her from the wedding?" Azure had been Veronica's ally all these years. "She'll stay with the kids until I get back."

I agreed to rush to Wisconsin to do what I could to help. I asked if she wanted me to call our parents. She begged me to. She had to handle the kids. She didn't know what to tell them or what to do. I had no advice for times like this although I did suggest she at least wait until they awakened in the morning to break the news. Let them finish this night's sleep in peace.

She gulped agreement.

Plus she had the police and the in-laws to deal with. Handling Edgar's family was like inviting the tornado into the storm cellar with you.

I gave her the best reassurances I could then hung up, called and woke up mom and dad, and told them the news. They said they'd start out first thing in the morning.

I'd do anything to help my sister. Unexpected death at any age can be tough, at an early age, a horror.

"Do you want me to come with?" Scott asked.

"Yes, thanks."

It was early April. He'd injured himself the first day of spring training. He'd had an operation on his shoulder the next week. Time would tell if he would ever pitch baseball in the Major Leagues again. He was into a six month rehabilitation stint.

We packed toothbrushes and clothes, grabbed my laptop, and were on the road in half an hour. I left a message on the school's absentee-call-in machine saying I wouldn't be in this Wednesday or Thursday. I had this Friday and all the next week off from school for spring break. You could use your sick days for funeral leave if the deceased was in the immediate family. Even if I'd had to take the days off without pay, I'd have done so without a moment's hesitation.

Four

Wednesday 6:07 A.M.

My sister lived in the Pleasant Valley subdivision of Harrison County. We arrived at the gates of the subdivision while the last shreds of night held on. I held up my identification to the camera so the guard could examine it and waited out the ritual: the house called, entry approved. In a few moments the gates rolled open.

Each lot was at least three wooded acres. High hedges and security fences kept neighbors at a distance. They lived in a semi-Tudor style near-mansion, all beams and stucco outside, six bedrooms and eight baths inside.

In front of their house, Porsches, Cadillacs, Mercedes, and a few cop cars nestled on both sides of the street and up their driveway.

The cop outside the front door demanded Scott and I show identification.

From the foyer, we entered the living room. The house felt to me as if there were two distinct atmospheres.

In the living room the décor was all my sister; warm, homey. Dominating the room were two nine-foot sofas with chairs perpendicular to them, both upholstered in some trendy, chunky fabric, sort of like burlap that looked as if it had begun to mutate and self-propagate. Equally trendy textiles in shades of brown, orange, red, and yellow were draped on nearly every surface. Genuine Navaho blankets purchased in Rough Rock, Arizona, hung on the walls. Large pillows in autumnal shades that matched the couches were scattered about in tasteful arrays. A deep gold carpet had light brown flecks mixed in. I knew the warmth came from my sister's sense of decoration.

Mordantly milling about amid this warmth were Edgar's relatives, my sister's in-laws. These people made the troll in the first Harry Potter movie look like a fashion model, making gray and doltish into a fashion statement, only bigger and uglier. Picture those creatures representing mucus in TV ads only bigger and you get the idea.

Although ugly might be too kind and too simple a word to use for their looks and demeanor. More cold emanated from them than from this past winter's worst blizzard. The government could solve the climate change problem by placing Edgar's relatives at strategic locations around the planet. Whatever other expression they might have, the cold that encased their personalities froze any ray of human kindness.

Their heft added dimension to their ogrish impression. They weren't bad because they were fat, and the fat didn't make them bad. They were evil and awful people who happened to all be overweight.

One odd, I hesitate to add, almost redeeming thing was Mrs. Grum most always appeared with a tiny lap dog clutched in her left arm. I never got that close, but at Edgar and Veronica's wedding I'd seen an obsequious toady of theirs accidentally get too close to the creature-- the dog, not Mrs. Grum. The tiny little thing had yapped and snarled at the interloper. Mrs. Grum hadn't taken the dog with her to the church that day. The dog was here now.

I thought her clutching on to the poor creature was kind of sad. What inadequacies or insecurities caused her to cling to the poor dog? Or was she just a neurotic twit? If clutching on to the dog gave her comfort and helped her with her grief over the death of her son, who was I to judge?

Each of the Grums was clad as if for an evening out at a posh country club. Then I remembered, they all must have been at the campaign headquarters, ready to be photographed in front of cameras. The Grums were a political power in Harrison County, which was at the epicenter of the current recall election, which I knew had taken place just that day. I hadn't heard the results, but it was clear from the way the Grums were dressed that they had all come directly from election headquarters

One of their great-great grandparents had been at the formation of the Republican Party in Ripon, Wisconsin. The Grums had been up to their nipples in Harrison County politics for decades.

Edgar's mother roosted in the center of the sofa that sat against the north wall. Veronica referred to her mother-in-law as the dragon lady. The morbidly obese woman ruled her family. She was the County Clerk of Harrison County and had been for years. She was also the social arbiter of the Women's Leisure Club which she ran with an iron fist. It was founded during the American Civil War by women whose men had gone off to fight in the Wisconsin 4th Regiment Infantry.

The women had met continuously since then, sometimes doing good, and sometimes being the backwoods equivalent of Peyton Place. In more modern times, their definition of modern being that which began before or during the Hoover administration, they'd become the stratified social hierarchy of the county.

My sister described them as, "The Harridans of Harrison County." Veronica avoided all contact with the women of the club.

The dragon lady's husband, Charles Dudley Grum, was a combination of bombast and bully, Harold Hill and Lord Voldemort, a Yankee peddler mixed with evil incarnate. He sat on the sofa next to his wife. His girth matched hers inch for inch. At the moment, he wore black, horn-rimmed glasses over dark soulless eyes, a vile colored suit on his immense bulk, and garish maroon shoes on gargantuan feet.

Both radiated hatred, disapproval, and disgust. To be fair, I don't think this was because Scott and I walked in. I'd rarely seen them have any other look on their faces.

The children matched the parental tonnage, their other two sons and their wives, plus various cousins, aunts, and uncles. Edgar being dead wouldn't really have fit in. I'd met many of them at least once, that occasion being Edgar and Veronica's wedding. I couldn't remember all their names. Edgar was the youngest.

In the living room some stood or leaned against the walls. A few sat on the edge of chairs. For one of the rare times when I'd been in the Grum family's presence, the younger son, Dewey, was not obnoxiously falling over everyone taking pictures.

I looked at them curiously. Not one of them touched another. Nobody reached out to comfort, hold hands. Maybe they didn't do that kind of thing with strangers around. Maybe they weren't a warm, huggy family. Nonetheless a son/brother had just died. I'd expect some kind of desire for human connection.

Mostly they looked sort of constipated.

You know the scene in westerns where a character walks into a bar and the piano music abruptly ceases and all conversation stops? That was what entering that room felt like.

At least they'd all assembled and rallied around at a moment of crisis.

Scott and I got cold stares.

No matter, I walked straight up to Edgar's mother and father, held out my hand, and said, "I'm so sorry for your loss."

I more than disliked them, but I knew basic common courtesy.

The old woman touched my hand for a millionth of a second, the husband for less than that. Scott's outstretched hand and murmured sympathy were met with stony silence. Perhaps they thought the mumbled thank you to me covered the both of us.

Much as I disliked them, they'd just lost their son. They were in the middle of a horror, and I needed to cut them a lot of slack. Was there a manual for proper grief behavior? No.

I needed to be less judgmental.

Five

Wednesday 6:12 A.M.

My sister entered the room. She wore an old sweatshirt over blue jeans. I remembered the shirt as one that her first boyfriend gave her in high school. It was too big for her then, was still too big.

We flew into each other's arms. I hugged her and murmured, "I'm so sorry," over and over. The fierceness of her embrace nearly caused me to gasp for breath.

I may have hated Edgar, but she'd loved him and married him.

When we unclinched, she hugged Scott and thanked him for coming.

She held both of our hands. Without ceremony, she said, "If I could speak to you." She led us deep into the house. We wound up in Edgar's office/den, which was on the far side of the house from the living room. I knew what she was doing, getting us as far away from Edgar's family as possible.

Veronica slumped into the massive, over-stuffed, vinyl-covered, brown swivel chair behind Edgar's desk.

The room was forty-by-forty and decorated in hunting lodge awful: heads of dead animals nailed to the walls, whole stuffed dead animals in various stages of agony with obvious wounds unconcealed by the taxidermists, probably at Edgar's request. Besides the former live woodlands creatures, a herd of huge bronze sculptures of various critters had been crammed into the room. The largest bronze piece was a grizzly bear that was over eight feet tall and must have weighed over eight hundred pounds. It stood two feet to the right of the desk. Near the door an eleven foot see-through canoe hung from the ceiling. At the rear were sliding glass doors that led to the backyard.

Edgar was a hunter. I'd heard he was an awful shot. Were the stuffed creatures purchased or genuine hunting trophies? I guess I didn't much care about the truth of that. I'm sure I was more sympathetic to anti-gun stuff and definitely far more pro-animal than Edgar was.

Scott and I had taken our traveling bags with us. We tossed our backpacks and placed the laptop computer on top of them in a corner, a six-foot-long bronze walking bear to the right and the grizzly to the left.

With proper lighting, small planes could have landed on the top of his desk. That is if it hadn't had a huge collection of junk nearly from one end to the other. On top of the desk right in front was a row of drinking vessels. Each had a picture of a deer: a personalized autumn deer coffee mug, a winter deer personalized travel mug, an autumn deer personalized gift tin, a winter deer personalized gift tin, a deer etched stainless water bottle, a sixteen ounce winter deer beer stein, a green engraved vintage deer coffee mug, a red engraved running deer coffee mug, and a stack of deer personalized ceramic coasters. Most of the pictures matched the deer personalized door mat just inside the door. The only significant part of all these to me, besides Edgar's name emblazoned on all of them, was that at least the pictures weren't of dead dear. All seemed pretty much frozen in life. Maybe the hunter hadn't quite got around to killing them yet.

Crammed next to the computer on top of the desk was a box that the outside label said held ten reams of paper. Scattered drifts of paper surrounded it, and random bits of paper stuck out from the top. The box seemed to have passed from containing new reams of paper, to being a trash bin.

The only actual open space on the desk was a small bit in the center in front of the huge chair. The space was big enough for a computer with a square foot of room to rest one's arms. In the far right hand corner of the desk was a picture of Edgar, Veronica, and the kids with a tent and a picnic table in the background. From the age of the kids, I thought it might have been taken in the past year or two.

I pulled a chair close, sat next to Veronica, held her hand.

She took several shuddering breaths then said, "I got back from, from… seeing Edgar… about an hour ago."

I put my arm around her. She leaned into me and said, "I'm sorry I lost it on the phone."

I thought if there was ever an appropriate time to lose it, the sudden death of one's spouse was one of them.

I said, "You know it's okay," and added, "Mom and Dad are on their way."

"Good." Mom would most likely be the one Veronica leaned on. Mom could be a rock.

I asked, "How are the kids?"

"They aren't up yet. That's what I have to do next, tell them. I think that's why I've been able to pull myself together. I've got to get them through this. I've got to get myself through this. I don't know how."

I said, "We'll do everything we can. Is there anything we can do right now?"

"Make it all go away."

"I would if I could."

"The police have been here. They said they would come back. They asked me where I was all night. They interrogated me. I'm frightened."

I said, "There's nothing to be frightened of."

"I don't know anything. The cops scared me. Are we in danger? Why was he killed? The police wouldn't tell me anything. I was here with the kids. He was at that stupid election thing."

Tuesday had been the recall election of the anti-human being governor. I'd followed the news about it closely in the papers and on the Internet. When we'd gone to bed, the results had been too close to call.

I said, "You don't need to be frightened. We're here. Mom and Dad will be here soon."

"I just don't know what to do. He was involved in that stupid election. They were going to party all night. I didn't care much about the damn election. I certainly don't care about it now."

"Is that where," I hesitated, "it happened?"

"I guess. I don't really care. I'm not sure I heard much of what the police said."

"My suggestion is that you call your attorney. Now."

"The family said they had someone coming over."

"Is this person your personal attorney?" I asked.

"No."

I said, "Do you have a personal attorney? One separate from theirs?"

Veronica said, "There's the woman who did our wills and the family Trust, but is that really necessary?"

I said, "It might be important."

She shook her head. "I'm just not sure."

I said, "At a time like this, especially since the police said it was murder, it could be vital." I didn't really want to remind her at this moment that the family members were always the most likely suspects, very much including the wife. Although with Edgar's family, the police had a whole raft of rotten, evil familial possible suspects to choose from.

She scratched her head. "I guess."

Scott said, "If it's easier, I can call."

"Would that be okay?" I asked.

Veronica said, "She's an old friend from college." She took out her cell phone and punched a few buttons, then handed it to Scott. I heard it ringing. He stepped to the other side of the room. Scott was so tall, the top of his head almost touched the jaw of a deer who looked stunned that Edgar could have been such a good shot. Right or wrong, the deer was dead.

I glanced out the windows to the backyard. I could see a small part of the outdoor pool and the upper swirls and turns of a mini-skateboard park Edgar had ordered built for his oldest son. Beyond these, newly budding tree limbs fractured the pale blue of the sky. The sun poured through the half-formed buds of early April. I could hear Scott murmuring into the phone.

Six

Wednesday 6:30 A.M.

I asked, "The police said murder?"

She nodded.

"Do they have a suspect?"

"I have no idea."

Scott walked over, held the phone out to Veronica. He said, "She wants to talk to you."

Veronica took the phone. Listened. Said, "Okay," several times. Clicked the phone shut.

"What did she recommend?"

"Not to say anything. I don't know anything. She said she'd get here as soon as she could. She said to wait to talk to the police until she gets here. I don't know when they'll be back. I don't care when they'll be back. I'm worried about the kids."

If worrying about the kids got her through the first stages of grief, it was okay by me.

She said, "What do I say to the children? How do I explain?"

I said, "I'm not sure. Tell them you love them. They're old enough to understand death. I wouldn't lie. I wouldn't go into gruesome detail, either."

"I don't know any gruesome details."

"Good."

She said, "I want you and my lawyer here when I talk to the cops again."

"Sure."

"And I don't have any cash." She pointed at the box in the middle of the desk. "That's what I was starting on when you drove up. The financial stuff is a mess. There must be bills to pay. I don't have any cash. I don't know about life insurance. Or how to pay the mortgage."

"You have bank accounts and things?"

"Edgar took care of all of that. I've got a credit card with a limit."

"No ATM card?"

"No. Edgar did all the banking. Wrote the checks. Paid the bills. Gave me cash when I asked for it. All the investing. Taxes. Everything."

"Where are the records?"

"He kept it all in there." She pointed at a door. "That's a room with files and things." She pointed to the box and the scattered papers on the desk. "I took out that box and tried to go through it. It's a mess, a total mess. I don't understand it. I don't have time to understand it right now. I need to deal with the children." She drew a deep breath.

"How can I help?" I asked.

She said, "He never went over financial things with me. I went in there earlier, there are a zillion more boxes of papers. I glanced in a couple others. Nothing is in order. Nothing is organized. What am I going to do? I've got to handle the kids, the funeral, and they said it was murder." She gulped. "Right now, I just need basic walking around money, and I've got to pay for the funeral."

I said, "You guys didn't discuss all this?"

"No. We're young. Who expects to die at this age? And to be murdered?"

"Did he have life insurance?"

"I think so. But do they pay off quickly enough for me to have money to live on?"

This was not the time to say, how can a modern woman let her husband just run things like a medieval fiefdom. She'd made her peace with him. I was not about to start a war with her.

"Do you want me to help you sort it out?"

"You're always so good at organizing things. You always know what's what. While I'm with the kids, will you start going over all that stuff? I'll need help anyway. I never was good with money."

"I'll give it a start, sort it out, then go over it with you."

"And when I deal with the Grum family, I want you, Scott, mom and dad, my lawyer, the police, the army, anybody with me." She shuddered then stood up. "I better get to the kids. I don't want them finding things out from them."

I knew who she meant by them, Edgar's evil family.

She continued, "It's nearly the time they wake up for school. Well, no school today."

"Good luck," I said. I stood and hugged her. "If you need any help, Scott and I are here."

"I know. Thank you."

She took a key out of her jeans. "This is for that room with the financial stuff."

I put it in my pocket.

Patricia, her youngest child, opened the door. Patricia was six. She wore pink pajamas with little blue and yellow bunnies dancing on them. Early morning sleep clouded her eyes. She said, "Mommy, why are Grandma and Grandpa here?" She noticed us. "Hi, Uncle Tom, Uncle Scott."

We nodded hello.

She went to her mother and hugged her.

"Are your brothers up?"

"I don't think so. Don't we have to get ready for school?"

"No school today. Mommy has to talk to you." She took her daughter's hand.

"What's going on?"

"Let's go find your brothers."

At the door she turned back and said, "If you two want to

stay in here, that's fine. In fact, it might be better." She didn't elaborate, and I didn't ask. She had huge problems to deal with. If she meant for some reason we were to guard this room, or if she meant this as a safe haven from Edgar's family, or if she meant the two of us would be more comfortable, or maybe she meant nothing by it, or maybe she thought all of them might be true. Maybe she was just trying to get through the next five minutes without sobbing hysterically so she could deal with her kids. Nobody was memorizing what she said. Nobody was going to hold her to what she said, not at a time like this.

Veronica and Patricia left together hand in hand. Moments later we heard a soft tapping on a distant door. She was knocking before entering.

Seven

Wednesday 6:51 A.M.

Scott closed the office door then sat down on the maroon leather couch. I sat in Edgar's chair. It was extra large, built for the heavy-set man that Edgar was.

Scott waved a hand at the assembled dead animals. "If I was going to build a shrine to killing innocent creatures, this would be it. If this was an English manor house, and we were in a British cozy murder mystery, the dead body would be in this room."

I glanced at the silent, mouth-open-as-if-in-mid-screech, bronze wolf. "It is a creepy place."

Edgar's older brother, Barry, manipulated his bulk into the room. He didn't knock. He looked neither of us in the eyes as he said, "Everybody's pretty hungry." His prominent nose was very red.

I wanted to say, you aren't crippled, get your ass into the kitchen and make something yourself, or unbend far enough to rush to a fast food place and get a to-go order for everyone.

Barry's shtick in the family, as far as I had experienced it, was to be master of the snide-aside. His forte was the mumble-under-the-breath not-quite-in-a-stage whisper comment such as: "How can he be qualified to be president? He's never learned to march in cadence?" Or this, "That's not an American car they bought. It better run perfectly."

Political debate as theatrical asides? Discussion of policy issues as snide slogans or outright calumny or deliberate personal attacks? Not a whiff of a syllable of significant issues, discussed devoid of emotion and approached rationally.

I never quite figured out the point of what I called Barryisms. Was the other person supposed to hear them? If so, were they to rush over and prostrate themselves at his feet and declare themselves converted to his way of thinking because of his self-proclaimed brilliant but barely heard bon mots? Were they designed to provoke someone into calling him on his ludicrous nonsense, to provoke a fight, to compel acquiescence? If they were designed to convince someone to come to agreement with him, they seemed pointless.

Pointless never bothered a Republican.

My sister had made peace with all of the Grums years before. I was not about to start World War III with them while she was overwhelmed with her loss.

"Where's Veronica?" Barry asked

"With the children."

He said, "We could ask her about food."

I was incapable of a civil response at this moment. Scott leapt into the breach. He said, "She's talking to the children. She's telling them what happened. I think we'd best leave them alone for a while."

"Oh. I guess."

Scott said, "I'll check the kitchen in a few minutes, and we can put something together."

Barry nodded. "I hope she's going to pray with them."

Blank stares from Scott and me.

"That's what helps at a time like this, praying to God. She and the kids have to put faith in Him."

Except for weddings and funerals, I hadn't been inside a church in more years than I could count. And if he wanted to chat with an invisible being in the sky, that was his business. I repeated today's mantra to myself. He'd just lost his brother. I had to give him some slack.

Scott murmured, "It's a tough time for everyone in the family. We'll all have to be supportive." Neutral and faintly positive, with not a hint of snark. The man is a saint.

As Barry turned to the door, I said, "Veronica told us the

police claimed Edgar was murdered."

"Well, I'm sure the police were probably hysterical. And I'm sure Veronica was confused. I'm sure we'll get this all sorted out."

Barry gave us a vinegary smile as he sidled out of the room.

Scott watched the door close then said, "Waiting for me to get into the kitchen is gonna be the longest few minutes of his life." He turned to me. "I feel so sorry for Veronica and the kids."

"Me too."

He came and took the chair I had been in next to the large swivel chair. He took my hand.

Scott said, "Barry or any random Grum can make murder go away?"

"Too bad nobody murdered him."

"You're upset. About what? Not Edgar being dead. I know you."

"I'm upset for Veronica. The Grums will make this harder for her and the kids, not easier. You'll see. I don't like them."

"Me neither."

I said, "I didn't follow Barry's parting crack. Hysterical police? I find that hard to believe. And Veronica confused? About murder? Nobody makes that kind of mistake. What's he up to?"

"Veronica told us the police said murder. Even Edgar didn't deserve that."

I blurted before I thought. "The man deserved to be tortured and die miserably." I looked Scott in the eye. "I don't believe I said that."

"You feel it. No point in denying your feelings."

"I know I'd never say any such thing to Veronica or the kids."

"I know. And be careful what you wish for." He then quoted from Tolkien, Gandalf on the worth of the life of Gollum when Frodo expresses the wish that Bilbo had killed Gollum when he had the chance in the caves in the Misty Mountains. Gandalf said and Scott quoted, "And some die that deserve life. Can you give that to them? Then be not too eager to hand out death in the name of justice."

I said, "You know I agree with that, but Edgar was such a shit."

"I know. The question is who would kill him?"

I said, "I presume most people who came into contact with him hated him. Except maybe his family and a whole lot of them sure didn't seem like they were all that fond of him either, or of each other for that matter. If the police were looking for people who hated him as the killer, they'd probably need a list of everyone he'd ever met."

"Veronica loved him."

"Are you defending him?" I asked.

"No, of course not, but he'll have had friends. If you're that rich at the very least somebody is eager to suck up to you."

"That's not friendship."

"But it might be close enough. For someone as awful as Edgar, maybe that's all he had, or that's what he was used to. Maybe he chose to be that way, which is really sad."

I felt a twinge of guilt. "I shouldn't be speaking ill of the dead?"

"You're recognizing reality. It just sounds kind of jarring, but if that's all he had, I do pity him." He sighed. "I wonder if it would help if we knew details about what happened."

"We can try the Internet." Scott got my laptop from next to the bronze grizzly. Supposedly the giant was some kind of family heirloom. Yeah, this family would have a bronze, angry grizzly as a keepsake. Next to it was its companion, a three-feet-high, on-all-fours, four-foot-long, brown bear.

Standing on the other side of the desk from me, Scott moved some of the junk on the top of the desk to the side to make room. He placed the laptop in the now empty space and began to boot it up. I moved the keyboard and computer monitor on the top of the desk toward me. As soon as I pressed the mouse, the screen came to life.

Scott pointed at Edgar's computer. "Why didn't the cops take that?"

"I would if I were a cop."

The computer immediately opened to the last page it had been on, a porn site.

I said, "He didn't shut it down so it went back to the last place he'd been. Here's something ordinary." The site was called Mona Moans for You.

Scott came around the desk and stood next to me. He gazed for a moment. "A straight site. We needed confirmation he was heterosexual?"

"If he was the last one using it. I think Veronica's got her own laptop, and I vaguely recall her telling me the only other time I was in here, that the kids weren't allowed entry to this room. So it was probably him, and judging from this he was pretty heterosexual."

"Why did he need to look at porn?" Scott asked.

I shrugged. "Why does anybody? Because it's there? Because he can? I know for sure I am not going to speculate about its significance in terms of his and Veronica's sex life. I'm not going to go there. Dead or alive I never want to think about Edgar's sex life."

Scott pointed at the list of bookmarks at the top of the page. One read 'tits' another 'legs'. A smorgasbord of anatomy abbreviations. I clicked on the show all bookmarks tab. A list of hundreds popped up.

Scott peered at the screen and nodded. "Relentlessly heterosexual."

"I'll try to care." I tapped the tip of my finger on the screen. "The real question is the one you asked. Why haven't the police taken the computer? Why aren't there police swarming all over this place? Why is there only the one guarding the door?"

Scott shrugged. "We don't know anything about the circumstances of the murder. For all we know, they have a suspect in custody, someone who has motive, means, and opportunity."

"You'd think they'd have mentioned that to Veronica."

I got my laptop carrying case from next to the grizzly bear and took out my flash drive. I stuck it into Edgar's computer.

"What are you doing?" Scott asked.

I worked as I spoke. "I'm going to save what's on this computer. Something odd is going on here. The cops should be here, not us. They're not. I don't trust the Grums. Maybe I shouldn't do this and maybe Veronica would be angry if she knew, but I don't like this. If I was a cop, I'd want this information. I don't trust any of these people."

"Seems like a bit much," Scott said.

I closed the site and then clicked out of the Internet. The desktop appeared. It was filled with photo icons. These were labeled by name: Susie, Sharon, hundreds more. Turned out Mona was not the only site Edgar perused nor were her pictures the only ones he saved. Further icons on the desktop showed pictures of downloaded videos from porn sites. They were alphabetical. Above Mona were Mandy the Randy and Luscious Laura. Good to know idiot porn names knew no sexual orientation. I took my flash drive and fitted it into the USB port.

"Are you sure about doing that?" Scott asked.

"In the middle of all this other crap, somewhere on here could be financial information. We can look at it later. The cops could take it away any moment. I'd rather be careful."

"Are you supposed to take another guy's data?"

"Two things. He won't care. He's dead. Plus Veronica asked us to help." I highlighted all the desk top items and then dragged them to the zip drive. I had 64 GB space on the drive so I wasn't too worried that everything on the computer would fit. After I downloaded all these I would check the documents folder and move everything there over.

I concentrated on Edgar's computer for a few minutes. Data began to transfer. While the computer and flash drive made friends, I said, "I don't like it when cops don't act like what I know cops usually act like."

I watched as Scott established the wireless connection on our laptop. He clicked over to Google and called up the Milwaukee papers. Huge election news headlines proclaimed the candidates to be within twenty votes of each other.

Useless, I thought. If it was close, the Republicans would know how to steal it: think Florida in 2000, or the special election for judge in Wisconsin. We liberals knew how it worked. You either won by a whole lot, or the Republicans would find a way to fuck you over.

Scott found one breaking news squib outlined in yellow about a possible tragedy at the governor's campaign headquarters, no details.

Eight

Wednesday 7:26 A.M.

I pointed at the door Veronica had indicated. "We should start with the stuff in there that she asked for help with. She said she needed money. I can give her some for now, but she claimed she didn't know about the family's finances."

Scott said, "In this day and age? That sounds kind of medieval."

I shrugged. "She said she didn't know how she was going to pay for the funeral. There's not much else to do at the moment. I might as well start now."

"I'll help," Scott said.

We used the key Veronica had left me.

I was reasonably familiar with end of life details: insurance papers, powers of attorney, and that kind of stuff. Years ago Scott and I hired a gay lawyer who was familiar with what needed to be in a gay couple's wills, and with all the things a gay couple needed to have to ensure each other's future in case one of them died. There were a lot of legal papers to go through and sign. Including simple things like power of attorney for medical decisions, power of attorney for financial decisions, pre-paying for our funerals, investments, who inherited precisely what, who was the beneficiary of every single thing. Scott was listed as the person for me in all these matters as I was listed for him. We especially made sure we had the kinds of things we could wave in the face of legal and medical personnel if they gave us hassles about end of life decisions.

We entered the room. It was a size between a regular closet and a walk-in closet. A tiny desk in one corner had a straight-back wooden chair in front of it. Except for that space and a few feet between them and the door, the room was filled with boxes; floor to ceiling, side to side, with barely enough room to open the door more than half way.

I looked at Scott. I said, "It's always best to begin at the beginning."

I took down the top box from the first stack on my right. He took one from the top of the heap in the middle of the floor. We each took our box to the large desk. I carried my box around to the back and pushed aside more of the paraphernalia from the top of the desk to the far sides. The stuff from the box Veronica had started on, I put to the far left side. Scott and I put our separate boxes on the half of the middle closest to us.

Scott paused before opening his box. "Maybe we should go through the desk first. He might have kept the most up to date or most important stuff in there."

I agreed.

I started with the center top drawer. As I looked through his desk I thought perhaps I'd find something that redeemed Edgar as a person. A picture of him with a warm fuzzy puppy? Edgar serving food to the homeless in a shelter? And if I found something, would that redeem the life of a mean spirited, racist, sexist, homophobic son-of-a-bitch? What would redeem such a person?

Unbidden into my imagination came the old joke. A man dies and shows up at the pearly gates, and St. Peter asks what good work have you ever done for your fellow man. The guy thinks for a long time and finally says that he once gave twenty-five cents to a homeless man. St. Peter calls out loudly to the Lord asking what he should do with the guy. There's a long pause and a then a great voice says, give him back his twenty-five cents and tell him to go to hell.

I wondered if that joke would have even more resonance with me if I believed in heaven, pearly gates, St. Peter, and/or god. Probably not.

But the center drawer confirmed the mundane: pencils, pens, erasers, scissors, paperclips, markers, transparent tape, stapler.

Drawers only on the right: the top one had an unopened ream of blank copy paper and a box of manila folders, the second different sizes and colors of blank note pads. In the largest drawer on the bottom were three thick books on computer programming followed by two books on how to build guns.

I flopped each book out on top of the desk. Page after dense page of instructions on building computers, programming computers, and making guns, but nothing of financial significance to help Veronica at this moment.

Edgar read these? I had no notion of his IQ level. Certainly, from the bigoted and ignorant comments he made, he showed no inclination to use any intelligence he did have in the service of sense and reason. And really, when someone says they don't believe in evolution, how can you not think they're an ignorant rube?

The gun books were fascinating in a can't-look-away-from-a-train-crash way.

"Check these out." I showed them to Scott. "Maybe he built the gun that killed him."

Scott said, "That's ghoulish and scary."

"Did he go around armed?"

Scott said, "The few times we saw him, I never noticed a gun."

I opened the box I'd gotten from the storage closet. On top was a brochure from a local pizza place for a dollars-off bargain. I checked the expiration date; four years ago. The next item was a receipt printed out from a porn site for 39.99 for one month on Mona Moans For You. The date was six months prior. It was a payment for a one-month non-recurring membership.

I held it up and showed it to Scott. I said, "He was definitely straight."

Scott said, "Not as comforting a thought as we might like." He glanced at the picture. "She looks nice in a big breasts kind of way, if you like big breasts."

I said, "I'm indifferent." I checked the bookmarked sites on the computer. "It matches one of these." I examined the desk top. "She's on here, too. I'm just not sure I care."

The papers quickly began to settle into logical patterns. Bills: we put these in chronological order by company. Receipts: from the local fast food restaurants to exclusive Parisian three star restaurants and a million places in between, again time order by venue. Travel brochures: mostly from hunting lodges around the globe. Coupons: for discounts on anything from pizza to airlines, to the local grocery store. He clipped coupons? Whatever for? He could probably buy the whole restaurant, but coupons he had.

Early in the process of sorting, the computer and the zip drive concluded their successful relationship. I pocketed my zip drive and let the computer rest.

For an instant I thought about hiding the porn receipts, then dismissed it. Fear of porn in the face of death, a nonsensically absurd notion. Besides, Edgar wouldn't care anymore if someone found out; he was dead. Veronica's opinion of him might change? That wasn't my problem. I wasn't going to alter reality. Who knew what would or would not help?

The desk top was soon filled with receipts set out by category, venue, and year. We began to make piles on the floor. I even used the grizzly bear's out-stretched arms. Scott placed some of his stuff on the bronze closest to him, the wolf whose head was up, mouth open, howling soundlessly at the moon.

Most of the brochures and the coupons we dumped into a trash can that quickly began to overflow.

A half hour in and Veronica had still not reappeared. I expected her back any moment. Telling your children about such a tragedy must be horrific. I could only imagine what my sister and her kids were going through. I was tempted to find her and see how she was doing. If there were books for what to say and do at a time like this, I didn't know about them. Even if there were such books, there wasn't time to read them and get their advice.

I presumed she'd be explaining to them, comforting, reassuring them. Sudden death was bad enough, but murder?

I didn't want to disturb a moment of such profound intimacy. To make the presumption that any intrusion of mine would be of help was on a level of arrogance I'd never want to display. I was less than thirty feet from where she was. If she needed help, I could get there in seconds.

I wished I knew of a way to make things better for her or them. There wasn't, really. Just to be here and help, offer assistance, and do things like sort through tons of crap.

I stopped at one point and said to Scott, "Why aren't the cops doing this?"

"You're asking me impossible questions. I have no answers."

"I knew that," I said.

"Sorry."

I asked, "Are we just sorting this stuff and the cops come in here and use it to prove someone guilty. We're doing their work?"

Scott added, "Or we find something that proves he was in some criminal conspiracy that got him killed?"

I could hope.

The fourth box in had insurance information.

I sat in Edgar's chair and began to read through the stacks of dense prose. A whole lot of them were from businesses who offered accidental death life insurance policies. You paid a minimal fee and got a payout if you died in an accident. Did murder qualify as an accident? I clicked onto the Internet and Googled double indemnity. The site I read claimed that such policies did pay out in the case of murder or accident, as long as the murder was not done by someone who benefited from the policy. Edgar had five of these. Veronica was the beneficiary.

I used manila file folders I'd found in the top right-hand desk drawer. With a fine point marker, I labeled one insurance and stuck those forms inside. I began another for investment companies, a third for bank accounts.

Five minutes later Scott said, "Why are there voter registration rolls in here for Harrison County?"

"Huh?"

He flipped through a stack of print outs that might have come from a laser jet printer in the early nineties. "These cover from nineteen forty-four to nineteen ninety-two." He glanced into the box and took out the next stack of papers. They were about as thick as a ream and a half of paper. He flipped through the first few and the last few. He said, "These go from ninety-two to this year."

"Strange."

"No stranger than hunting lodge brochures."

Forty-five minutes in, I found the tax forms from five years before. It was a start in organizing the income folders, making it far easier. Any company they had income from would have sent a form of some kind, normally a 1099. If he was making money from businesses that didn't send tax forms, I think he and now Veronica at least peripherally, were in trouble. Taxes were due late next week. My guess was Veronica would need to find Edgar's accountant or hire one of her own.

NINE

Wednesday 8:44 A.M.

I'd just placed the first investment form into the tax folder when the door to the den burst open. Edgar's father, Charles Dudley Grum, marched into the room.

"Where's Veronica?" he demanded. His voice was nearly a shout.

I said, "She's telling the children their father is dead."

He added a snarl to the loudness of his voice. "What's taking so long?"

There was a timetable for announcing the death of a parent to children? How cruel? How absurd?

I didn't really want to deal with this guy right now. Then I reminded myself, for it seemed like the thousandth time already, that he'd just lost a son, and he deserved a lot of slack.

At their wedding, Edgar was drunk from before the ceremony began. He swayed at the altar. I remember glancing at the family across the church aisle. The gargantuan Mrs. Grum slopped over the edge of the pew across from my mother. My sister's moments-from-officially being mother-in-law's gargantuan face radiated hate. Not disapproval, hate.

When I met him, I thought Edgar was a fool. When I saw him at the wedding, I thought he was a drunken fool. My sister loved him. Who was I to tell her he was a disaster? And she wouldn't have listened. She was in love.

During the entire reception, her mother-in-law sat in a corner and barely seemed to alter an ounce of her posture. The dog didn't move much either. Didn't the poor thing ever have to relieve itself? The alternative was too odious to consider. I felt sorry for the poor critter.

It wasn't the drunken Edgar or my sister's hate-filled mother-in-law, I found most offensive at the wedding. It was Charles Dudley Grum, the father-in-law, whom I found most odious.

At the reception when Scott and I began to dance, one of Edgar's dad's minions came over and told us to stop. I knew it was a minion from someone who talked to me later.

Scott's dancing is a sight to behold. The man is all grace and athleticism on the baseball field. Put him on a dance floor to any kind of fast music, and he looks like a man in the midst of electro-shock therapy in a video where someone keeps pressing the pause button, kind of spastic jerking on steroids. On the other hand slow dancing with him is a joy. His body swaying, dipping, and dancing next to mine, up against mine, pure bliss. And yes, our doing so at such an event is still a political and moral affront to many. Good.

We'd even taken dancing lessons at one point. The lessons didn't do an ounce of good for his dancing to rock and roll.

I'm afraid I committed one of the great sins at that moment of attempted minion intervention. I was neither afraid, intimidated, or much interested, that was normal. No, the great sin was that I laughed at the minion attempting to remove us from the dance floor.

We didn't stop dancing. If guests were offended, they did not rush out of the reception screeching in horror. In fact, they all seemed to live through it. So the minion stuff was odd, but not the oddest.

That came at the height of the dinner, prime rib and lobster. Charles Dudley Grum got up to make a toast to his son. He was at least as drunk as the younger man, if not drunker. Picture an enraged bull swaying like a cobra, eyes pink, nose red.

Prior to this my sister kept telling me that her future father-in-law was a charmer. Up to then I'd missed that part of his personality. What happened next did not add the notion that he was charming to my list of things I thought about him. Perhaps all who knew him and his family were charmed by their reported wealth and reputed influence in local politics. At the reception, I didn't note anything that resembled charm in anyone in Edgar's family.

Charles Dudley Grum was at the podium in the middle of the head table. He held a randomly screeching microphone and lurched back and forth worse than a drunk trying to walk down the aisle of a moving train.

Well, I wasn't married to him.

It's what he said that I found most awful, weird, offensive. He talked about my sister as, "the little woman who could now keep house the way a woman should," and, "the new addition to a family that knew how to keep traditional values sacred," and "that she'd married into a family that knew how to pray and keep things holy."

You think I'm making this up? It got worse.

He talked about what a fine man Edgar was despite his wayward youth. Then he began listing all the wayward youth things his kid had done. Beginning with a disgusting toilet training incident, moving on to drunken teenage puking, then with him, daddy Charles Dudley, being called to settle run-ins with school authorities and with the law.

Weird, odd, obnoxious was bad enough, but the eternal recitation was boring beyond belief. My parents and the rest of my family sitting at our table had frozen smiles plastered on their faces. The entire rest of the audience, except Scott next to me, were laughing and cheering and carrying on as if Charles Dudley Grum was announcing the last triumph of the idiot right.

Except, of course, Mrs. Grum, whose stony expression altered barely a whit. At the best of times her face looked as if someone had recently shoved a baseball bat up her butt, thick end first. At that moment her expression looked like maybe the bat had been replaced by a smallish cucumber. I remember wondering if this slight change meant that she was amused, possibly even having a good time? I'd hate to think she was as astonished and disapproving as I was. I'd hate to think I shared any of the same emotions as she. Such thoughts might introduce the notion that she was human. At any rate, she didn't try to interrupt or stop her husband.

Edgar, instead of being embarrassed or angry, began cheering his dad on at the end of each incident. As in, "Yeah, dad," or "You tell 'em dad."

My main thought at the time was that at least I wasn't marrying him.

After they were married, Veronica and her husband moved near his family in Wisconsin. At the time, he had a job in a law office there as a clerk.

Edgar, in my sister's version, had tried breaking with the family. He'd quit the clerk job, become a financial planner, and been laid off by that company. His family had upbraided him for being in trade, for losing a job, for not being as successful as the rest of them.

The unofficial version I'd gotten at their wedding from a drunken cousin. She'd told me that even the family couldn't put up with his incompetence, or at least they stopped putting up with his incompetence when he started costing them money. Nothing criminal, she insisted at the time, just rampant stupidity.

Most recently, he'd signed on to work temporarily in the county repub office and the anti-recall campaign.

Scott and I never went to my sister's for the holidays.

In fact, other than a few lunches, I rarely saw her although we talked on the phone frequently. We'd been close. She'd rant about her in-laws, but she loved her husband. There wasn't much to be done, and there wasn't much I could suggest. Nor was I being asked for suggestions.

Shutting up is an underrated virtue.

Ten

Wednesday 8:47 A.M.

Charles Dudley Grum planted himself in the middle of the room.

In response to his demand for a time frame for breaking horrific news to children, Scott said, "I'm sure she's doing the best she can."

Edgar's father glared from one to the other of us, finally fixed his eyes on me.

He said, "What are you doing?"

I looked up from the tax planner document I'd been about to inspect.

I was not about to justify myself to him. Nor, simply because he asked a question, was I obligated to answer it. Instead, I asked, "How are you and the rest of the family doing?" Scott tossed the coupon booklet he had in his hand into the trash and came around the desk and stood next to me.

Mr. Grum said, "You have no right to be going through those things."

I said, "Is there anything I can do to help you right now?"

He said, "You will leave this. Go. You will not interfere in this family."

Before he walked in, he couldn't have known what we were doing. We hadn't started sorting until after Barry Grum's earlier visit. I wondered why he'd come in here in the first place. I didn't have a lot of patience with these people in normal times. Usually, by this point I'd have told him off. I kept my voice calm.

I said, "I will leave what go, precisely?"

He waved a hand at all the boxes and papers. "I will tell

Veronica that you don't wish to do this, that you will put all these papers back, and that you don't wish to be bothered."

Very quietly, I said, "You don't speak for me."

He stamped around the room bumping into a few of the larger animals. He slammed his fists down on the desk. He shoved fistfuls of paraphernalia and papers from the desk onto the floor. Throughout, he bellowed and screamed at full volume various versions of, "Get out. Go away."

There was way more emotion being exhibited here than was called for by the simple truth I'd stated.

I stood up. The man was out of control. Did he need a sedative, a mountain of them? Did he take blood pressure pills? He looked like he needed a whole bottle's worth. He looked a heartbeat or two short of a stroke. I was more worried about him collapsing than I was about making points about how absurd he was, or demanding to know who he thought he was that he could command me at will.

He grabbed a stack of papers that were on the top of the heap in the box Scott had been going through. The top ones were hunting lodge brochures. He leaned across the desk, waved them in my face, and finished his rant with, "Nothing. You have nothing to do or say. You will do what I say." He planted his fists on top of the desk. His chest heaved as he gasped for breath.

I'd dealt with far too many idiot administrators in my time to put up with this. I took a breath to begin an angry response. I didn't get the first syllable out. Scott put his hand on my arm and said, "Maybe you should sit down, Mr. Grum. Can I get you something to drink? A glass of water? Should I call a doctor? Or call 9-1-1? You don't look well."

Scott's deep, calm, thrumming voice brought me to my senses. This was no time for me to be out of control. Charles Dudley Grum might not need me, but Veronica did.

Scott's voice had no such soothing effect on our attacker. Thrusting his hips against the desk, he bent toward us, his clenched fists mushed onto the top of the desk, concentrated on his breathing. Scott and I stood silently. Finally, Mr. Grum had enough breath to say, "You can get out and not bother this family anymore. Do as I say!"

In deference to his presumed emotional distress over his son, I replied in my softest voice, "You have no power over me."

"What I say goes in this family, in this county."

I said, "I'm sorry. I don't know what we're talking about. Is there something I can do to help you at this terrible moment?"

Again, he turned very purple. He sputtered. Again, he began to pace and shout. "How dare you? You're not in charge here. I've done exactly what this family needs. I know exactly what this family needs. I've made all the decisions. I will make all the decisions."

"What decision are we talking about?" I asked. "Your son is dead. I'm sorry for your loss."

The inkling of horror crept into the back of my mind. Had he made the decision to murder his son? Too ghastly, too inhuman; then again, he was a Republican. I so very much didn't want it to be true that the Grums somehow could be involved in the death of their own son. It was just such an awful thing to contemplate.

Mr. Grum tried to launch his vast bulk around the desk. He sprawled on top of it for a few moments. All of the rest of the papers and junk on top of the desk went flying. Some of the ceramic souvenirs broke into bits on the rug. It took him a few moments to control his rage and get himself righted on his feet.

Next he tried to rush around the desk to attack us.

We tried the simple expedient of not moving.

The older man couldn't get at us by going around to the left because the chairs were in the way. He tried the right, but had to stop because he had trouble fitting his gargantuan self between the desk and the grizzly bear.

His feet crunched on shards of the broken paraphernalia he'd swept onto the floor. He kicked at several of the larger bits.

Mr. Grum was breathing too hard. He swayed, shuffled

sideways, grasped the desk for support.

I said, "Do you need us to call 9-1-1?"

He gulped breaths for several minutes. We waited. His face turned from awful purple to deep red. Then he began screaming again, "You're just some faggot interloper who we've had to tiptoe around for years."

I thought of matching him scream for scream. The screamers usually think that once they're screaming and you're not, they've won.

He waved a fat finger in my direction. "We aren't going to put up with you anymore. You're history." He swayed, clutched the desk for support. I'm afraid the thought flashed through my head that if he had a heart attack or a stroke, should such a thing eventuate, I would not weep.

I wondered if Veronica and the kids could hear him, or maybe Mrs. Grum and/or their kids might come rushing from the living room in support.

In the softest, most measured tones I could summon, I said, "You will, now and forever, treat me and mine with dignity and respect. You do not get to play plantation master with me, now or ever."

Scott didn't interrupt me or try to shush me, and I got no warning touch of his calming hand. As we met this threat, I felt his shoulder press against mine in solidarity. That touch was enough and more than enough to remember at that moment how much I loved him.

As I stared at Mr. Grum trying to control himself, I wonder what the hell was going on here? Was he some kind of enraged, mad fool? Or a poor, desperately wounded schlub who had lost his son and didn't know how to deal with the loss except to hit out at anything in his path, a wild animal too blind and grief stricken to deal any other way?

Mr. Grum continued drawing deep breaths.

Scott said, "Mr. Grum, we are deeply sorry for your loss. This must be the hardest thing a parent could possibly go through. Whether we like each other or not, Tom and I are here to help Veronica and your grandchildren and your family through this difficult time. We'll be happy to do what we can."

Mr. Grum responded to this compassion with, "You can help by getting out. Now and forever. Veronica is not our blood. We have a family Trust. We are here to protect our interests. The Trust is very clear on what happens when someone dies."

I'm not sure I cared about his family Trust. It didn't bother me that he didn't want me involved in his grief and sorrow. That was none of my business. I did know I cared about Veronica and helping her through this. A rampaging bull elephant he might be, but perhaps if he raged at me, Veronica might be spared some grief later. And what was this crap about not being "blood"? Was this son-of-a-bitch planning to leave her destitute? He wouldn't want his grandkids out on the street, would he? Hard to tell, he was a Republican after all.

We were interrupted by a tap on the door.

Eleven

Wednesday 9:03 A.M.

The door opened. A woman peered into the room. She balanced a briefcase and a cup of coffee in one hand and held the door handle in the other. She said, "I was told Veronica was back here."

I said, "She's still with the children."

The woman came into the room. She was in her mid-to-late-thirties, slender, and wore a white shirt and a dark gray pantsuit. She said, "I'm Enid Achtenberg, Veronica's attorney."

Mr. Grum said, "We don't need any outside attorney. The family has attorneys. You're not wanted. Get out."

"You're Mr. Grum," she said.

"Yes, so what?" His voice was still at bellow level.

Nobody else from the family had rushed in to see what was going on. Maybe the rest of them were used to bombast beyond all levels of decency, or he was the one in the family who did the bidding and commanding and they didn't dare interfere. Although, according to Veronica, Edgar's mother ruled the roost.

Ms. Achtenberg said, "I'm here to see Veronica at her request. I can wait in the car."

I said, "I'm Veronica's brother. This is my husband Scott. We were here when Veronica called you." I touched Scott's arm. "Scott was the first one you talked to. You are welcome to wait for Veronica here with us."

Ms. Achtenberg said, "Poor Veronica. Those poor kids."

"You can't ignore me," Mr. Grum said. "You don't get to say who stays or goes in this house."

Before I could say, neither do you, Scott said, "Is there

anything else we can help you with, Mr. Grum?"

The gargantuan hulk pointed at each of us in turn. He gulped and blubbered, made inarticulate noises. Finally, he stormed out the door.

Ms. Achtenberg clicked it shut behind him. She came over to the desk, placed her coffee on it, and put her briefcase on the floor.

I pointed at the heaps of stuff on the floor. "Mr. Grum seems to be intent on making a mess." Scott and I bent down to pick up papers and paraphernalia. Achtenberg lent us a hand in cleaning up the Grum-induced chaos.

As we worked, she said, "He's a hell of a piece of work."

I said, "The whole family is nuts."

She scanned the mess Mr. Grum had created on the floor and said, "Veronica's father-in-law seems to have anger issues."

We picked up the larger intact pieces of junk and put them off to the side. The larger smashed pieces we deposited in the trash can. The smaller bits and pieces would need to be vacuumed. We placed the papers back on the desk.

Finished cleaning, Scott and I sat behind the desk. Achtenberg took a comfy chair on the opposite side. She said, "Veronica always talks about you, how close you are. You've been a big help to her over the years. She says you both are good guys."

I said, "Married into this family, she needed all the friends she could get."

She looked at Scott, "How's your shoulder?"

"Healing okay, thanks. The doctors have some hope."

"Good, and thank you for taking a stand for the working people in this state."

Scott said, "Just a link in the chain."

The stand she was referring to was Scott's activities on behalf of workers. Most professional athletes have unions and some even make statements supporting working people. Scott had issued statements, come to the state for rallies, and contributed substantial money to their causes. I'd joined him in many of these activities, but he's famous and I'm not, so his presence was significant and mine wasn't.

Scott's fame can be a pain in the ass. Even if this injury ended his career, he had what some said were already Hall of Fame numbers. Fans can be a nuisance. In public, usually a ball cap pulled low over the eyes and a pair of sunglasses disguised his identity from all but the most discerning. Our favorite restaurants helped by seating us as far from prying eyes as they could. Leaving huge tips didn't hurt either and quite often people are willing to go out of their way to please a star.

I said, "How long have you known Veronica?"

"We first knew each other at the University of Iowa. We've kept in touch over the years. She and I meet for coffee, not as often as we'd like. Maybe three or four times a year. I'd never met old man Grum until today. I'd only seen him at the wedding and that was years ago. This morning, she called you first?"

"Yeah. She called and we rushed up here. We arrived about dawn."

The door opened.

Twelve

Wednesday 9:21 A.M.

Veronica stepped in. The women saw each other and hurried into each other's arms.

When they unclenched, I asked, "How are the kids?"

Veronica hesitated. "I think. I guess." She dabbed at her eyes with a tissue she held crumpled in one hand. She shook her head. "Numb. We're all numb. I asked what they wanted to do. They want to go to their favorite pancake house to eat. They need to eat something. I'm going to take them to eat."

"Do you want us with you?" I asked.

"No. I think it should just be me. I want them to be able to talk if they want to. They're getting dressed. We'll leave in just a minute."

Achtenberg asked, "Just a couple things before you go."

My sister halted with her hand on the doorknob.

Achtenberg asked, "Do you have guns in the house?"

Veronica's hand flew to her throat. "The police told me he was shot."

"Yes. Did Edgar own a gun?"

Veronica's hand swept around the room taking in all the stuffed dead animals and lifeless representations of woodland critters. "For all this, he's got an arsenal. I made him keep them in a storage shed out in the back. I wouldn't let him have them in the house. It was the first fight after we got married. Then when we had kids, I made sure he had it double and triple locked. I was not going to have an accident with those things."

"You never touched them?"

"Never. I don't know what kinds he had. I didn't want to

know what he owned. I've never fired a gun."

Achtenberg said, "Good."

"Are they saying someone with one of Edgar's guns…?" She couldn't finish.

Achtenberg said, "I'm covering all the bases. I want to anticipate what the police might ask."

Veronica nodded. "I've got to get to the kids."

"Anything we can do here?" I asked.

She came over to the desk. "Yes, keep those people out of here. Before you showed up, Edgar's family had already been talking about the family Trust. About inheritance. About the will. Already talking about it! I hate them! I hate them! I hate them!" She was breathing almost as hard as her father-in-law. Ms. Achtenberg put a hand on Veronica's shoulder.

Veronica took a huge breath, calmed somewhat. "Their son is dead, and they're talking money. I'm going to need help fighting those people. Enid, can you go over our family papers with my brother and Scott? I know you can't be here every minute, but the more people on my side who know how this works the better."

Enid said, "I have your permission to talk to them freely?"

"Yes." She pointed to the closet. "Our family stuff is supposed to be in that room. I know I made Edgar get copies of all the family Trust documents. Even that was a fight. They accused me of trying to steal the family money. It was one of the few times Edgar stood up to them. He said as long as he was part of the family Trust, he should have copies of everything."

Achtenberg opened her briefcase and took out a one-inch-thick packet of paper and handed them to Veronica. "These are the documents from your file. I stopped at the office on the way here. This might save us some time. These are the documents I worked on for you and Edgar."

Veronica pointed to the closet and said, "Our copies must be in there with everything else." She handed me the stack of stuff Achtenberg had just given to her. Veronica continued, "That room is a mess and there doesn't seem to be any order to it. If you have the time now, I think it would be better if you go over your copies with them. Those people are worse than vultures who haven't fed in a month. I need allies." She hesitated. "What about the police? I can leave, can't I? With my kids? To go eat?"

Enid said, "Yes. If they ask, I'll explain where you are." In walked my mom and dad, Veronica's kids, several strangers, and Mr. and Mrs. Grum and her little dog, too.

Mom had several large boxes of pastries in her hands. Dad had two carrying trays with coffee with small packets of cream and sugar scattered among the coffee cups.

Mom and dad would know to bring food at a time like this.

THIRTEEN

Wednesday 9:32 A.M.

The kids looked dazed and confused. Patricia ran to her mother, grabbed her around the waist, glanced up at us, and then stuck a thumb in her mouth, a reversion in the face of unfathomable crisis. I didn't blame her. Would that such simple gestures could solve all of our problems.

Two of the strangers wore ill-fitting sports coats and sported not-very-concealed weapons. The tall one in the brown coat and pants demanded everybody's name. A third stranger wore a dark gray suit, with a pale yellow shirt, and a yellow tie with dark gray stripes.

The room began to seem crowded what with the cast bronze and iron beasts, whole stuffed dead critters, the heads of dead animals, and now the large herd of humans.

Achtenberg planted herself between the interlopers and the rest of us. One of the new guys towered over her. The other came to about her height. The tall one had demanded our names. Achtenberg said, "I'm Enid Achtenberg. Who are you and why should we give you our names?"

Good for her. This situation was out of control.

Mrs. Grum said, "Arrest them all."

An image of the Red Queen in Alice in Wonderland flashed through my mind, "Sentence first -- verdict afterwards." This was making less and less sense. Assumedly the new guys were cops, or were they private security personnel working for the Grums, or they were random people off the street who happened to be wearing guns?

The tall guy said, "I'm Detective Brendstin. This is Detective Adlow."

Achtenberg said, "I.D.s please."

I liked her.

They took out I.D.s and flashed them for a second, put them away.

Achtenberg held up a hand, "Again please, gentleman."

Brendstin looked like he was holding himself in from reaching out and throttling her. Adlow, much older than the taller detective, kept his eyes down. Maybe he was embarrassed and chagrined, which would be a new development among this crowd.

The third stranger in the black suit said, "I'm Albert Warner, the Grums' attorney." He handed Achtenberg his card. She didn't bother to look at it.

She waited a few beats as the detectives glanced at each other then dragged out their badges. Achtenberg actually examined the detectives' IDs, took out a pen and paper from her briefcase, and wrote down information from both badges. She didn't hurry. She didn't take her time. Just a professional doing a sensible job. I really liked her.

Mr. Grum reached to grab the paper she was writing on. She jerked it away.

An unchagrinned Mr. Grum said, "There's no need for this. My lawyer has been meeting with the police."

"Why?" Ms. Achtenberg asked. "Is he a suspect? Does he have information related to helping find the killer?"

Warner said, "I'm sure if we all just sit down and talk about this, we can work things out."

Ms. Achtenberg asked, "Work what out?"

An excellent question. What the hell was going on here?

Detective Brendstin said, "We need to question everybody about the murder." Maybe he was reasserting his need to control the situation. If he was supposed to be in charge, he wasn't doing a good job of it so far.

I said, "The children need to be protected from all this."

The three kids had clustered around Veronica. They stood silent and wide-eyed.

My mom said, "We'll take care of them." Mom's a brick. She and my dad ushered the kids into the hall. The three kids were very used to my mom and dad so the comfort level was sufficient to cause less disruption than might have been.

Veronica stepped into the hall with my mom and dad and the kids. Mr. and Mrs. Grum evinced no interest in their grandchildren.

Mr. Grum pointed at Scott and me. "These two don't belong here. They were out of control earlier. They have no status and no place."

Out of control? I was having a Kafkaesque moment, presented with a complete distortion of reality. It wasn't just his opinion. It was a complete misrepresentation of what had gone on.

Scott said, "Mr. Grum, why would you say something that was blatantly false and provably not true? Tom and I were both here. You have no witnesses."

Mrs. Grum spoke, "I was here. I heard and saw it all. Those two were out of control."

Scott, who always tried to see the best in people, just stood there with his mouth agape.

Enid Achtenberg said, "When I walked in, Mrs. Grum was not here. When I walked in, these two gentlemen," she pointed at us, "were calmly standing behind the large desk." She pointed at Mr. Grum, "He was breathing so hard and had turned such an awful color, I was seconds away from using my cell phone to summon paramedics."

Detective Brendstin asked, "Why would Mr. and Mrs. Grum claim such a thing if it were not true?"

Achtenberg said, "And at a time like this! I agree. It makes no sense. Maybe you should ask them since it is provably false."

Mr. Grum said, "These people don't belong here. Officers you need to do your duty."

This was getting nuttier every second.

The door to the hall opened. We heard Veronica telling the children in the hallway, "I'll be with you in just a few minutes. I have to talk to these detectives. Go with Grandma and Grandpa. We may have to stay here instead of go out." She thanked my mom and dad and returned to the room. Veronica stood to my left and slightly behind Scott, Achtenberg, and me.

Mr. Grum said, "We really need to get this settled and wrapped up as quickly as possible."

Achtenberg asked, "Have they arrested someone?"

Brendstin, the bigger detective, said, "No."

"Do you have a suspect?"

"No."

Mr. Warner said, "Do we really need to bother the family at a time like this?"

Not bother the family in a murder investigation? I began to get a feeling that I was lost in unreality, very much like Oz but with no charm, no magic, and no heroines or heroes.

Brendstin said, "We have some questions."

Achtenberg said, "What exactly do you need, detectives?"

Veronica took my hand.

The cops said, "We need statements from everyone."

Achtenberg said, "I am not an attorney for anyone here but Veronica Grum. Is she under arrest?"

"No."

"I understand you interrogated her earlier."

Brendstin said, "Yeah. We talked with her."

Achtenberg said, "Then that should be sufficient. She won't be talking to you any further. Certainly not until she has had time to confer with me."

Mr. Grum said, "We're trying to find out who killed my son."

Achtenberg said, "We all want to know that. We all also know that the most likely suspects in a murder are the family and acquaintances of the deceased. Now, I know what my client is going to do. She is going to be silent." She pointed at Scott and me. "These two gentlemen just arrived after being called by my client. They can't possibly add anything to your investigation."

Brendstin said, "We gotta talk to everybody."

Mr. Grum said, "We need to minimize any scandal. We have to all cooperate." He pointed at Achtenberg, "She has no official standing in this family. Who invited this lawyer here?"

Veronica spoke up, "I did. I will do precisely what she says."

Achtenberg put a hand on Veronica's hand. "In a few minutes my client is going to return to taking care of her children. I think those three youngsters have to be our major concern. They've just lost their father. Detectives?" She used a tone that dared them to disagree, more authority in it than all Charles Dudley Grum's bombast.

Mrs. Grum said, "We'll take the children to breakfast."

Veronica spoke immediately. "No, I want them here with me."

Mr. Grum said, "Well, really, you can't keep them away from us."

Mrs. Grum's voice rumbled. "Edgar is looking down at you from heaven. Would he like seeing you acting like this?"

Veronica began turning nearly as purple as her father-in-law had been a few minutes ago.

Achtenberg broke in. "My client will be making all the decisions regarding her family. Her decision is for them to be here with her. That should be sufficient for all involved." She glared at the Grums, then turned her stare on the detectives.

None of them raised any objections.

"We should all leave this room," Mr. Grum said.

Veronica said, "No, Tom and Scott are going to stay here." She placed her hands on her hips and glared at them. She was adamant and there was nothing they could do.

The Grums wanted us out, an excellent reason to stay. Their presence in the house was somewhat understandable. Their insistence on us leaving this room was totally suspicious. Their obvious connection with the police, beginning to be worrisome. Something was in this room they did not want us to see: a key to the murder, a key to the family's finances, a secret drug stash, the lost treasure of the Incas, one of the stuffed animals was secretly crammed with treasure, or hints to how they kept power and stole elections in Harrison County? I suppose I could speculate pointlessly and endlessly.

Veronica, Scott, and I stood stock still in the room. Achtenberg motioned to the cops and Warner, "Could I see you for a minute, in the hall? And maybe the Grums could wait in the living room." Her calm intransigence was met with grim acquiescence.

As they were leaving, Achtenberg turned to us, "Wait for me, please."

Warner and Achtenberg were talking a mile a minute as they pushed through the door.

When they were all gone, Veronica let out a sigh. "I've got to get to the kids."

"Mom and dad will handle them until it's time to go."

Veronica said, "We're staying here. I want the walls of my home around me, and who knows what my in-laws will try next."

"Good idea to stay," I said.

And if she'd decided to leave, I'd have said, "Good idea to go." Support for her was paramount, not choosing to believe I knew best about what she should do or say. If she wanted opinions, she'd ask.

Fourteen

Wednesday 9:58 A.M.

A few moments later Achtenberg returned. She, Veronica, Scott, and I ensconced ourselves in the dead-animal den.

Veronica said, "This is a nightmare."

Achtenberg said, "I'm sorry for how awful this has been for you."

Veronica turned to all of us. "I don't understand what is going on."

I said, "The cops are acting oddly. The attorney for the Grums consulted with the police about their investigation?"

Achtenberg nodded. "That's certainly the impression I got from all that."

Scott asked, "The Grums have that much power in this community?"

Achtenberg raised an eyebrow. "Are you kidding? Murder and politics in this county? They don't have "that much power" as you so quaintly put it. They have all the power."

Scott asked, "To actually cover up a murder, to direct a police investigation?"

Achtenberg said, "I talked to my one contact in the sheriff's department as I was driving over. He was terrified to talk to me. Terrified. Something is not right. All I got from him was that the murder happened at the campaign headquarters, and that it was a single gunshot to the head."

Veronica gasped.

I asked, "Do you want us to stop talking about this?"

Veronica wiped her tissue over her forehead, got another one from the box on the desk, pressed it to her face. When she finally looked at us, she said, "I just want to get through this. I want to know what is going on. Are you saying they...they...that sounds like an execution."

Achtenberg took her friend's hands. "When I was out in the hall with the cops they were oddly aggressive about your movements, Veronica. I mean, yeah, the wife is always a suspect, but there just seemed something off kilter about it to me. At the same time they seemed awfully deferential to the Grum family."

"Could they have enough influence to steer a murder investigation?" I asked.

Achtenberg said, "Yes."

Veronica said, "They wouldn't do that."

I wanted to shout, yes they would, don't you get it yet? What I did say was, "We need to examine every possibility. We don't want false accusations starting."

The thought struck me that maybe the family had started making accusations, had already tainted the cops, the investigation, or leaked bizarre nonsense to the media. I had no doubt they'd accuse Veronica if it served their interests.

Veronica stood up. "I have to get to the kids. I don't have much money."

I handed her all the cash in my wallet.

I said, "We found at least one bank that Edgar had funds in. The account had both your names on it." I dug out the statements we'd found from First State Bank of Harrison County. She glanced over them. I asked, "Do you have the check book for that, an ATM card?"

She shook her head.

"Scott and I will look for them."

Veronica put her hands to her face. "I can't handle any more of this. You guys handle all that money stuff, please. I've got to be with the kids." She stood up, squared her shoulders, marched to the door, opened it, paused, turned to us, and said, "I want the Grums out of my house."

"We'll help," I said.

Achtenberg said, "Let me handle it."

At the door, we met my mom and dad and the kids. Mom said, "We were just coming to see what was going on."

Veronica said, "We're for sure staying here."

I said, "We're going to invite the Grums to leave."

My mother said, "Good."

For her a very strong comment.

But when we got to the living room, all the Grums, their lawyer, and the detectives had departed. The same or similar lone cop car sat in the driveway.

Veronica, my mom and dad, and the kids headed to the kitchen.

Achtenberg, Scott, and I returned to the office.

Fifteen

Wednesday 10:00 A.M.

The three of us sat and looked at each other for a moment.

I said, "This is screwed up."

Achtenberg said, "If I know the Grums, it's going to get worse." She shook her head. "I'll never know what Veronica saw in him."

I said, "I completely agree. She must have complained about him."

"Mostly she defended him. When we had coffee, she'd say that he rebelled against the family. That he wasn't like them. That he wanted to get out from under them."

I added, "I never saw any evidence of that."

"Nor did I." Achtenberg sighed. "They met because of me. I will always regret that."

"How'd that come about?" I asked.

"A bunch of us friends were going out. Veronica and the rest of us were in The Evil Hawkeye bar in Iowa City. One of the women had a blind date. Turned out to be Edgar. She saw him for what he was and was trying to ditch him. Veronica and he met. And the rest is misery. And yes, I know, she loved him." Another sigh.

I said, "Well, really, you weren't directly at fault."

"For the misery of her life, even a glancing sort of responsibility is enough for guilt." She shrugged. "Love. Who knew?"

We both nodded. Scott handed out napkins and small slices of Kringle to Enid and me and took one for himself. It was pecan, the best kind. I swallowed it in two bites. Mom had remembered to pick up the Kringle from Racine. Count on mom to get the best pastry ever invented at a time like this. I took a sip of coffee from one of the cups mom and dad had brought in earlier. I felt I needed both caffeine and sugar at that moment.

Scott asked, "What did you mean, if I know the Grums?"

She said, "You know them, right?"

Scott and I gave summaries of what we knew about their role in the county.

After we finished, Achtenberg said, "That's the Veronica version, mostly true. There's the private, rumored version."

"What's that?"

"Vileness through the decades, the kind that doesn't make headlines. For example in the fifties and early sixties the Grum family and their cronies led the fight to keep this county white, and if not all-white, then very segregated. Another example, in Chicago, the Democrats went to Daley for inside help. In Harrison County the Republicans went to the Grums for the same thing. People around the Daleys might go to jail, might be convicted, but the Daleys were never indicted, arrested. Same with the Grums. They always kept their noses clean. Politicians were bought off, deals were made, problems swept under the carpet, but I have no specifics. Certainly no proof of criminally indictable activity. If anybody does, I've never heard of it."

Scott said, "I've read a number of history books on the Civil Rights movement in the fifties and sixties. None of them mentions marches or demonstrations here that I remember."

As we talked I offered more Kringle around. Enid declined. Scott and I took more. You had to scarf down Kringle when you got the chance. You never knew when you might be facing your last chance at Kringle.

Achtenberg said, "My dear, it was then, and it is still going on. Nowadays the Grums try to be more circumspect. They work very quietly, deviously – a little zoning change here, a required lot size law there. Federal money comes in for high-density development, but poof, the money disappears. An Interstate highway moves a few miles this way or that and somehow where it goes or doesn't go always seems to redound to the Grums' benefit or help with their racist inclinations."

Scott said, "And they get away with this?"

"The most recent lawsuit against a perceived racist move by the County board was filed five years ago. It will probably be going on for at least five more years. They fought change then. They fight change now. Doesn't mean it doesn't come. Just makes it harder."

We spent half an hour going through Veronica's papers and the family Trust documents we'd found so far and devouring the rest of the Kringle and coffee. We agreed that after Scott and I sorted the rest of the mass of papers in the closet, we'd go over what we found with both her and Veronica. When we were finished, Achtenberg nodded in satisfaction. "As far as I can tell, Veronica should be okay. If this copy of the Trust is up to date, Veronica does inherit some, but a great deal more passes directly to the kids."

"The kids get that kind of money? Patricia is only six."

Each child got over five million dollars.

"No, Veronica is the trustee in conjunction with Mrs. Grum."

"Like equal voting stock?" Scott asked.

"Sort of. It's not clear who has the final decision. Veronica could be in some trouble, but I don't think a lot."

"We found some insurance policies. There could be more. Would Veronica get that money?"

"If she's the beneficiary."

She was.

"How about bank accounts?" I asked.

"Depends whose name is on the accounts."

"I don't know if we found all the policies or all the accounts."

"Keep looking. The Trust is clear on a lot of the contents. You saw the list. For instance, a quick glance shows that most of the sculptures in this room are in the Trust, but not the boxes of stuff in that closet. When you find more information on all the accounts, the sources of income, and the deed for the house or documents on it, we'll know more."

I pointed at the grizzly. "That's a family heirloom?"

"The document we do have is incredibly specific about what belongs to whom, but it's ten years old. How much of the money is Edgar's? If his name is on it, and it is not named in the family Trust, it's now Veronica's. His will is clear. This house and land are his. None of the money and property in the family Trust have any connection to Veronica. Just her kids."

"So they can't throw her out?"

"No."

"But she's going to need income to pay the bills, the mortgage."

"Look carefully at the investments you found. Are they in the Grum Family Trust or in Edgar's name?"

"We'll sort it out," Scott said.

Achtenberg stood up, picked up her purse and briefcase. She said, "Good. I trust you guys. Meanwhile, I'll see if I can find out what the police are doing. I'll be back this evening."

Sixteen

Wednesday 11:00 A.M.

Scott and I spent the next hour sorting papers. We talked some at first. One of the first things I said was, "What was that not our "blood" crap?"

"Sounds mostly like they're trying to protect their money, and it's an easy shorthand for hating a relative or two."

A lot of the work was mindless, really, especially once we had a system going. At first often, but then less so, we'd consult with each other about the placement of a particular item.

Edgar's bank records indicated he had numerous accounts in a bunch of different banks, some of them with addresses in the Cayman Islands. I took a sheaf of statements from one bank and showed them to Scott.

We paged through six months of them from one bank. At the end, I said, "I don't get these. Where did he get the deposits to his accounts if he had such lousy jobs? If they were electronically deposited, there'd have been records. If he was depositing them with cash, why and where and who was he dealing with in that much hard cash? Why aren't cops looking through his financials?"

Scott said, "Somebody must know something about them, although Veronica says she doesn't."

"It could also be as innocent as him having investments that gave him regular interest or capital gains payments." I fanned the stack of bank records. "These don't say where the money came from, just that it existed."

"Do we care where it came from?"

"I don't unless it has some effect on Veronica."

Scott swept his hands around at all the papers. "Makes you think."

"About what?"

"Death. What it will be like when we're old. When we're sitting on rocking chairs on a porch waiting for the sun to set. When we die. I don't know if I'd want to live without you."

I got misty eyed. I walked over to his side of the desk and pulled him close. I said, "It'll be a long time before we're sitting on rockers on a porch at the Old Gay People's home."

"Forever with you sounds good."

"Sounds perfect to me."

We embraced. His warmth and strength were always a joy to me. His smell was intoxicating.

Then back to work, box after box, mounds of papers getting higher and higher.

Maybe the saddest thing I found was in the bottom box in the front on the farthest right of the closet. It contained papers and memorabilia from Edgar's childhood: birth certificate, report cards, class photos, Valentines received, high school diploma, letters of recommendation to colleges. In second grade he'd won third prize in a spelling bee contest. The most consistent thing in his report cards were the checks in the sections, Does Not Work and Play Well With Others. Some things never change.

I said, "This is sad."

Scott came over and looked.

I said, "This is it? This is the sum total of the honors he received?"

"You don't have to win a lot of honors to be a good person. The vast majority of teams don't win the championship."

"I know that, but the high point of your life is in second grade? And that was third place?"

"Maybe there's more."

"I hope so." I pulled more memorabilia out of the box. One was a certificate for third place in the county checker championship when he was in sixth grade. I said, "This is just sad more in kind of a nostalgic way rather than a you-didn't-win-a-championship way."

"Well he married Veronica. That had to be a good thing."

"That's true. I wonder where the wedding stuff is. Or probably Veronica has that somewhere."

Seventeen

Wednesday 11:10 A.M.

Scott and I took a break from sorting papers. We found the rest of the family in the kitchen. The two boys sat at the table with electronic game devices in their hands. Patricia sat in my mom's arms. They were discussing dolls and flowers and dresses. Dad was washing dishes while Veronica was wiping and cleaning.

The phone on the kitchen counter rang. The Caller ID said it was the gate keeper. I answered. He said, "I've got five more deliveries. I can't keep all this stuff here."

I asked, "What deliveries?"

"Food, flowers, gift baskets. Mr. Grum said to hold them here. I don't have room for all this."

"Can you bring them to the house."

"All of them?"

"How many are there?"

"A bunch. They've been arriving for a couple hours. People wanted to stop in too, but Mr. Grum said not to let them in. I think they were Mrs. Veronica Grum's friends."

I said, "Mr. Grum is no longer here. He was never in charge. I am. Bring them on up. If you want, I'll come down and help you with them."

If they were friends of Veronica bearing gifts, I thought they might bring her some comfort. If she didn't want visitors or the gifts, we'd keep them out. It was certainly not Mr. Grum's decision to make.

I put my hand over the receiver. "Your friends have been stopping by. Bringing food, gifts. Do you want them to come to the house?"

She thought for only a second or two. "Yes, having people around will help, people I know and who are friends."

She grabbed a paper towel and dabbed her eyes. So much for Grum's isolationist's nonsense. I told the gate keeper Veronica's wishes.

Scott and I met the guy at the door five minutes later. He had a van full of gift baskets, flowers, even two casseroles. We stored the food in the fridge and the other stuff on the counters. The kitchen had a twelve-foot-by-three-foot island in the center.

Scott collected cards and names and began a list. Scott would remember that Veronica would need these if she wanted to send thank you notes.

EIGHTEEN

Wednesday 12:02 P.M.

People, casseroles, and condolences began to accumulate. A few of the visitors brought their kids, which turned out to be good. They knew Veronica's children and could help keep them occupied without constant, direct adult supervision.

Sometimes they arrived without benefit of security checks. I learned these were from the neighborhood.

Scott and I went back to paper sorting. About an hour later I was on a bathroom break. The living room and kitchen were filled with men and women bustling about organizing, eating, drinking, cleaning, or comforting Veronica. At least one Grum cousin, aunt, uncle, or daughter-in-law that I knew was in there with them.

I ran into Azure Grum in the hall. We exchanged sympathetic greetings. Azure was the one at the wedding who spilled the beans about who the minion had been sent from to try and stop Scott and me from dancing. While talking with her at the wedding, she'd given me all kinds of fairly useless and perfectly nasty gossip about the Grums.

Azure was short and thin. She'd married into the family so she wasn't in imminent danger from the Grum family fat curse. She wore a white sweater over a long-sleeve, gauzy-white summer blouse, and baggy jeans.

I said, "Thank you for coming over in the middle of the night."

"Thankfully the kids didn't wake up. I'm always willing to help Veronica." She beckoned me down the hall out of ear shot of the others. She said, "I feel so sorry for Veronica. She had it tough in this family."

"How so?"

She looked back toward the kitchen, nodded toward a room nearby. We entered a room which was a mini-movie theater with a wide screen at one end, large comfy chairs facing it in the middle. The shag rug was green and the walls painted gold. The plush velvet covered chairs were in plaid patterns of green and gold. Heavily curtained sliding glass doors led outside. Yes, the curtains were green and gold.

The room had a Green Bay Packer shrine on the wall opposite the screen. The pictures went back to the days of Curly Lambeau and George Whitney Calhoun and the founding of the team, plus photos and/or portraits of all the team's quarterbacks from Norm Barry to Aaron Rodgers. I knew this because my nephew, Gerald, their middle child, had spent one long hour explaining it to me while Veronica, he, and I had been waiting for Edgar before we could leave for a family outing.

That was another thing about Edgar. The world ran on his time, and be damned to the rest of you.

I suppose I would have been more sympathetic if his time was being used to perform emergency brain surgery on widows and orphans from war torn countries. If anyone had dared to put him remotely close to a position of power, he would be more likely to have started the war.

The sad reality was the family could be sitting in the SUV ready to leave for something, but Edgar might decide that moment was time to refold the towels in the linen closet. The rest waited until he was done with this easily postpone-able activity.

Azure and I entered, took seats. She carried a small purse in one hand and a glass of orange juice in the other. She held it up to me. "You want a mimosa?"

I declined.

She said, "Hell of a thing."

"Murder is that."

"Can you imagine? Murder! In this family! They won't be able to hush this one up."

"This one? There've been others?"

"This family hushes everything up. Everything. From simple stuff, like how old you are or who was pregnant before they were married, to political scandals. In the county and in the state for that matter."

"Edgar had that kind of power?"

She gave a short laugh and looked toward the doorway that led back to the kitchen where the dim murmur of voices continued unabated.

She took a sip from her drink and leaned toward me. "I shouldn't tell you this."

"It's okay if you don't."

"Edgar didn't have that kind of power. His family does. Has and always will. Edgar was a screw up." She looked toward the doorway again. I couldn't imagine they could hear us, but I could imagine the paranoia the Grums could spread. She nodded toward the sliding glass door. "Let's step outside." Outside she put her purse and drink down on a glass-topped table.

From our vantage point we could see that the backyard contained a mini-skateboard park, a thirty-by-thirty flagstone patio, with the biggest damn outdoor grill set up I'd ever seen, and an in-ground pool currently covered in winter plastic.

She pulled out a cigarette and matches from the small purse and asked, "You mind?"

"Your lungs."

She lit the cigarette and blew the smoke away from us. She added pollution to a cool early afternoon with bright blue skies. It was warm if you stood in the sun.

She asked, "Have they tried praying at you yet?"

"Not directly."

"They're just praying fools. Those people pray at the drop of a sin. They use prayer as a weapon. If you are not praying, you are somehow less than them."

"They probably think Scott and I are beyond redemption."

She said, "Well, the truth is, this whole family is screwed up."

"I've noticed some oddities."

"I married into it, like Veronica. I've always felt sorry for her. I'm a cousin-in-law. These folks are loony birds. My husband is sane. We have as little contact with the rest of them as possible. He got out. He moved to Milwaukee and opened a coffee shop near the U of W campus in Milwaukee."

"Not a sane one among the others?"

"Just Veronica. She was a saint. Where she got that kind of patience, I'll never know. All the Grum sisters and sisters-in-law hate each other. You should see them at big holiday events. Cat fights. Bitch fights. Punches and hair pulled and pushes into pools. It's fun in a sick way, if you're at a distance." She took a puff on her cigarette. "And the summer reunion!"

"Reunion?"

"Every summer, the whole goddamn family gets together at some huge farm in northern Wisconsin. Veronica avoided the other in-laws. She'd only go if she knew I was going to be there. When we did attend, we hid in the woods or stood as far in the back away from them as we could."

"I only saw them once all together at Edgar and Veronica's wedding."

"That was a hell of a scene."

"Does Mrs. Grum ever smile?" I asked."Tell a joke? Let her hair down? Not that she has to. She certainly does not have to conform her life to my standards, but she just looks so unhappy every time I've seen here. And I don't think I'm the cause of that effect. What exactly is she waiting to approve of? Or is there nothing that would appease her? Does she ever laugh at a joke?"

"Mostly I've seen her reign in that Buddha-like silence. She doesn't even cuddle or coo to that stupid dog. The poor thing might just as well be a stuffed creature as a breathing animal."

"Why don't any of them rebel or get out?"

"Too stupid? Too desperate?"

"Desperate for what?"

She took a slug or her mimosa. "Money? Inheritance? The family Trust is supposedly this convoluted thing that you only inherit if you suck up to mommy and daddy dearest on alternate Tuesdays in all the months that have an r in them."

"It's that nuts?"

"My husband tried to explain the Trust to me once. I got a headache, and he didn't know all the real down and dirty details. I'm not sure who does. Except maybe Warner, their attorney. He makes my skin crawl. I've never seen anyone whose eyebrows stick out so far, not outside of the movies. He must have them waxed."

"I only met him briefly. Veronica's lawyer dealt with him."

"Achtenberg? I know her. She's good."

By now I knew some of the details of the Trust but decided revealing them to her was not my choice to make.

"So Edgar was stuck."

"I'm not sure he ever wanted to become unstuck, but he didn't have a lot of choice. The man couldn't hold a job."

"But why did he have to work if he had all this family Trust money?"

"He was stupid? He was desperate? He was afraid they'd cut him off? That last is the most likely. I do know the longest he ever worked one place was seven months."

"I thought he started as a clerk in the family law office."

"Sort of. Depends on which version of the truth you want to believe."

"Version?"

"Either he left because he was declaring his independence from the family." She puffed on her cigarette. "Or he was an incompetent boob who couldn't even manage such a low stress job. Or neither. Edgar and the truth were not good friends.

Maybe he tried to get out, sort of."

"How's that?"

"He always had deals. Investment deals. Stupid deals. Million dollar stock for a penny or penny stocks for a million. Some stupid shit. Once he wanted my husband to put ten thousand dollars into some land/condo scam in Texas."

"Your husband was going to say yes?"

"I had to put my foot down. Honestly! Why people couldn't see his nonsense, I have no idea."

"People always lost money?"

"I never heard of one that made money. Then there were rumors of pyramid schemes, like Bernie Madoff."

"Did he do actual criminal things?"

She said, "I never saw proof, no. He just seemed like such a sleaze when it came to money, especially other people's money."

"Veronica didn't see all this?"

"She's your sister. What did she tell you?"

"Not much."

"Maybe independence sort of depends on a pay check, doesn't it?"

"Was he totally dependent on his family for money?"

"That I don't know."

"We found a ton of coupons among some things Veronica asked us to go through. He was that broke he needed to clip coupons?"

"He'd never starve with mommy and daddy around. What he needed to do for day to day basics, I'm not so sure."

"It sounds like an awful life."

"Depends on your perspective. Remember, besides money, the family has pull and power. He only has his current job because of the family's influence." With the toe of her shoe, she stubbed out her cigarette on the flagstones then continued, "At any rate, most recently he'd signed on to help with the Republican campaign to destroy democracy in Wisconsin. That recall campaign needed as many workers as they could get. The public hates all of the Grums."

"Then how do they have so much power?"

"The Grums always believe that they can get anything they want and with all the money they've got, they aren't far wrong. It's never 'we were wrong', it's 'we didn't get our message across'. Translation, we didn't spend enough money on slick advertising geared to the rubes to get them to buy our snake oil. This time I think they were scared. Even with all that cash advantage over the opposition, they were working like mad."

I'd seen the attempt to push idiot ideas concealed by false advertising in zillions of Republican campaigns. Never, ever tell the truth about how they were going to screw the American people. I had one friend of mine, a die-hard ideologue, who said that not telling the truth was an important part of their tactics. He claimed they knew people would never vote for them if they knew the truth: just wave the flag, hate the homosexuals, praise god, and pass the ammunition. Unfortunately, that still worked.

"What did he do for the campaign?"

She lit another cigarette, took a long pull on it, stared back toward the rest of the house, then leaned toward me. "That family was in charge of making sure there were enough votes to keep that loon Mary Mallon in office."

"They have that kind of power?"

"Oh, yes, my dear, they do. You've heard the story?"

"About the election?"

"Oh, yeah. The Grums and their rich buddies had it settled. By hook, and if need be, most definitely by crook, they'd have enough votes. If it was close, the Democrat would for sure lose. Votes would be found. They'd wait until all the tallies were in from certain precincts in Milwaukee County, Madison, and any other Democratic stronghold. Then they'd release their final votes or find final votes."

"How?"

"You remember Mayor Daley in Chicago in 1960?"

"Sure."

"Same thing."

I'd heard about the accusations for years and even read up on them somewhat, that Daley had stolen the election for Kennedy in Illinois in 1960. The story was Daley had released his last precincts after the final Republican precincts from downstate had been released. I'd also heard another version, that Daley had learned his lesson from those very same downstate repubs who'd done the same thing for years - wait for Chicago to report and then release their precincts with, amazingly enough, just enough votes to overcome Chicago's advantage.

The truth about 1960? There was litigation for years. Repubs had a history of trying to delegitimize any Democrat and his or her win. No matter how wild the accusation, the argument back was always that the Democrats had always done the same thing, the usual false equivalency argument.

The key was the election had to be close. A landslide either way made these shenanigans moot, and the recall election couldn't be closer. When I'd checked on the Internet this morning, accusations of chicanery, illegality, and deception on both sides flew back and forth.

She said, "Orders had gone out from the highest level. Win this one or else."

"Who's the "highest level"?"

"Not the Grums."

"Not?"

"They're local. Important if you consider Harrison County important. The Grums look down on everyone around here but usually the Grums know their place in the pecking order that is wealth in the Republican party and this country."

"But the results I saw on the Internet an hour or so ago said the Democrat was ahead by ten votes."

She tittered, patted my arm with one hand, took a puff on her cigarette, smiled, and said, "I'd say by about the middle of this afternoon, they'll announce thousands of found votes."

I feared she was right. "You know this for a fact?"

"I know this county. I know Republican politics in this state. If Governor Mallon doesn't screw it up, they might pull it off. In a worldwide stupidity contest, I'm not sure which of them would win, Governor Mallon or Edgar. You know they dated?"

"Recently?"

"Edgar may have been many things, but a philanderer he was not. At least I never heard. This was years ago. When he was in college."

"Isn't she a lot older?"

"And he was a grossly fat pig. Your point?"

"They were in love?"

"She was certainly in love with the Grum money. With him?" She shrugged. "She broke up with him long ago. Eventually she married someone from a family even richer than the Grum's, a first cousin of the Ducharmés. She won her first county-wide office not long after that unholy union. And now, poof, years later, the booby prize, Governor of Wisconsin. Or as we call it, doing the bidding of the rich."

I'd heard of the Ducharmés. They were among the billionaire oligarchs determined to make sure laws were passed and tax breaks were given in local, state, and federal legislatures to make themselves and their cronies even more wealthy billionaire oligarchs.

"How does stealing the election involve Edgar?"

"He's a screw up. You know how some people, especially an awkward teenager, can't seem to walk across a room without tripping over their own feet?"

"Yeah."

"Edgar turned awkward and inept into a lifestyle."

I understood awkward and inept and had some sympathy for it. Unfortunately, I was not immune myself, although Scott was usually pretty indulgent of my gaffes. Plus, I taught teenagers, most of them the very definition of awkward.

"But how does him being awkward and inept lead to him screwing up stealing the election?"

"Idiotic, unfounded, mad rumors have been flying around this county. Everybody knows the election is rigged for the Grums. If there's any hitch, it'll be because of Edgar. Trust me. Soon they'll report enough votes for the Governor to win." She put out her cigarette and pulled out another one and lit it.

I'm glad I wasn't her lungs. She continued. "All I know is what I heard through the family grapevine. He worked in that campaign. I heard he bragged that they'd win no matter what." Another shrug. "If things go wrong, it has to be his fault. Even though he's dead, it still could be. Although they'll hide their cheating and any screw up."

"The newspapers don't investigate?"

"They either own the local papers or intimidate them."

"How do you intimidate a newspaper?"

"Whoever has the most money wins. You know that."

All too true. I asked, "What about reporters from Milwaukee, or nationwide?"

"They get here and all they see are cows grazing peacefully in the fields."

"If it goes wrong, and it's Edgar's fault, doesn't that mean they'd have had to give him something important to do?"

"Who knows? The family was nuts. Daddy just indulged him constantly."

"You really think they'll steal it?"

"Don't you?" She took a gulp of her drink. "I have no proof and no direct knowledge, but you'll see. Although, you do know there were problems for the campaign?"

I said, "We read that it was vicious and both sides spent tons of money."

"They may have both spent money, but the Governor's side had tons more of it to spend. A reporter who had infiltrated the campaign was found dead. There were rumors of suicide and/or murder."

I said, "There's a doubt it was suicide? The Grums are powerful enough to make a reporter disappear? They can cover up a murder or a suicide?"

"Paranoia runs deep on both sides. Maybe the reporter knew too much or someone thought he did, which is just as deadly. The Grum motto is, if necessary and possible, crush any threat."

I said, "This whole thing sounds insane."

She said, "Welcome to my world. And remember, it's not insane to them. It's business as usual to them. And as for cover-ups, you'd think they'd want to find out who killed their own son."

I asked, "Would they kill their own son because he screwed up stealing an election?"

She paused several moments to think, took a puff on her cigarette, took another drink, finally shook her head. "They are awful and vile, but I don't think they're that awful and vile. I don't want to think they are that rotten." She shuddered. "No, Edgar was a screw up, but murder?"

I found this tough to believe, too, even of desperate and despicable repubs. I looked out at the bright morning, listened to birds chirping, felt the soft wind on my face.

She continued, "Maybe he screwed up stealing it. Maybe he screwed up covering it up. Remember, the family doesn't control the recall election. They're doing bidding."

"They'd do the bidding of someone who told them to kill their own son?"

She looked doubtful. "They're hateful. Exactly how hateful I've never dared try to quantify. I don't think they'd actually pull the trigger. Or order it pulled. But if someone behind them was threatened, that person certainly would."

"Rumors through the family grapevine, not proof?"

"No, not proof. I can see. I can listen. I can speculate. It's mostly crap in this family." She blew out a lungful of smoke. "Hell, I don't know. They're so nuts and so desperate, who knows what they're capable of. I'm here to support Veronica. I better get back."

"Why'd you tell me all this?"

Instead of putting her cigarette out on the flagstones, as she had done before, she mashed it into the ashtray with short, sharp jabs for emphasis. She leaned close and spoke with an intensity I knew the Grums could inspire. "I hate this family. All of them. Except Veronica. That old witch, old lady Grum, tried to stop my marriage. To her nephew! A nephew! What business was it of hers? She is evil incarnate. Talk to anybody who knew them."

"Anybody specific?"

"Not in the immediate family. On the periphery. Those who still have a grasp on reality."

She stood up and walked to the door, turned back as she opened it. "Trust no one in this family. No one."

"Including you?"

She left.

Nineteen

Wednesday 2:00 P.M.

After finishing with Azure, I was in the kitchen getting a drink of water. My younger brother, Darryl, rushed into the room. "You guys have gotta see this."

"What?"

"On television. Hurry. The Governor is announcing they found eleven thousand more votes in Harrison County."

On the flat screen TV in the living room, Governor Mary Mallon stood behind a bank of microphones. A squib at the bottom informed us that this was breaking news. Mr. and Mrs. Grum, Warner the lawyer, and a herd of other people I didn't know clustered around her in the background. The looks on the faces of the assemblage struck me very much like that of vermin being exposed to the light.

They were in a room with a row of American flags in front of blond wood paneling. Mallon's voice sounded a screech or two higher than the wicked witch of the west. She was saying, "I have complete confidence in the Wisconsin electoral system and complete confidence in the honesty of the election officials in Harrison County."

Mrs. Grum stepped forward. She clutched the poor damn dog, which seemed to be attempting to cower between her gargantuan breast and right armpit. Did she have no sense to leave the thing at home? Mrs. Grum said, "The vote count was wrong by eleven thousand votes because I accidentally tapped the wrong key on the computer when I was entering totals. That's all it was, a simple human error."

Mr. Grum shot forward, "We are in the middle of a family tragedy. We won't be taking any questions. I'm sure the police investigating our son's death are questioning the violent elements in those who have been in the streets trying to destroy our elected officials."

I shook my head. This vilification of the teachers protesting cutbacks was another attempt by the right to shut down the First Amendment rights of everyone who disagreed with them.

I remembered the rush to judgment after the sad events that had occurred in Columbine, and the way the right had jumped on incorrect information, then never made any attempt to engage on the issues that had caused the tragedy in the first place. Anyone who spoke against them was instantly vilified in their attempt to destroy, hurt, defile, or maim their opposition.

At least there was no mention of suspicion against Veronica in Edgar's death, yet.

Governor Mallon immediately stepped back in front of the microphones. "We all feel for the Grums' tragic loss and understand how this tragedy could have triggered a simple mistake." She paused a moment while the Grums shuffled off. When they were gone, she resumed, "We'll have people here to explain the voting procedures and processes."

A unseen reporter shouted, "What about the murder of the reporter, Zachary Ross?"

Mary Mallon smiled just like the villain right before she injected the deadly poison into her helpless victim. She said, "Those questions need to be addressed to the police."

More reporters shouted questions.

Mallon's smile got wider, the alligator just before it snapped its jaws shut. "You people are out of control. This press conference is over." She turned and marched away. The others behind her followed.

The screen cut to a newsroom. The commentators on the local Milwaukee station asked each other all kinds of questions. They already had a guest spokesperson on who was from Mallon's staff. Freshly scrubbed, perfect teeth, and obnoxiously blond, she violently defended the Grums. She prefaced each of her comments with the caveat, "This is such a terrible time for the

Grums. We need to remember common decency and not subject them to an inquisition after Mrs. Grum has already admitted her mistake. The voters have spoken, the recall was defeated, and the opposition needs to get over itself."

Sitting next to her was an unkempt schlub, hair awry, teeth badly aligned who viciously attacked the Grums. Could a media outlet be more blatantly obvious in its attempt to give a visual that helped their side? He agreed that this was a terrible time for the Grums and that they deserved sympathy for their loss, but said, "At the same time we must get to the bottom of this vote count irregularity. The Republicans in Harrison County need to get a spokesperson out here who can answer a few basic questions about how the votes were tallied and how Mrs. Grum could have made such a colossal mistake so easily."

Twenty

Wednesday 2:07 P.M.

Scott, Mom, Dad, and Veronica entered the room. Veronica said, "Can you guys take care of the kids? Mom and dad are going with me to the funeral parlor." Her clutch on our mom was very similar to the way Patricia had clutched onto her. "We'll be back in an hour or so. I've got a million things to do. I tried to make a list. I've got to call the cleaning service, and a caterer for food after the funeral." She handed me the list.

"You don't want to do it at a restaurant or the church?"

"Definitely not a church and no restaurant. I want to be in my own home. The kids will feel better here. I'll feel better here. If it's in my home, it will feel like the Grums have less control."

I promised to get started on the calls. Veronica, mom, and dad headed for the funeral home.

Scott told me he watched the press conference streaming live on the Internet in the office. He left for the grocery store with the kids. He has a magic touch with children. I don't know if it's his fame, or maybe how tall he is, or his aura of gentle, firm command, but whatever it is, he has a natural affinity for putting children at ease. It sure worked with Veronica's kids.

My brothers Lionel and Darryl stayed in charge of the steady stream of people and food. A few politicians were introduced to me. I didn't recognize them or their names. I spent some time in the office making calls. When I finished them, I began setting up a spread sheet on the computer based on the financial data we'd found so far. I also dug back into the mess. We were barely a third of the way through with the boxes.

What I really wanted was a nap. But I was more worried about Veronica than I was my lack of sleep.

Scott walked in about three.

“The kids okay?” I asked.

“Holding together as best as possible. After we got back from the store, I set them up in the movie theater room watching a movie. We’ve got enough groceries for the moment. You want me to help you in here or go help Lionel and Darryl? There’s people starting to show up again.”

“I’m working on doing a computer summary of the balances of all the different accounts I’ve been able to find so far.” I showed him the screen.

He glanced at the columns of names of businesses and numbers. Doing the numbers required clear logic and organization not a lot of math skills. For that I had a calculator. Putting things in categories and time order seemed to fall naturally.

I said, “I’ve got a lot more of this to do. Darryl and Lionel are out there on their own.”

“I’ll check on the kids then go help them.”

I told him the news I got from Azure Grum.

Scott said, “Edgar was an incompetent shit. Stop the presses.”

“Somebody’s got to fill that role in society. Better him than us.” Scott left.

Twenty-one

Wednesday 3:30 P.M.

I took a break from the office and joined Scott on duty at the front door. "Everything okay?" I asked.

He nodded. The bells chimed, and Scott opened the door to a tall, slender man with hair going slightly gray at the temples. I ushered him into the living room.

He stuck out his hand. "I'm Harold Avery." Scott introduced me.

Avery said, "You're the baseball player married to Veronica's brother." He looked at both of us. "I remember all the headlines when you got married. Congratulations, that takes balls."

What do you say to that kind of thing? I'm glad you approve? As if I cared if he approved or existed. I said, "Thanks."

He glanced toward the rest of the house and lowered his voice. "I was told Veronica was near the point of a breakdown. I'm her physician, her gynecologist."

Breakdown? What the hell was going on here.

I said, "She's at the funeral home making the arrangements. She's upset and grieving as anyone would be at a time like this, and I'm not a physician, but I don't think she's near a breakdown. Who told you she was near a breakdown?"

"Mr. Grum called."

"I'm not sure Mr. Grum is hitting on all his reality cylinders."

He lowered his voice, "You got that right."

I said, "You know the family?"

He looked toward the kitchen, where intermixed with genuine well-wishers were various Grums. He glanced around and nodded his head toward the outdoors. "Let's step outside."

We walked out the front door and to a side yard. We sat in the gazebo. We could still see the front door and who came and left. Plus we had a partial view of the mini-skateboard park, the backyard shed, and the covered out-door pool. The afternoon was cool and pleasant.

He said, "Edgar hated his family."

I said, "I didn't know him that well."

"We grew up together. The Grums live on the other side of this subdivision. My family lived next to them. I went to school with him for twelve years. We were best friends. His parents and my parents did a lot of social events together with that stupid woman's social club."

"Why is it stupid?" Scott asked.

"Best example? As kids both families would go to flower shows. Either his mom or mine were the head of the Women's Heritage Society. It was one of their biggest fundraisers of the year. Still is. We were so bored."

"But you were Edgar's friend," Scott said.

"For my part. When we were kids. Nowadays, not so much."

"Any particular reason for that?" I asked.

"Yeah. Edgar was a jerk. You don't always see that as clearly when you're ten as when you're twenty. The real problem is the Grums are pigs. All of them." He shook his head. "His and my parents are still best friends. Both families have lived around here since before the Civil War. There were some intermarriages way back when. He and I are very distant cousins so I can't really avoid Edgar."

"If you don't mind my asking, was there one particular incident that ended the friendship?"

"We were best friends. 'Were' is the operative word. The major break came when I went to med school at John Hopkins. There wasn't a fight or anything. Calls didn't get made." He sighed. "Friendships end, but we hung out together all through grade school. I was even his roommate in college freshman year for a while." He glanced around the yard. A man and a woman I didn't know were knocking at the front door. Another car was pulling up. No one was remotely close to being in hearing distance.

I thought this was strange - as if we were members of the underground in 1942 Paris meeting in Pierre's at the third pillar from the left, a cigarette dangling from one side of our mouths, speaking in harsh whispers, a waitress with a stiletto concealed in her bra. What did these people think was going to happen if they spoke the truth out loud? Then again, Edgar had been murdered so who knew what dangers lurked in these suburban Republican hearts?

"Did Veronica know you and he were once buddies?"

"I like Veronica. She is a saint to be married to him. We never discussed her marriage. She came to me for her once-a-year checkups. I was her doctor for the babies. As far as I could tell she was happy with him. Who was I to dump on her marriage?"

"Did he get along with his family?"

"Depended on the day, week, month, year. Sometimes he'd be angry with them. Sometimes he'd be running to them for money or protection. He did it when we were kids. My parents told me he did it as an adult."

"What did he get angry about?"

"You know he was the youngest?"

"Yeah."

"Everybody thought he was a yutz and a fuckup."

"Was he?"

"Pretty much, but who likes it when your family tells you that?"

"His friends didn't?"

"If he had friends, they were friends with his money, not with him. Or friends who wanted to be close to his family and their money. Governor Mallon is an excellent example of that."

"How so?" I asked.

He leaned back in the uncomfortable white wrought-iron bench.

"They dated in college. She was a grasping pseudo-intellectual back then. Hasn't changed much. She broke up with him when she found somebody with more connections and more money."

"She didn't mind that he was younger?"

"Does money have an age restriction?"

I smiled. "What turned people against him? Or what was the yutz factor all about?"

"The best example I can think of is Edgar's deals."

"Deals?"

"He always had a deal he was working. Always. He constantly tried to get people to invest in deals. That's why he went into that investment banking. He was going to make deals. Huge, big, mega-buck, super profitable deals." He sighed. "Like everything Edgar touched it turned to shit. He wanted me to invest a hundred thousand in a land deal in Texas. He justified people losing their money by saying it was okay that they lost their money because he lost twice as much as they did. He was awful at business, led his clients into making stupid investments, or he tried to get his friends to buy into stupid investments. He was a menace. That's why he lost his job at that investment company. He was costing them clients and money."

"It's kind of sad."

He nodded. "He always had his mom and dad to run to when he was stuck. And he did. The sadder parts were the little things."

"Like what?"

"He didn't have a lot of basic social skills."

"That I noticed."

"But he always had his parents to fall back on then and now as an adult. They gave him a job in the anti-recall campaign."

"What was he doing for them?"

"I don't know specifically what he did. Whatever it was he

probably screwed it up." He shook his head. "This county is a mess. You heard the nonsensical press conference the Governor had with poor Beulah Grum next to her?"

We nodded.

"I don't like Mrs. Grum, but it was sad they made her stand up with the governor. She just lost her son. None of it made any sense. Even I know the election was stolen."

"How so?" Scott asked.

"Arithmetic."

"Arithmetic?"

"Yep. Totals don't add up. Look at every county in the state. You get the average turnout for the election, nearly fifty percent. So the average turnout in Harrison County would be about a hundred thousand votes. Amazingly, in a few key precincts the turnout would have had to have been over seventy-five percent. It will be as far over that as they need it to be."

Scott frowned. "They expected to get away with this? Can't someone check?"

"So far they have gotten away with it. And who's going to prosecute? The Republicans control every office in the county. Statewide they stripped the Secretary of State of all oversight of elections. The Attorney General in the state is a Republican."

He pointed to a gentleman with swept back silver gray hair walking up to the front door. "See him?"

I nodded.

"Buster Fanning. He'll stay about four minutes. He's not here for Veronica. He's here to be seen by the Grums. Once he realizes there are no major Grums, powerful, influential Grums, he'll leave."

The front door opened a few mintues later and, as predicted, Buster Fanning hurried down the walk.

"No one knows this stuff?" I asked.

"Someone probably knows the truth. I've never seen that

someone come forward, and by this time the truth would be so twisted, it wouldn't be recognized as the truth." He stood up. We followed suit. "You're right. It's just sad. I know once when we were little we found this old fort about two miles from here. We rode our bikes. Someone had nailed stuff poorly together, used rope to tie stuff together. Edgar used an old knife to cut the ropes. Used the edge of the knife to rip out all the nails he could. He did all the destruction, and I admit I didn't stop him. The cops were called. It was his word against the kid who built it. Some kid our age. Not in our social set. Not as rich as us. I backed up Edgar's story. I still feel awful for that. The poor kid didn't have much, just this crummy fort, and Edgar had to ruin it. And I lied for him. I was a shit. I've tried to be better."

"Why are you telling us all this?"

"The last time I saw Edgar, he said there was something funny about this election."

Scott said, "He confided in you even though you weren't close any more?"

"Edgar and social nuances didn't go well together. It isn't likely that he noticed our relationship had changed. No, that time we talked, Edgar kept hinting he could really screw things up for a lot of people. And they'd better watch out, and he better get some respect. We were at some annual country club charity event. His brother, Barry, eventually corralled him and shut him up."

"It doesn't bother you that the election could be stolen?"

"I'm not political. They so desperately care about who is in charge so they could make more money. I went to medical school, which is not as respectable to them as making fountains of money off the backs of hard-working Americans."

"What could Edgar do to screw things up?"

"Edgar was big on using veiled threats, always was even as a kid. He never followed through on them. Whether or not he was serious this time, I have no idea." He shook his head. "As an adult I pretty much kept away from his family and mine. I met

Veronica before they got married. She's a good person. I think Edgar genuinely loved her. She seemed to be a good influence on him, but I was only her doctor. Today, I was worried when I heard she was out of control. Have her call me if she wants anything for herself or the kids. I can prescribe her a sedative, and maybe I'll check on the kids."

Avery turned to Scott, ducked his head, and sort of blushed. "Can you autograph something for me?"

"Sure."

Avery left. Scott stayed to help with the crowd, and I went back to the office.

Twenty-two

Wednesday 4:25 P.M.

I was there about twenty minutes when the office door crashed open. Veronica grabbed the rebound and slammed it shut. She leaned against it, shut her eyes, and breathed deeply. Her voice started as a whisper and rose to near a shriek, "I hate them. I hate them. I hate them. I hate every bone in their bodies. I hate the air they breathe."

I hastened to the door and took her hand. I opened the door quickly and looked up and down the hall. If anyone had heard, they weren't putting in an appearance.

I helped her to a seat then asked, "What's wrong? Did the Grums do something?"

She shuddered, drew deep breaths. Finally calm enough, she said, "If those people pray at me one more time, I swear." She got up and paced the length of the room, slapped at the grizzly, and turned to face me. "We walked into the funeral home, and right in the entryway, the first thing they wanted us to do is pray. When the funeral director met us, we had to say a prayer with him."

She sat and rubbed her hands across her face for a moment then looked at me. "I've never gone to a funeral home to make arrangements for a funeral. I've never even thought about it. It was a good thing mom and dad were there." She wrapped her arms around herself. "When we arrived, the dragon lady was already there. After praying, she began to decree and declare what was going to happen for the funeral. It was awful." Her voice began to rise. "And Edgar's father. He was with his odious wife. He told me I didn't have a choice. I had to have the funeral their way."

I held her close. I never understood this whole shtick about "my-funeral-is-better-than-your-funeral." And is somebody taking attendance at funerals? The stupidest question I've ever heard is, "How would you like it if no one came to your funeral?" Well, I suppose I wouldn't care much. I'd be dead. And so the living are supposed to count up the mourners? Whoever has the most mourners, wins? Wins what?

"What did they want?" I asked.

"They wanted this god awful extravaganza. They wanted a Christian rock band. They wanted singing groups. They wanted praise Jesus songs mixed with eulogies by every relative they have."

I asked, "I know eulogies, but how does this praise Jesus stuff work?"

She said, "The preacher gives a combination sermon eulogy then someone sings a song. Next somebody gets up and does another eulogy. Then another song. I don't want to hear all that shit."

"How long does this song/eulogy extravaganza last?"

"Hours."

"Really?"

"Really. I went to one of Edgar's uncle's funerals. In this gargantuan mega-church they had huge screens, stadium size screens, immense flat screen things, hooked up to computers. They showed pictures, every picture in his life, huge twenty-foot pictures of a dead person, rotating from screen to screen, interrupted by songs from groups, some live on stage, some taped, but all shown on those damn screens. They sang endlessly."

"Funeral dirges?"

"No, praise songs to god."

"Huh?"

"As in, every other word was praise and all the other words were Jesus."

"That's it?"

"There might have been other stuff. It was numbing after about ten seconds. It was awful. Maybe it comforted the afflicted. Maybe it pleased the Dragon Lady and the Dictator." Her body twitched and shuddered. "Thankfully mom and dad were there today."

"What did they do?"

"Dad looked at the old bitch and her despicable husband and said, 'if that's what Veronica wants, fine. We are going to do what she wants. This is a hard time for all of us, for you and your family, but we will do what Veronica says. I'm sure we all want to do what is best for Veronica and the children. Don't you agree?'"

I knew well my dad's trick of ending an oration on our errant behavior with a question that suggested you would be unreasonable to disagree with his last statement. It was a trick I'd most often heard from Margaret Thatcher, a politician my dad would be loath to be identified with.

Veronica said, "Mom chimed in right away. You know how she can be. She said, 'You're absolutely right dear. I'm sure no one could disagree'. The Grums could have overwhelmed me at a time like this, but mom and dad put an end to their nonsense, and mom and dad didn't scream, or shout, or carry on, nothing at all like the Grums." She drew a deep breath, reached for a tissue from the box on the coffee table, dabbed at her eyes. "Thank god for mom and dad."

"They can be wonderful. It all worked out?"

"It's going to be a simple ceremony, the way I wanted it."

"Did she have the dog with her?"

"Yes."

"I feel sorry for it."

She managed a grim smile.

I said, "What I don't get is how they can just barge into the funeral home. You can't just co-opt someone else's funeral. How did they think they were going to get away with that?"

"They know the funeral home director, family connections,

political connections. It's this damn county and who knows who. The Grums just tried to take over. They led him to believe they were in charge of the funeral. The first five minutes were pure hell. I was in shock. I'm still in shock. Numb. Daddy was a treasure. Thank god that's over with so I don't have to talk about it or think about it."

Dad was the quietest of all of us, but it did no good to cross him for all his mildness.

I said, "Good for mom and dad. I talked to Azure Grum earlier."

"She's the best of them. Drinks a little much, but in this family, I can't blame her."

"She mentioned Mary Mallon used to date Edgar."

"Mallon is dangerous. She'd date a corpse if it would help her career. She knew the Grums had money and power. It was just a way for an in when she was younger. But she married a Ducharmé. She may be vile, but she has the instincts to go where the most cash is." She crushed the tissue and wedged it between the paws of a dead beaver on the coffee table.

"Did Edgar ever talk about Mallon?"

"Maybe a long time ago. It wasn't a big deal."

"I checked on the kids before I came in here. I kept it together in front of them. I don't want to think. I want to keep moving. Am I broke? Am I indebted to the goddamn Grums?"

"This is preliminary. We still have a lot of boxes to go through." I went over all the financial records we'd found so far. Showed how I'd set it up on a spread sheet on the computer. I increased the font size and then printed it out when she didn't seem to understand. By printing it out, she could hold it in her hand. This seemed to help her.

I asked her the same questions I'd asked Scott earlier. "Where did he get the deposits to his accounts if he had such lousy jobs?"

I showed her the bank statements.

"I don't know."

"If they were electronically deposited, there'd have been records. If he was depositing them with cash, why and where was he dealing in that much currency?"

"I never saw that much cash."

I found her lack of knowledge appalling, but I kept my mouth shut.

When we finished she said, "I'm not broke?"

"Far from it."

"I get the house?"

"For sure."

"And I can get money? Yes, I know you told me this stuff, Tom, but I'm just saying it again to reassure myself. I'm going to have to learn so much. And taxes are due next week."

"He's got an accountant listed here. Or if you want a different one, you can probably find one who could file an extension. You could call the one Scott and I use or find one locally. If you want, I can call ours and make an introduction, get you started."

"Yes, please do."

She slumped against the back of the chair, sighed, and said, "Thank you. Thank you. I could never have done this financial stuff."

I said, "Scott helped." I didn't say, sure you could have, you're tough, you're smart, sometimes you just have to deal with crap.

"He's a dear. You have such a good marriage."

"You never complained about Edgar."

"I did the best I could."

I let it drop. "Among the stuff we found were books on building guns. Did he go about armed?"

"As far as I know, he only carried a weapon when he went hunting although he loved the new concealed weapon law here in the state."

Twenty-three

Wednesday 5:15 P.M.

The rest of the afternoon was a swirl of activity. No cops and none of the major Grum players put in an appearance. Maybe the funeral home fracas had stopped them. Friends of Veronica's and relatives of ours appeared along with minor politicians of all sorts, Republicans and Democrats, state reps, state senators, county board members, library board members. Many of them seemed to expect Charles and/or Beulah Grum to be present. Many said, be sure to convey our condolences to the Grums. I hope most of them were sincere. I hoped my cynical interpretation of their presence was untrue, "make sure the Grums know I was here to get my suck-up points."

About six I wandered into the kitchen. Someone had ordered buckets of chicken from a local place, and these were set out with the tons of stuff that had been brought in during the day. Scott and the kids were not in evidence. Around sunset I went to look for them.

Twenty-four

Wednesday 7:00 P.M.

I found Scott and the kids in the backyard. Floodlights illumined the darkening scene. Clutching a tattered stuffed panda, Patricia sat on a swing. Her brother Gerald gently pushed her. I saw David, the oldest, swoop to the top of the skate board ramp, twist, and swoop back down. Then Scott swooped upward and did a flip and landed smoothly. Scott and David wore helmets, knee pads, and elbow pads.

I walked to the edge of the mini-skateboard park. It looked sort of like a swimming pool but with more curved sides and extensions of curving cement above ground as well.

David had a look of intense concentration. Scott was trying to explain a trick to David and suggesting he take several smaller steps first in learning to do what Scott just did.

I was going to suggest that if Scott's doctor knew what he was doing, or if the team knew how many clauses in his contract he'd just violated, he'd be in huge trouble. He wasn't that far removed from his surgery, and he was certainly risking doing harm to his rehab, or reinjuring himself.

Then again, I was not his mother, but his lover.

David was thirteen. On the cusp of serious criminal delinquency. He'd caused trouble in school since first grade.

Veronica and Edgar always rushed to his defense. It was the school's fault. It was the teacher's fault. It was the other kid's fault. Every time, somebody, anybody else, started it.

In third grade he'd almost been expelled. You don't get almost expelled in third grade unless you are perceived as a serious danger to others.

Every bone in my teacher's body screamed out that this kid

was in serious trouble. He would graduate into an uncontrollable teenagehood unless there was some kind of serious intervention. Teams of therapists would be called for.

One of the oddest things was that with me he nearly always was a fawning suckup, eager to be as touchy huggy as about a four-year-old. I knew I didn't have the capacity to help him.

In public he was a hellion. The stories in the family were infamous. When he was eight, the family was out at a restaurant. The kid was whiny, crawly, clingy, the kind of behavior that might be normal in a two year old who hadn't had enough sleep. At that restaurant Edgar grabbed him by the arm and dragged him outside. Each of them were screaming and flailing at each other, arms flying, legs kicking, fingers pinching and gouging, the two of them in a ghastly familial wrestling match as they stumbled out the door. I thought both of them needed serious help.

Once I'd tried to gently steer my sister into a more realistic mode with her kid, but I got instant defensiveness and let it go.

I talked to my parents about the whole thing. Mom said she'd talked to Veronica a number of times about David. Mom's a peacemaker of extraordinary dimensions. Veronica had rebuffed her, defended her kid, her own behavior, and her husband's.

Scott, for some reason, was able to work his magic with this one as well. It might have gone back to when David was little, and we were baby-sitting and the kid woke up in the middle of the night with some kind of fluish/stomach problem. Scott knew exactly what to do. A little warm Coke, singing him some soothing songs in the middle of the night in a darkened room, and the kid slept peacefully through the rest of night.

I stood at the edge of the skateboard ramps. I said, "That was pretty spectacular." Pause. How do you tell someone who is actually getting along with a totally recalcitrant child to stop it. I said, "That's not dangerous?"

David said, "It was cool."

Scott said, "It's getting late, and we should probably be getting ready for dinner. Your mom is probably concerned with how you're doing."

They were standing at the bottom of the biggest declivity. Their skateboards were turned on one end as they leaned against them. Scott must have borrowed one of David's. Patricia and Gerald came to join me in spectating.

"Will you teach me more, Uncle Scott?" David asked.

"Only if your mom says it's safe."

"Awww."

"You know I won't go against what your mom says."

"I know." But the kid didn't sound as petulant as usual. How does Scott do that?

They climbed out. Gerald asked, "Can I carry that, Uncle Scott?" He gave the skateboard to Gerald.

Gerald took it in one hand and held out the other. Scott took it, and they held hands as they began to walk. Patricia rushed to Scott's other side. He stopped, reached down, and pulled her up with his left arm, his non-pitching arm. The three of them walked toward the house.

Gerald was the quietest of Veronica's kids. He always seemed to be watching, hoping for a nod of approval, or a kind word.

David climbed out of the skateboard track trough and looked up at me. He said, "My dad built this skateboard park for me."

I said, "That was good of him."

David said, "He built it, but Uncle Scott just spent more time out here with me this afternoon than my dad did in three years." He brushed dirt off his long sleeve sweatshirt. He said, "I wish Uncle Scott was my dad." He hefted his skateboard and walked to the house.

It was a heart-stoppingly affectionate thing to say, or maybe a heart-wrenchingly awful comment about what a shit his dad was, or a sad kid trying to cope with his loss in any way he could.

Twenty-Five

Wednesday 8:00 P.M.

After we grabbed something to eat, Scott and I got back to work on the files. We still had stacks of boxes left to go. Nothing I'd found since my meeting with Veronica gave me reason to worry about her financial situation, safe so far.

When we were alone in the room, the first thing I said was, "I'm glad you were able to help David with all the skateboard stuff, but I worry when you do tricks like you did."

He said, "It was kind of dumb. There's no need for extra worry at a time like this. I made a bad decision. Yes, I know I was breaking seventeen different clauses in my contract."

"I wasn't going to report you to the contract police."

"I know." He came over to me and took me in his arms. "But you worry about me, and I appreciate it. It's not like I'm sacrificing our living standard for a reckless moment."

"I know."

"But you're annoyed."

I said, "I try to be less rigid about holding to guidelines that make no sense." This was in reference to what I called 'mom rules'. These were the dictums drummed into us by our mothers when we were kids that in retrospect as adults, seem kind of nuts.

"And you've gotten better at it."

"And I didn't say anything."

It was his turn to say, "I know. And I promise not to do it again."

"Thank you."

We embraced. He is so nice to come home to. And his arms are always home.

Enid Achtenberg walked in about nine. Veronica was with the kids putting them to bed. The last few well wishers were helping clean up – with Mom and Darryl, in the kitchen, with Dad and Lionel in the living room. The distantly related Grums who were in attendance had been among the first to leave.

Enid met with us in Crippled Critter Central. Scott and I sat in separate chairs behind the desk. Enid sat in front of it. We had boxes neatly labeled and organized alphabetically by company all along the floor. Every paper in each was filed by date with the most recent on top.

She began, "I found out a few things. I've got to talk to Veronica when she's done with the kids. How is she holding up?"

"Keeping busy. It's been crazy all day."

Achtenberg pointed to the no-longer mess. "You guys have been busy."

"Not even half done."

I showed her the further Trust documents we'd found and the insurance papers. She knew which pages to go to in the Trust that were the most important.

She held a stack of papers out to us. "This is the Grum Family Trust which is different from the Trust documents we looked over earlier. This one is fairly clear."

"How so?"

"When Mr. and Mrs. Grum die, and if Edgar has predeceased them, the money does not go to Veronica, but to her kids."

"Is that normal?" Scott asked.

She shrugged. "I've seen lots of different things." She shuffled to the important sections. "This is the most recent." She read through two pages. "It's pretty ordinary. There are a few odd things that go back to the family upon his death."

"I know," I said. "The grizzly goes back to the Grums."

Achtenberg said, "And a few other things. There must be an antique china set somewhere. If a moving truck drives up looking for the grizzly, it goes."

We went over a few more papers and confirmed the opinion that I'd already given Veronica. She was going to be okay.

I said, "Some of it doesn't make sense." I showed her the bank deposit stuff.

She said, "It could be innocent."

I said, "Or he could be a crook. He got murdered for some reason."

Achtenberg said, "And sometimes people die for no reason at all."

"Did you find anything out about what the police have?"

She took a deep breath. "Some. The guy who found the body is Mike King. He's a private investigator from Chicago. Mrs. Grum wanted the investigator arrested for killing Edgar."

"Did they?"

"Even the police here need proof. I think."

"Why was he around?"

"He was hired by someone, I don't know who yet, to find out how the Governor's side was going to steal the election."

"They had proof?"

"He was supposed to get proof."

"One of the family members told me that one of the campaign workers died, a reporter. I checked the Internet. Several bloggers insisted the Grums must have been involved. None of the bloggers offered any proof."

"I know those rumors are believed by the recall campaign. I have no facts or data either way."

We filled her in about what we had found out from Azure Grum and Veronica's gynecologist.

Scott asked, "Could it possibly be true that they've covered up murders before?"

"I know Azure Grum a little. She's drunk a lot. A friend of

Veronica's for sure, doesn't like her in-laws. Her husband is a decent, quiet man. But murder? I just can't imagine. Although imagining the Grums doing awful things isn't hard to do."

I asked, "Do the police think the investigator did it?"

"The cops were on the scene fairly quickly. The investigator had a gun which he was licensed to carry. They already know his gun hasn't been fired recently. Also, the investigator had no gunpowder residue on his hands."

Scott said, "But Mrs. Grum claims that he did it?"

"Maybe she's just making it up? Who knows? What I did find out was that Edgar was shot execution style. That's all I've been able to find out so far. The police are keeping very quiet."

"Isn't that kind of usual in this kind of case?" I asked.

Enid said, "They're hunting for suspects."

"They'll need to look at everybody who ever knew him."

She sighed. "We already knew Edgar was a menace and most, if not all, members of the Grum family are evil incarnate. Nobody has any actual facts that point to a murderer."

"Assumedly the cops are going over the surveillance tapes from the headquarters, and the news station's video footage from Tuesday night and Wednesday morning."

"There seems to be about a three-hour time frame in which the murder could have been committed. People were in and out of the hotel, the ballroom, and the headquarters next door all the time. It's all one huge convention complex. They've got over three thousand people from the ballroom itself, plus the guests from the hotel not connected to the election, and the people from the floors that housed business offices, and the people who worked at the hotel. It will be impossible to pinpoint where everyone was. If they get one suspect, they could narrow it down with the footage. Maybe."

Scott said, "All the areas have video coverage?"

"That's another problem. Just some areas."

I had a notion from the modern spy/thriller movie, where one guy sitting at a computer goes through thousands of hours of video footage from a zillion cameras in a major city, and it takes him five minutes to find the person he's looking for. Bull phooey. And here, how would they ever get all the names of all the people they saw?

"What happened to the private investigator?"

"They questioned him for hours. His prints weren't on the gun. The video footage with him on it shows the murder had to have happened before he got there."

"Anything about the gun?"

"Unregistered, possibly homemade, they're waiting for forensics on it."

"Homemade? We found gun making manuals." I got them out of the desk drawer and showed them to her.

Making guns at home never crossed my mind as something I would be interested in doing.

Scott asked, "Did Edgar carry a gun?"

Achtenberg shrugged. "I don't know."

"What's the deal with the dead reporter?"

"I don't know."

Veronica entered. She took one look around the room and shuddered. "I'm tired of the goddamn dead animals. Let's get out of here."

In the Green Bay Packer trophy room, she collapsed into a chair. "The kids are in bed. I don't know if they're asleep. I don't know if I'm going to be able to sleep."

Achtenberg filled her in on everything she knew and left a half hour later.

TWENTY-SIX

Thursday 12:05 A.M.

My sister and I were alone again in the Green Bay Packer trophy room. It was just after midnight. The last well wisher had left. My parents had gone to bed. We were staying at the house as were my mom and dad. Scott knew I wanted to talk to Veronica. He would be as he always was at home or when we traveled, naked in bed, reading a book.

My sister and I sat next to each other on a couch. Embers smoldered in the fireplace.

She sipped from a glass of Merlot.

My sister whispered, "I loved him. God help me, I loved him. I don't know why. I know people never understood why I loved him." She gulped. "From the first I saw the person he wanted to have become if he'd had a loving family and upbringing."

I tried soft shushing noises, patting her arm. I was not about to demand details and proof of whatever bits of him she saw whether it was hidden kindness or generosity of spirit, or whatever it was that led her to see this. She had seen it. She did love him.

"Edgar was sweet. He was always sweet to me. He brought me little gifts. I got flowers even when there wasn't a special occasion. He was thoughtful. He loved me." She began to cry.

She leaned her head onto my shoulder. I put my arms around her. She wept.

After her tears had eased, I took a box of tissues from the coffee table and held them to her. She grabbed a few and wadded them up and wiped at her running nose.

She said, "I hate his family. All of them."

My sister had never been a hater. More a reconciler like my

mom.

"Every single one of them should rot in hell. They are bullying, obnoxious pigs."

I didn't tell her that I thought her husband hadn't fallen far from the family tree. I opted for, "It must have been tough marrying into them."

People might fight with their in-laws, but Veronica had never hinted at this much anger. Had she been suppressing it all these years? That couldn't be healthy. Grief could be adding to her anger.

"That woman ruled and commanded, and they obeyed and demurred. Beulah Grum married into that family, but her people, the Felches, have actually been in the county longer. I've met a few of them. They add to the cold and distant familial ghastliness. They all look like refugees from that sinus commercial." Another mucus memory connected to the Grums. She took another sip of Merlot.

"Did you know," she asked, "half my life revolved around keeping away from the Grums, especially my kids? We'd vacation on holidays to Disney World or resorts like that or go on cruises, anywhere his family wasn't. Sometimes his family organized these gigantic get-togethers on cruises to various parts of the globe, and we couldn't get out of them." She sipped from her wine. "I took every opportunity I could to make sure we were not even in the same time zone as them. I didn't want my kids to be like them."

She refilled her glass of wine from the bottle on a green and gold tile-topped coffee table in front of us. She sipped from her wine and took a deep breath, leaned back close to me, and said, "Edgar hated his family. I did too. They were awful. They are awful."

"You kept quiet all these years," I said. "That couldn't have been easy."

She whispered, "They killed him."

I caught her eyes. "Who?" I asked.

"That family. All of them. He was happy until this last year. He lost his job at the finance company he worked at. With the downturn they let over half the staff go."

"Has he been acting normally lately? Anything unusual happening?"

"Not that I noticed. He's been busy with that stupid campaign, not coming home until late every night."

As quietly as I could I asked, "Didn't he lose a lot of jobs over the years?"

She said, "After he left that law clerk job, he just wasn't a good fit." She listed three of them.

"Did you ever discuss why he left so many jobs?"

"He said he was always moving up, or they weren't paying him what he was worth. He was finding himself."

I thought, what bullshit, but she had bought all his excuses.

She continued, "They coerced him into working on that campaign. He'd come back late every night. He wouldn't talk."

I didn't offer any alternatives about why he might be late. Maybe he was cheating on you. Nor did I mention the folders with porn pictures on the desktop nor the hundreds of bookmarked sites.

"He'd curse the family. As the day of the election got closer, it got worse. He got more and more tense and more and more crazed. You have to find out who killed him."

"The police are working on it. I don't know anyone here. I have no contacts."

She leaned close, gripped my arm, spoke in whispered gasps, "They killed him." I'd never heard anyone so passionate and so fierce. "The police are in it with that goddamn family." Either she knew enough about the history of the county or had been alert enough to notice this through the chaos of the day or maybe a bit of both. She may have been blind about Edgar, but I never thought Veronica was stupid.

She put her wine glass down and clutched my arm with both of hers. "His goddamn family killed him. You have to find out who did it, and what they did, and how they did it, and you have to make them pay, and they better pay and it better hurt."

What else could I do? I promised to help.

I asked, "Did he say what he was more crazed and more tense about?"

"No. That damn Grum family secretiveness took over. It's a disease with them. Did you know when one of Barry's kids, you know which one is Barry? Edgar's oldest brother?"

"He came into the room right after you left first thing this morning. He's the one with the very red nose."

"Yeah, him. Well, Barry's son, the day he turned eighteen, he signed up for the Army. He got sent to the war in Iraq. So Edgar asked at one family get-together about how to contact his son, Oswald is the kid's name, or how to send him a package, a letter. And Barry said there was no way they could send him things."

I said, "Maybe he was in a secret organization or undercover."

"Ha! I found out the truth from one of the other mothers one time when I couldn't get out of going to one of those Women's Heritage Society meetings. The mother had a son in the very same unit. Slept two beds away from Oswald. That family called, talked, everything. They sent gifts, packages. It's just nutty secretiveness. They all hate each other."

How sad, I thought. I was lucky, I guess. With all of our quirks, mom and dad and my family looked pretty normal especially compared to all this.

"Who in the family could I talk to?"

"Why them? They're all terrible."

"I've gotta start somewhere." I told her about the conversations we'd had with Azure Grum and her gynecologist.

She shook her head stubbornly. "They didn't understand Edgar."

I said, "There were the regular deposits to the bank that have no explanation."

"I don't know where they came from, but Edgar was not doing anything illegal."

"Did he get family money?"

"Not that I know of. They kept him on a short financial leash. He had little actual money of his own. They wouldn't let him at the family Trust money. I think he gets bits of money from the family Trust periodically. Maybe that's what those are."

"Do you know anything about his investments?"

"I know he was always trying to make a deal. He had millions of deals. I'm not sure they worked out. He'd be all enthused about one, then I'd never hear about it again. I figured he gave up, or lost money, or his family made him stop, or they were part of what the family was doing."

I said, "And give me the name of the other places he worked."

"He had so many jobs."

"The ones you can remember."

TWENTY-SEVEN

Thursday 1:00 A.M.

I trudged up to bed. We were in a second floor corner room farthest from the others.

When I opened the door, Scott was as I expected him to be, sitting up, propped on a cloud of pillows. He had a book open and Bose Quiet Comfort headphones on, which were connected to his iPod. He was probably listening to a Danny Schmidt album, a new favorite singer for him. I stood in the open doorway and watched him for a moment. The covers were pulled to his waist, but drooped on one side revealing the first hints of his lower torso. The golden hair on his chest shimmered in the soft light of the reading lamp next to the bed. His torso expanded and contracted with each soft breath as his eyes scanned the page. Watching him calmed all the jangling of the day. I realized how tired I was and was reminded for the millionth time about how much I loved him.

When I closed the door behind me, he looked up, smiled, took off the headphones, put a marker in the book and closed it. He was reading *The Metaphysical Club* by Menand, a book about the effect of the American Civil War on the development of philosophical thought in the years after that conflict ended.

Scott asked, "How is Veronica?"

I began undressing. "Holding up as best anyone could do at a time like this. Mom and dad being here make a big difference."

He was watching me undress. I turned full frontal toward him. I didn't put on a show or make it a production although sometimes he liked that too. It was just a moment I know he liked, as I did watching him. One of those small moments of intimacy long term couples know about each other.

"And you?" he asked.

"Tired."

I dumped my clothes in a random pile where I stood. His were folded neatly on a chair. He glanced for an instant at his. He looked at me and said not a word. If you've been married as long as Scott and I have, I occasionally actually remember not to be as big a slob as I am in my natural state. I picked them up, hung things on hangers or folded them neatly.

Each guest room had its own private bath. I brushed my teeth then crawled into bed next to him. He placed the book on the nightstand.

I said, "She wants me to investigate the murder. She doesn't trust Edgar's family."

"She's right about that."

"And she doesn't trust the police."

Scott said, "I still don't get the Grums having that much power. Even in Chicago, you've got to be kind of circumspect. Cops don't just bow and scrape in front of people or get them to bow and scrape to you in front of witnesses."

I said, "Who gives hints and commands to police in the presence of others?"

"Someone who doesn't care that other people are hearing it," Scott said. "Which means someone who is totally confident of their influence and power."

"Or a moronic twit who is trying to cover up the fact that he or someone in his family killed his kid."

"There is that. Those people are awful." He rearranged the bed covers and moved himself so our legs touched then he said, "That election stuff was incredible."

I repeated the left's mantra. "If it is close, they will always find a way to steal it."

Scott said, "I checked on the Internet about what the gynecologist told me. There are some web sites that agree that the math for the Grums doesn't add up."

"How so?"

"The percentage of turn-out and the total votes around the state averaged forty-nine percent. That's what it was until the announcement at the press conference. In Harrison County the turnout was announced now to be at eighty-one percent."

"So?"

"The eighty-one percent happened in only three heavily anti-recall precincts. The anti-recall precincts in the rest of the state averaged forty-nine percent, as did the pro-recall precincts."

"Oh."

"The upshot is the Republicans in this county have come up with eleven thousand missing votes. More than enough to win the election for their side."

"Rigged?" I asked.

"Of course. Will they get away with it?"

I shrugged. "What do you think?"

Scott said, "I almost felt bad for Mrs. Grum at that press conference. Having to be there dealing with politics instead of her own grief. Who would be such a brute to require her attendance?"

"I sort of did too, but she's been in public life long enough in the electronic age."

"No, I meant having to do that kind of thing with her son murdered a few hours before."

I asked, "Why didn't they have some flunky on stage? Why did she even wind up being in front of the media? There's got to be more than one repub in this county who can talk to the press."

"Maybe because she's in charge of voting?"

"I don't care. At a time like this with her son murdered? Who gives a crap about an election?"

He asked, "Are you going to investigate the murder?"

"I will do what I can for Veronica. There's going to be enough people in and out of the house that I can talk to." I related what Veronica had told me a few minutes before about what she'd seen in Edgar. "Despite what she told me, I still don't understand why Veronica loved him."

He touched my arm. "We find someone with whom we can share the dark places of our hearts with. If we spend time toting up their good points and bad points and comparing them with our own, well, I think that way lies madness. No, my sweet dearest, are you sure there's any point to speculating on the nature of love?"

"Well, no. It just amazes me."

Scott said, "She was in love. There was or is nothing to be done."

I agreed then added, "Veronica confirmed that Mallon dated Edgar."

"I'm not sure I want to think about that much less begin to envision it."

"Republicans must have sex. There's always more of them."

"And his dad indulged him and his mom ignored him?"

I said, "That's what we've got from our sources so far. Doesn't help solve who killed him. Yet. If he was a brat used to getting his way, maybe someone tried to thwart him. Maybe Edgar had to fight to get his way, and it got out of hand."

"Yeah, but he's dead. Not someone he was trying to thwart."

I said, "Thwarts to the left of me. Thwarts to the right of me."

He smiled. "Volleyed and thundered. So you're going to investigate?"

"Talking to these people will be a start. Look what we got today without even deliberately doing it. I'd like to try and go to some of his old jobs and see if I can't find some people there to talk to. Of course, at the rate people are coming here, it may make our job…" I raised an eyebrow at him. He nodded yes. "Our job easier. If I can thwart this family in the slightest way, I will. If they're guilty of a crime, I'd love to get them all thrown in jail."

Scott said, "I tried not to think about this next thing."

I feared his next thought.

He continued, "You know when Mister Grum was yelling about him being the decider…?"

I looked in his eyes and asked, "We didn't have the same thought?"

"That maybe he decided his own son needed to be dead."

We looked at each other in silence for several moments. I said, "They are evil, awful, vile people, but I don't want that to be true."

"Me neither. It's amazing we both thought of it."

I asked, "Is that what being married means?" I snuggled close to him.

He said, "This election was so vital that they'd be willing to kill their own son? I just can't believe that. I don't want to believe that."

I agreed.

He took a deep breath then said, "You know what I think was the most amazing thing?"

"What?"

"When Mister Grum claimed we were out of control. Is he that blind to reality?"

"Obviously so."

"Or is he just used to telling any lie and being believed."

"That too."

"And his wife lying to back him up."

"Totally nuts."

"And Azure Grum and Harold Avery looking over their shoulders?"

"That was more nuts. What the hell kind of hold do the Grums have on these people?"

"Same thing with that crap about Veronica's gynecologist being told she was near the point of collapse. Why?"

"The answer to why is easy. Somebody is trying to screw over, or cause suspicion of, at the very least tarnish, Veronica. Tarnishing her doesn't make a lot of sense. Then again, we aren't getting a lot of sense from the Grums right now. Although the killer gains if she comes under suspicion."

We both began to repeat the mantra about giving them slack at the time of losing a son. We stopped, shook our heads. Things were not connecting.

He slowly rubbed the tips of his fingers over the hair on my arm. He said, "You know the Grums have money to buy off half the planet, but we are not poor. We are not without contacts. We could call our attorney in the morning. He might have some connections up here. We may or may not have as much money as this whole family, but what we've got should be enough if we get in a short term cash-for-cash race."

I said, "If it's as simple as cash, you're right, but this could involve not just cash, but cops, politicians, egos, and right wing insanity. Plus Edgar's death. I'm not sure we're fighting just cash, but we've got to start somewhere. You're right. We should call our attorney in the morning."

I rearranged the covers around us. "Nobody much noticed how famous you are."

"Kind of a relief. Edgar's family was familiar enough with me. The cops, who knows? They were busy, and Achtenberg was polite but not excessive. That was nice."

"Did you hear what David said outside while you were walking with Gerald and Patricia into the house?"

"No, what?"

"He wished you were his dad."

We held each other's eyes. With one hand, I caressed the top of his right ear, his hair. I said, "I'm glad I know you. I'm glad I love you."

I put my head on his chest, my arm around his waist. He smelled so good, as he always does.

He said, "I love you."

"Do you think lightning would come down from heaven and strike us dead if we had sex in this house?"

Scott nuzzled my shoulder. "If Mrs. Grum is right, Edgar could be looking down at us right now from heaven."

"Would he be checking porn sites from there or watching random people screwing in his house?"

"I've never understood how that "looking down from heaven shit" is supposed to work." He nibbled my earlobe.

"Should we wave?" I asked. A vision flashed through my mind of a heaven with railings crammed with people craning their necks to get a view of what was going on down on Earth. Did they observe when their loved ones were taking a dump? Or did they see a sort of Super Bowl highlight reel of people's lives put on for them by a department of angels who spent their time editing people's lives? I thought the whole thing was just nuts.

Scott said, "If I believed in heaven, he wouldn't be in it." He turned out his light. He was humming 'Stormy Weather' as we reached for each other. I can't ever imagine being too tired to be close to him.

TWENTY-EIGHT

Thursday 3:00 A.M.

Sometime later I was nearly asleep when I heard a loud crunching sound. I swung my legs onto the floor and listened. I heard a loud crack. Scott sat up beside me.

He whispered, "What was that?"

"It came from outside." We threw on T-shirts, jeans, and shoes. We stopped in the kids' playroom and picked up a couple of baseball bats. No one else in the house put in an appearance.

Together we made a complete circuit of the downstairs. This took about fifteen minutes in the mansion-sized house. We found no evidence at any of the windows and doors of a break-in or attempted break-in.

In the kitchen we turned on the lights for the backyard. Their glow illumined about fifty feet out from the house. We skulked outside, stood at the edge of the light at the end of the patio, and peered into the darkness. I hefted the bat. I whispered, "You see anything?"

He shook his head. "We're exposed here against the light."

We moved into the shadows on the side yard, the light to our left. A few owls hooted, a slight wind rustled to the newly budding tree and bush branches, but we could see nothing that might have caused the noises.

Scott said, "That sounded like a human doing something, not something that occurred naturally."

"It's not going to do us much good stumbling around in the dark."

We listened for several minutes, but the sound did not repeat itself. We went back into the house, turned out the lights, and went back to our room. We kept the bat with us.

If there were other suspicious sounds in the night, I slept through them.

Twenty-nine

Thursday 6:00 A.M.

Thursday morning I left Scott in our room exercising with two mini-dumbbells. We were ritualistic about exercising and with major rehab, he was extremely faithful in following the doctor's orders. The dumbbells were the smallest available. He had a series of repetitions that he did with each arm. He'd build up to heavier weights over time. I'd gotten far too little sleep, but things needed to get done.

Before I left, I stood next to him where he sat on the floor and waited until he finished a set of repetitions.

I leaned down and kissed him on the lips while I let my hand linger on his crotch. I sighed. Long day today, and I was tired from the very early start and long emotional day yesterday.

First, I checked the Internet. I found the Wisconsin papers were filled with the news of the Grums' announcement at the news conference of the newly discovered votes. I wondered where they'd found time to come up with them what with the death of their son, or if they'd had it well planned for a very long time. News of Edgar's death made the papers, but the articles told me nothing new.

Second, I called Todd Bristol, our attorney. Early as it was, no doubt he was in the breakfast nook of his high-rise condo on Lake Shore Drive in Chicago. He would be fully dressed and ready for work. I often thought he slept in his courtroom attire: charcoal suit, trousers held up by black suspenders stretched over a white shirt, black socks, black shoes. He wore a perfectly knotted tie and glasses with thin gold rims. His live-in housekeeper, a twenty-three-year-old college student, would be serving him very strong coffee, black, and a piece of unbuttered toast.

I told him everything. He said, "I'm sorry for your loss.

If it is appropriate, convey my sympathies to your sister." He harrumphed, took a sip of coffee. "As to the investigation of the moronic son-of-a-bitch who married your sister, stay out of it."

"Excellent advice."

"You're going to ignore it as you usually do."

"Do you know anybody up here who might be able to balance influence with the Grums?"

"Hmmmm." He thought several moments. "I shall check. Be careful. What you say about the police sounds ominous."

I repeated what Scott said the night before, "We have money, not like they've got money, not like the Ducharmé brothers, but..."

He interrupted. "Money! My dear, few people can even dream about the mountains of cash they have. All the money Scott and you will ever make is but a drop in the bucket compared to what they have, and money isn't all they have. It's handy to be rich, but they know how to be vicious in a million ways. You, as well as anyone, should know that. They can destroy you. It doesn't take a direct attack or a frontal assault. For example, with Scott, all it would take would be rumors among homophobic sports writers who just happen to put the most vicious possible spin on an innocent story, an innocent comment, or an inadvertent comment. They have a thousand ways to cut you into little pieces, and their little hands wouldn't get the slightest bit dirty." He chuckled evilly. "That's just the kind of fight I like, certain defeat against impossible odds. I will get to work on it for you."

Thirty

Thursday 6:30 A.M.

I headed for the kitchen. No one else had put in an appearance. My family and the cleaning crew had done a great job on the downstairs. The very light beige kitchen cabinets gleamed. The floor was spotless. I checked the dishwasher. The stuff inside was clean so I put it away. I filled the coffee maker and pressed "on" and got out gold ceramic mugs from the cabinet. Found sugar, regular and diet, cream, synthetic and real, set them out, then began hunting for simple breakfast things, cereal, bread for toast, milk, juice, eggs, bacon.

I didn't hear noises from other parts of the house. Much of the rest of the family were in hotels and motels. They were scheduled to arrive early. If we had to, we'd have enough of my people to match the Grums relative for relative.

David Grum walked into the kitchen. He wore black and gray madras shorts, black sandals with black ankle socks, and a black T-shirt with the stark white logo on it of an obscure rock group I'd never heard of. I said good morning. He mumbled a sleepy, "Wha's up?"

Scott entered with Patricia in his arms. She clutched him around the neck. David said a respectful, "Morning, Uncle Scott."

"Morning, how are you holding up?"

"Okay."

"Did you sleep?"

"Yeah. Some. What's going to happen today?"

"We'll try and keep things calm for you. Most probably your mom will talk to you."

Gerald entered. I took breakfast requests. Scott offered to make pancakes. He and the kids worked together.

Veronica appeared as the kids were finishing their meal. She wore a mauve warm-up suit.

She said good morning, hugged her kids, and asked them, "How are you doing this morning?"

The boys mumbled okays and all rights. Patricia just kind of clung to her.

Veronica hugged Scott, got Patricia settled, and eased herself into a chair. I put a cup of coffee in front of her. She said, "Thanks."

A few minutes later my mom and dad appeared. Dad said he'd start on gate duty. Someone would always be on duty in the dead animal office/den. Whatever it was that was in that room that everyone wanted, we weren't taking chances on them getting hold of it first. The problem with gate access and the Grums was that they lived in the same subdivision and didn't have to go through security before appearing at the front door. They probably owned the gate.

When everyone else but Scott was gone, I asked Veronica, "How are you holding up?"

"The kids seem okay. If they're okay, I'm okay."

I asked, "What did you need us to do today?"

"I've got a million things to do, more calls to make. The wake is Saturday. Sunday is Easter. The funeral is Monday. Edgar usually takes the kids to church most Sundays. I've got to get set for that. Will Patricia want to see the Easter Bunny? Will she even think of it?"

I said, "We'll help with whatever you want us to. We've got more boxes in the office. If you're going to have people in, we can help with that."

"I like having people around. I'm not as frightened when there's lots of activity."

I said, "We'll be here as long as you need us and do whatever we can."

She went to shower and get dressed for the day.

Scott and I made our own breakfast and began to clean the mess from the morning meal.

Scott refilled the dishwasher. At one point he asked, "She wants all those people around?"

"I guess so."

"I'm not sure that I'd want the chaos. Then again, I've never thought about it. I don't think about being without you."

"I don't think about living without you."

Around eight my mother rushed into the kitchen. "Your father says Governor Mary Mallon is at the gates."

My younger brother breezed into the kitchen. "Don't let her in."

"You can't keep the governor out," Mom said.

"Sure you can," I said, "but let's ask Veronica what she wants."

Veronica was summoned to the kitchen in the time honored Mason household way. My younger brother stood in the kitchen doorway and yelled up the back stairs, "Hey Veronica, get in here."

My mom said, "Hush, now. Don't be like that at a time like this."

Perhaps my family wasn't totally devoid of cluelessness either.

Veronica came in. Patricia trailed close behind her.

Dad said, "The governor's at the gate. She says she's come to pay her respects. Do you want me to let her in?"

Veronica looked at me, then mom, then dad. "What do I do?" she asked.

"Is she a friend?" Dad asked.

"No. She dated Edgar ages ago, and I've met her once or twice. She's quite close to the Grums."

Mom said, "What can it hurt? She's come to do something decent."

Veronica said, "Okay."

Dad punched the kitchen-extension, intercom button and gave them permission to enter.

Veronica said, "The Grums encouraged her to run for office. What is she doing here? I have too much to do. I have too much to think about." She pulled in a deep breath, stood up straighter. Here's where mom's training about dealing with guests paid off. Plus, Veronica had all of us with her, strength in numbers. We trooped to the foyer.

The governor entered first. I'd seen her on television. Back when Edgar and Veronica got married, she'd been a state senator who I'd never heard of. She'd been at the wedding, but I didn't remember her from that event.

I hadn't taken the slightest notice of her until after she was elected, and she began attacking the workers of Wisconsin and blaming the teachers for the state's problems.

She marched in leading an entourage of cops, politicians, and assorted flunkies. Detectives Brendstin and Adlow were at the very back. Brendstin exuded annoyed and frustrated glares, like he was forced to be here and wanted to be arresting and torturing people. Adlow looked at no one, held himself nearest the door, like he wanted to be a thousand miles away.

Men and women with cameras, microphones, tape recorders, and pads of paper in hand oozed and eddied among the others. Barry Grum sidled in as well. He lurked in the background near the detectives.

My, my, I thought, an invasion. Planned.

Mallon walked straight up to Veronica, held out her hand, and said, "Veronica, I'm so sorry for your loss."

She was about two feet from me. I could see the dye job on the bits of her natural hair that cascaded halfway down her back. Her pale complexion, contrasting with the starkly-dark hair, made her seem corpse-like.

Veronica took her hand, said, "Thank you."

"Is there anything I can do? Anything at all that my staff or I can do at a time such as this, we'd be happy to help."

I saw Barry Grum moving his bulk around the crowd toward the hall that led to the rest of the house. My younger brother had been delegated to den/office guarding.

I thought he might need assistance so I eased myself around the crowd. I followed Barry. Scott was right behind me.

Barry didn't bother to knock on the office door. He barged right in.

My brother turned from where he'd been standing at the sliding glass doors staring out. Darryl said, "Can I help you?"

I said, "Barry, is there something you need?"

Barry looked at all three of us. "I wanted to find something personal of my brother's so I could use it during my eulogy."

I said, "Anything particular you're looking for?"

"Maybe something from when we were kids."

I guess a fairly legitimate thing, but why in here? What was it in here that was so vital to them all? I wasn't going to give him stuff from the box from Barry's childhood, not until Veronica and her kids had a chance to pick what they might want of memories from the recently departed.

My Dad appeared in the doorway. "Barry, the governor and her people are in the kitchen getting something to eat. Would you care to join them?"

We trooped out leaving my younger brother on guard.

The crowd accompanying the governor clustered around the kitchen island. Baskets of food were opened and their contents placed on platters. Coffee came from the giant urn on the cupboard next to the sink. Someone had dropped off several platters of already cut up fruit the day before. These were put out along with plastic knives and forks. My mom was chattering away with the governor about her husband and children. Veronica was busy finding enough cups for the multitude. I joined her.

"What is she doing here?" she muttered.

"You're not honored and dazzled?"

"I'm frazzled, frustrated. It was a mistake to let her in. For a few minutes this morning, I want time to be with my own tears. I want time with the children."

We turned back to the crowd. Mallon's bright smile conveyed all the sincerity of a hangman about to push the lever for the drop. She said, "You know, Veronica, while these nice policemen came with me, why don't you talk with them for a while?"

My father, perhaps one of the most non-violent of men in the universe, immediately stepped forward and placed himself between all of them and us. The calm and quiet with which he addressed them was deceptive. I've learned the trick from him, the quieter he spoke the more angry he was, and as his voice lowered, it became more and more unlikely who and that which had angered him would triumph. He said, "Nobody is talking to anybody about anything. Today is going to be a day of quiet for this family. And when Veronica's lawyer is here, her lawyer will speak for her."

Mallon said, "I just meant..."

My father, impressed by few and certainly not by this witch, interrupted her, "No, Governor, what you mean is, we're sorry for your loss, is there anything we can do to help?"

Mom, me, Scott, and my brothers clustered around dad. Veronica stayed behind us. Her kids, drawn by all the excitement, were behind her.

A man in his late thirties stepped forward and said, "I'm Theodore Apht, the governor's spokesperson, and of course, that's exactly what the governor meant."

She couldn't speak for herself? I'm not sure Mallon quite understood what just happened, but her aide did. Mumbled sympathies emanated from all involved, and the moment of tension drained away. For a few moments Veronica clutched onto my dad the way Patricia clutched onto her.

Scott's voice dropped into the ensuing silence. "What are the police doing?"

"I'm told they're concentrating on the thugs who have been demonstrating against the people's elected representatives," was Mallon's reply.

School teachers as thugs rushing to the streets had been the characterization they'd been using for months. I knew she never described the gun-toting Tea Baggers as thugs. I'd followed her anti-intellectual rants on the Internet. As a teacher I took her irrationality personally, and her blaming teachers for the economic downturn infuriating.

I asked, "Do they have any facts indicating one of the demonstrators was at the hotel?"

"I'm sure the police are checking every angle. They need to be aware of how evil the opposition has been. We've received numerous threats."

I wanted to say, "I'd like proof of that," or, "didn't the police follow up on the threats at the time?". I didn't.

I wasn't eager to have her in the house, but it wasn't my decision to make. As long as she stuck to comforting Veronica, I would hold my tongue.

Barry Grum spoke up, "These people in the streets have been out of control and prone to violence. We know Union thugs have led this movement. People responsible will be questioning those thugs. The leaders of this movement are violence prone."

Scott spoke up, "That strikes me as evil and irrational. I hope the police are doing better than that."

Scott? Mister keep everything calm? Mister don't antagonize the enemy?

"They always look at the family as well," Barry said. He gave Veronica a mean glance.

"Then have they interviewed you, your brothers, cousins, aunts, and uncles, and your mother and father?" Scott asked.

The governor stepped in. "I'm sure the police are doing everything they can. No one can control what the media says."

Scott said, "Yes, you can. You try to control it every time

you give a press conference, every time your press spokesperson leaks information to the press, every time you or one of your representatives appears on a talk show."

"Who are you?" the governor asked.

I intervened. "A member of the family."

Things were getting very tense.

My mom asked, "Are the police close to an arrest?"

The governor said, "I don't know."

My dad asked, "What about the person who found the body?"

Apht, the spokesperson said, "The police are following all possible leads."

The two cops remained in the background. The young, burly guy, Brendstin, scowled continuously, lips pursed, brows drawn together. Adlow, the older man, mostly hung his head and didn't meet people's eyes. Something odd was going on there.

Scott asked, "Why are there reporters here with you?"

Mallon looked like she just guzzled a good dose of vinegar.

Scott continued, "I saw some of them on the news. Why aren't they asking you about the charges of stealing the election? Why are they even here during this time of family tragedy?"

My mother said, "Why don't we all have some more to eat?" She pointed. "There are so many delicious things. Does anyone need more coffee?"

Much of the herd lurched in the direction of the goodies on the surrounding counters. The governor followed suit. Once she moved, most of the others resumed wolfing down the proffered provender.

Enid Achtenberg strolled in.

Then Barry once again headed toward the doorway to the rest of the house. My brother casually planted himself in his path.

Barry tried to brush past him. He stood like a rock. In seconds my dad was beside him. The cops approached Veronica. She turned very pale.

Enid got between them and her.

Achtenberg said, "We met yesterday. I'm Mrs. Grum's lawyer. Can I help you gentlemen?"

Scott joined my dad and brother barring the access to the rest of the house. I joined Veronica and my mom. The herd in the kitchen were on their own.

Detective Brendstin said, "We had more questions."

Enid asked, "About what?"

"Mrs. Grum's whereabouts when her husband was murdered."

Veronica gasped. My mom hurried the kids out of the room.

Enid said, "She already told you where she was."

"We wanted to go over it again."

Enid asked, "What's to go over? She said she was home asleep."

"Why wasn't she at the election headquarters?"

Veronica opened her mouth as if she would answer. I placed a hand on her arm.

Enid smiled. "My dear detective, how kind of you to be interested. Really, I can't think of a more useless question. How are you doing with the investigation?"

"She needs to answer our questions."

Behind us I heard Barry Grum say, "Get out of my way."

Scott said, "This isn't your house. You aren't in charge. My guess is the real reason for the governor's visit was to get you into the house."

Barry said, "How dare you?"

Scott said, "Not a difficult insight. What is it in that den that you all want to get hold of so desperately?"

"Detectives," Barry Grum shouted, "arrest these people."

Enid laughed. "On what charge?"

Silence.

Governor Mallon's voice came from the kitchen doorway. "We have to go now."

Poof and the mob shuffled out the door, trailing reporters behind them.

We all looked at each other, at their departing figures, and kept our mouths shut until the front door closed.

Lionel said, "There's got to be something in there they want."

My dad said, "So let's search the place."

Lionel asked, "Search for what?"

That stopped us. Scott said, "What would they want so desperately?"

"Money?" Lionel guessed.

"Something that proves their guilt," my dad suggested.

"Guilt for what?" I asked. "That they stole the election? Proof of who killed Edgar?"

Lionel said, "This sounds kind of hopeless, and whatever it is, could be anywhere in the house."

We searched over, under, around all the critters, nothing. We moved all but the larger pieces. If something was hidden under the grizzly, they were going to have to get an industrial crane to move the damn thing. They must have dragged the huge bear in through the sliding glass doors or, who knows, maybe they built the house around the thing.

Nothing we found seemed to be something of value to the Grum family in terms of murder or the election. Nothing gave a hint to us that some kind of criminal activity was afoot, but we might not have recognized it. Scott and I would have to continue our vigilance as we went through the boxes.

The rest of the family left, and Scott and I resumed with the filing and cleaning. After two hours we had more bags of trash and a few more financial bits of information.

We took a break. Lunch was an almost quiet affair.

My dad asked as we were cleaning the mess from lunch and the morning herd of visitors, "Veronica, did you still want us to let people in here? Wouldn't you like some peace and quiet?"

"As long as the kids are okay, it's all right. Friends and food and talk are good. And some of the people bring their kids, so David, Gerald, and Patricia have someone to talk to."

I thought it was nuts and a switch from what she'd mentioned earlier, but it was up to her. I didn't expect extreme consistency from someone under the stress she was experiencing.

The rest of them left. Scott and I were alone in the kitchen cleaning the Mallon crowd mess and the lunch dishes, like an old married couple working together at cleaning the messes others had made. At one point I said to him, "I was a little surprised when you made comments to the governor."

He tossed a cleaning rag into a trash container under the sink then looked up at me. "She hit the limit on my temerity index. How often do you have the chance to confront absolute evil?"

Thirty-one

Thursday 1:00 P.M.

Early that Thursday afternoon my dad and I had time to stroll out to the gun shed. Veronica had given us a set of keys, and pointed out which ones opened this building. Scott was back in the dead animal den guarding and sorting. Mom, Darryl, and Lionel were on greeting duty.

The day was filled with high clouds. While walking across the lawn, my dad said, "I can't believe the Governor. That took a hell of a lot of nerve."

I said, "They wanted something. Veronica told me how grateful she was to have you and mom there at the funeral home. She said you were great."

My dad let out a snort that was kind of between a snarl and a bark. "Wasn't hard. When they're that stupid and that mean. You just have to remember who you are and what you want. Those people are too stupid to live."

My dad was one of the mildest of men. He caught my raised eyebrow.

"What?" he asked. "A little truth seems to be needed around here. These people are a menace to the universe, and I'm not talking about their politics. Anybody that stupid and that unwilling to deal with reality needs to be beaten with sticks."

I said, "I can't believe Veronica is letting all those people come to the house."

"She's like your mother. If there's stress, they want to keep busy. If they've got a problem, they want to talk. The bigger the problem, the more people they want to talk to. Your mom's been that way from before I married her."

"I'd want peace and quiet."

"That'll come," my dad said. "Veronica will be remembering this her whole life. For now the crowd is a comfort." He shrugged.

The so-called shed was the size of a three-car garage. It was built of brick and had one door and no windows. The locks had scratch marks, and the door jamb on one side and the hinges on the other looked as if someone had tried to pry them open with a crow bar. My dad and I examined them. He said, "Somebody tried to get in here."

"I thought I heard something as I was falling asleep last night. Scott and I went downstairs and examined all the doors and windows but couldn't find evidence of tampering around the house. We turned on the lights for the backyard and came out on the patio, but we couldn't see anything."

My dad said, "Ghost of the Grums?"

"Not a bad guess, especially if we were in the middle of a gothic horror novel, but we've got no proof."

Dad said, "The Grums are a gothic horror."

I found the keys for the triple locks. I paused before I opened it. "How can the police not have sealed this? This makes no sense."

My dad said, "Not the first time since we've been here that's happened." He shrugged. "Maybe they have the gun."

"We didn't see anything about that on the Internet, and you'd think Achtenberg would have mentioned it."

Upon entering I reached to my right, felt along the wall for a switch, found it, and flipped it on. My first notion upon entering the so-called storage shed was that it was way better than my first apartment, twice as large, better lit, and with more furniture. The carpeting was all-weather ordinary, green and gold. A few display cases displayed guns.

The main difference between my first apartment and this shed were the wall decorations. I had bricks, boards, and books. This had racks and racks of guns. I knew a little about guns because I'd been in the Marines. Each displayed gun had a little cards next to it labeling what the gun was, its provenance and/or a brief history, how much it cost, and how many critters it had been used to kill, if any. He had a pair of 1911 .45 caliber Ithaca marine army service pistols, but with different handles, one ivory, the other ebony.

There were shotguns from Boos & Co., Holland &Holland, and J. Prudey & Sons. One of them was a gold-inlaid 12 bore. One rifle was an H.H. Sheikh Zayed Bin Sultan Al Nahyan Mosque rifle. I pointed this last one out to my dad. "Can this be real?"

"Why?"

"If it's real, it costs hundreds of thousands of dollars."

My Dad said, "So Veronica's rich."

"I haven't seen the guns on any of the lists in the documents we've found."

My Dad bent forward to read the card. "Why would you think it was fake?"

"Edgar was many things. Being a victim of a fake or trying to perpetrate one wouldn't surprise me."

My Dad said, "I think eccentric is one of the milder words I'd use for the Grums in general. Coupons clipped and guns collected?" He shrugged. "Who are we to judge?"

He was right about that. After we spent a few minutes glancing at the displayed items my dad asked. "You know what's missing?"

I shrugged.

"A bazooka."

"Huh?"

My dad said, "Wasn't he supposed to be a lousy shot?"

"Yeah."

"Well, to compensate, why doesn't he have extra fire power. Knowing Edgar, I'd presume he'd need a bazooka, or a tank, to equalize the odds between him and Bambi."

"You might be underestimating Bambi."

None of the guns mounted on the walls, and none of the shelves of boxes of shells told me who killed him.

My dad said, "There's a bank of switches here." He flipped several. Bright lights illumined the guns, racks of track lighting, spot lights.

One card said that the AK-47 on display was the one that had killed Osama Bin Laden. I pointed it out to my dad. "That can't be real."

"It's really a gun," my Dad said, "as to its provenance and history." He shrugged.

I asked, "How could you prove it was real? I wouldn't take what it says on that display card as proof. Can you buy this kind of thing from the military?"

"More likely he got scammed."

"The better question is why aren't the cops all over this place? Why haven't the cops been all over this place?"

My dad said, "What's this red button?" It was at the end of the row of switches he'd flipped. He pushed it. Racks of guns six feet wide slid sideways. The two walls behind them parted a few feet, it revealed a small room. The floor was a door like that on a storm cellar. Dad checked a newly revealed panel of switches. Flipped them, nothing happened. I saw another red button on the end of the row. Before I could say anything, he pressed it. Hinged on one side, creaking louder than the sound effects in a thirties horror movie, the door rose like the lid of Dracula's coffin. Steps led down.

I said, "Plot thickener if I ever saw it."

"Do we descend?"

"We're not doing anything illegal. We have permission from the current owner."

We had to duck our heads. The door at the bottom was not locked.

I flipped a light switch on the wall to my right. A six-feet-by-six-feet workbench rested against one wall. Again, absolutely everything was labeled. The walls here were corkboard. On them pieces of equipment were outlined in black magic marker. Then below each outline was a label of what tool was to be placed there. It looked like everything in the room had a color-coded laminated label. The tools all had pink labels, the guns yellow, the label maker had a green label saying "label maker".

"Edgar was this organized?" my Dad asked.

"Apparently."

The wall on the left had shelves filled with gun paraphernalia. There were plastic containers labeled and filled with barrels, chokes, stocks, sights, pads, muzzle breaks, trays and trays of different kinds of bullets in boxes. On the floor next to the workbench was an Armorer's Tool and Gun Parts organizer bag. It was nylon with about a million zippers, compartments, a sunglass case, side pockets, expandable mesh outer pockets.

Another wall had tools: a barrel nut wrench, a hay teeth wrench, armorer's wrenches in different sizes with different size holes, a torque wrench, several different sized rubber mallets, a metal punch. Camping and outdoor gear sat on the cement floor to the right of the door.

On the workbench there was what looked like a very large toothpaste tube labeled 'white lithium grease'.

One wall had a few guns displayed. One was a Barret 50 Caliber Sniper Rifle, which I knew could pierce an engine block from a mile away. If it hit a human, all that would be left would be a pink mist.

A small display case had several 45 caliber US Marine service pistols from 1911.

On the work bench a small card said Holographic Weapon Sight Eotech 3X Magnifier flip to side mount. Next to the card was what certainly could have been the described item. I knew people used such a thing instead of a regular sight. This kind magnified the target and crosshairs to, in theory, make your shot easier.

Dad summed it all up. "Why the hell did he have all this crap?"

I said, "What's weird is maybe he made the gun that killed him."

My Dad shuddered.

We heard steps on the stairs and turned to look.

A voice demanded, "What the hell are you doing down here?"

It was Barry Grum.

My dad and I turned to face him. I blurted the first thought I had. "What the hell are you doing here?"

His voice was filled with disdain. "We live in the same subdivision. We don't have to go through gate security. Veronica hasn't banned us from the house. You're not in charge."

I said, "From this moment on, you will treat us with civility and keep your tone and your language within the accepted realms of decency and politeness."

He said, "Fine." With the tone and sneer I would expect from his nephew David.

I said, "I accept your acquiescence, and will ignore your inability to do so with anything approaching civility." See, I could compromise with these assholes.

Barry stormed out.

"Something is hidden here?" I asked.

My dad said, "There has to be some reason these people keep cramming their noses into every crevice they can find."

We hunted through the place upstairs and down, lifted every tool, opened every box, examined every manual. For a half hour's work, we got nothing.

I summed up, "He built his own guns?"

"Appears so."

"But none of them are labeled as home made. I don't see a completed gun or a being-worked-on gun. Could all of this have been for show? He just ordered a bunch of gun making stuff, owned a lot of gun making stuff, but never got around to making a gun, and was lucky not to accidentally shoot himself or blow himself up?"

"People do strange shit. You know that."

I said, "I've just never seen it so blatantly displayed."

"People collect guns, which is not all that strange."

Thirty-two

Thursday 2:30 P.M.

Back in the house, someone had delivered liquor. People were drinking liquids and scarfing down food.

I found Veronica in the middle of a gaggle of women I didn't know.

I managed to get her aside for a minute.

"You okay?" I asked.

"It's so good to have all my friends around me. They are too kind. I'm grateful they've come to help. The kids are with their friends in the play room."

So much for worrying about her over-stressing because of the crowd.

I said, "We found a sort of secret gun making room down some steps out in the shed."

Veronica took a sip of wine, smiled at some women, and said, "I know nothing about it. That shed was built about the time he had the skateboard park put in. If he built guns, he didn't tell me about it."

Scott and I got back to sorting for an hour. I was exhausted. I saw his eyes drooping over a glossy covered pro-gun manifesto. We stuck it out. I wanted to be at least half through by dinner time.

Thirty-three

Thursday 5:00 P.M.

Just after five Todd Bristol called.

He asked how I was holding up and how the family was. I told him we were managing okay.

I asked, "Did you find out anything?"

"What I have so far is this. You've got the Grums and the Grums' lawyers. Frankly, and I know this is prejudiced, but I'd be more afraid of the Grums' lawyers than I would be of the Grums. The lawyers are professionals. They'd do vicious legal things to Veronica, you, Scott, your family, and probably their own grandmothers if any of you got in their way. Their firm is one of the biggest in the state. But even more, I'd be more afraid of the Grums' minions doing hatchet jobs. Doing what they think are the Grums' bidding."

"I see the Grums as pretty much in the minion category as well."

"And they may be. I guess most people must be a minion to somebody. Just remember minions tend to do stupid things to please their bosses."

"Murder their own son?"

"Never underestimate the stupidity of those who think they are in the 1% or of those who want to claw their way into being among the 1%."

"Any background on Edgar Grum?"

Todd said, "All I've got on him is that he was the family screw-up, but you already knew that."

"I think a lot of the Grums are prejudiced against us."

Todd said, "My guess is that it's not because you're gay they don't like you. It's because you're in the way."

"Or both, but what are we in the way of?"

"That my dear, I have no idea."

I told him everything that had gone on, especially the madness of the Grums in seeming to want to get into the den and perhaps the gun shed.

Todd said, "It has to be connected with the murder or the election."

I added, "Or both."

"They could be connected. You have any proof of that?"

"Well, no."

"I didn't think so."

I asked, "We've heard about a private investigator, Mike King, from Chicago. Supposedly some gay guy hired him to investigate election fraud. He found the body. You ever heard of him?"

"Mike King? *The* Mike King?"

"I don't know," I said, "how many Mike King detectives are there in Chicago?"

"He is very hot. Very successful. His operatives are mysterious and deadly."

"Is there anyone in Chicago you don't know?"

"When they are hot gay men connected with legal stuff in this town, I make it my business to know."

"What did you learn about the crime scene itself?"

"That it doesn't tell us much. He was probably shot around an hour before he was found. There were tons of fingerprints around, but people were in and out of his office all the time. Edgar loved to talk. It was one gunshot wound to the front of the head, just above right between the eyes. He was found leaning back in his chair, his eyes closed. The gun was there, wiped clean of prints. It is likely it is his own gun; at least others who worked there claim to have seen him waving it around. The police have been all over it. As far as I can find out they have found no clues to who did it from the scene."

"Don't they have surveillance footage?"

"Not for the campaign office. Anybody could have gotten in."

"Where were all the Grums during the time the murder was committed?"

"If there is surveillance of the Grums, and that's a big if, it has been destroyed, lost, stolen, gone into the ether. These people are very powerful."

I asked, "Can we stop the cops from getting in here to investigate?"

"You told me what Enid Achtenberg did. I'd have complete confidence in her. She sounds like she's worth her weight in gold and silver."

Dinner that night was a buffet made up of foods neighbors and friends had brought in. A few of the friends and neighbors stayed to help eat it.

I was almost too tired to chew.

All of them left by seven. Scott, Mom, and Dad, and I cleaned the mess.

We tried going back to work sorting, but I saw Scott's eyes nodding over another glossy-red covered pro-gun manifesto. I was trying to make sense of an insurance document. The words kept going in and out of focus.

We gave it up and went up to our room.

While we got undressed, we compared notes and comments on the day. Still wearing my gray boxer-briefs, I fired up the computer and put in Edgar's flash drive. I figured we could look for a few minutes before dropping off to sleep while gazing at the monitor screen. Scott and I looked at the various folders and saved porn icons. They gave us little insight into what might have happened to Edgar. If there was a clue to his death, I had no idea where to even start among all this gibberish.

We discussed our various encounters of the day.

Scott asked, "Barry Grum was nuts when he confronted you in the gun shed?"

"Pretty much."

We were too tired to make much of it. We crawled under the covers and went to sleep.

Thirty-four

Friday 6:00 A.M.

I was up early again Friday morning. Scott was exercising. I decided to take a morning run around the neighborhood. Normally Scott and I exercised together every day. Partly it was to stay in shape and try to look hot for each other, but mostly we worked extra hard so we could indulge in our chocolate habits with less guilt.

I set out through the subdivision. Widely spaced streetlights let me follow the serpentine, gate-guarded road. A few homes had front porch lights on. Some had powerful spotlights above the garage doors. Most were completely dark except for dim flashes of orange and red lights indicating security systems in place.

The moon was half full and the breeze was up. I should have worn a heavier sweatshirt, but I warmed up after about five minutes. One car passed me in the first twenty minutes, none after that.

It was nearly seven by the time I returned. Early dawn light illumined the trees, bushes, and homes. I showered, dressed, and headed downstairs while Scott finished his meticulous routine. I stopped in the kitchen to begin breakfast preparations. No one else was up. Out the kitchen window I saw a man in a dumpy suit crossing the lawn.

I was sure it was the older detective Adlow. In his right hand he carried a roll of Crime Scene tape. I wondered what was up, a new crime? I walked out the door off the kitchen and crossed the yard toward him. I caught up to him at the door to the gun shed.

I didn't want to come upon him and surprise him so from fifty feet away I called, "Hello."

He spun in my direction. I kept my hands where he could see

them. His eyes were tired with the detritus of humanity he'd seen all his cop years. I held out my hand for him to shake.

He said, "You shouldn't be here." He didn't hold out his hand or move toward me.

I said, "Has there been another crime?"

He didn't look me in the eyes. He stared out at the lightly wooded countryside, trees mostly barren, grass mostly gray and brown.

Now Adlow walked up to me. He asked, "Has anyone been in there?" He nodded toward the shed.

I said, "We were all in there. It wasn't off limits before. Detective Adlow, something odd is going on here. I know you don't have to talk to me or trust me."

He interrupted, "You're the one with the lawyer who says you can't answer questions."

I kept my patience intact. I said, "I guess we're all kind of wary when we see the Grums with an attack posse, makes people nervous."

Adlow glared for a minute then did another gaze off into the trees. Would he be angry because of my "attack posse" crack, lose his temper, arrest me. I sometimes wished I was better at keeping my mouth shut before I said things to piss people off. Scott says I've gotten better at it over the years. I wished I'd gotten even better about two minutes ago.

Adlow said, "I'm an honest cop and an honest Republican, but these people are fucking with my pension, and the investigation sucks. My wife has taught school for forty-two years. They want to fuck with her pension too."

I'd died and gone to amateur sleuth heaven.

He continued, "I got sent here to do crap duty because they don't trust me. Any moron can put up crime scene tape."

I said, "I know you don't have to tell me, but what the hell is going on?"

He said, "We are expecting a warrant, and we will have one. I know you don't have to let me in the gun shed, but it might help me feel a little more like talking."

I thought for a minute. Here was a chance to get inside information. Could it be a trap? For whom? I hadn't killed anybody.

I said, "I can get keys."

He nodded.

I hurried back up to our bedroom. Scott was just out of the shower. "What's going on?" he asked.

I said, "Adlow, the detective, is here. He might give me some information if I let him into the gun shed."

"You think that's wise?"

"It might get us information."

"You want me to come with?"

"Two of us there might make him reluctant to talk."

"Keep your cell phone handy. Call instantly if you need help."

I hurried back out. Adlow was examining the shed door. "Someone tried to break in."

"They didn't succeed. We heard them the other night and came out. We didn't see anyone. Maybe they made too much noise and scared themselves off, or they could have heard us and run."

He grunted and moved aside so I could unlock the door. We walked in. I didn't volunteer that there was a secret gun assembling room. I was only ready to trust him a little bit.

He walked around the room examining the guns. He found the switches for the basement room. He flipped them. The walls parted. I pressed the button for the storm cellar door. It did its coffin-creaking noise and opened. We proceeded down. Again he examined everything in the room. He touched nothing, inspected everything.

Finished, he took a three-legged stool and placed it so, as he sat on it, he could lean his back against the wall by the door. I took another stool and sat facing him. He said, "I'm glad your partner came to the rallies to try to save our pensions."

"You were there?"

"I went to as many as I could. My bosses aren't any bigger assholes than any other bosses. They aren't any more or less politically involved than any other cops, but these idiots in the legislature are insane. And that Mallon…" He shook his head.

He was talking freely. I was prepared to be silent until all the cows in Wisconsin stopped giving milk.

He continued, "The investigation is fucked. I don't know if I can trust you. I know I can't trust anybody in the department. I want this shit Mallon to lose. It's not my fault the economy went to shit."

I said, "No, it's not."

He looked at me briefly. He said, "I knew that."

"Who's in charge of the investigation of Edgar Grum?"

"It is not me."

"Not the other detective?"

His dark brown eyes held mine.

I said, "Who has the power to derail an investigation?"

"The Grums."

"The county clerk?"

"And her whole family. And the sheriff who owes his office to the Grums, as does every politician in this county. You do know the Grums hate you and your partner?"

"I didn't think we were even a blip on their radar."

"You are very much mistaken. Before we showed up in that room where you guys were on Wednesday, the Grums were adamant about you two guys. They wanted you arrested. For all I know they might have been planning to put you in the deepest dungeon and torture you and leave you for dead."

"Harrison County has dungeons?"

"I've never seen one, but that doesn't mean the Grums don't have them." He grumbled and shifted his weight. "I guess I'm exaggerating but not by much. They also tried to throw suspicion on Veronica."

"How?"

"Mr. Grum, his son, Barry Grum, but especially Mrs. Grum kept repeating the line about the wife being the prime suspect in any murder such as this. They don't like your sister, not one little bit. They talked about trying to get the kids away from her. The other day, I almost had to laugh when your lawyer stepped in. That Grum lawyer is a big shot around county government. The sheriff, the Grums, the lawyer, all of them are hip deep in some strange shit."

"But you keep working for the department."

"It's not a bad job if you can avoid the politics." He sighed, shifted his butt as if he had a hemorrhoid acting up. "But none of that has much to do with the murder as far as I can see. It's more relatives and in-law shit and that goddamn recall vote. There was something fishy about that whole campaign. You know a reporter who went undercover to work in the anti-recall campaign was murdered?"

"Yeah."

"I was in charge of that investigation for a short while. I got no cooperation from the campaign in the investigation. Zero. Zip. None. The poor guy might not have existed. Turns out, people liked the guy. It didn't come out until later that he was a spy."

"How'd you find that out?"

"Frank Smith. An old guy who won the lottery and put a lot of money into the recall campaign. Smith was a maniac about the whole thing. He demanded a full investigation. Called me every day after it happened. He called my boss to get him to put pressure on me. Big mistake. The people behind my boss, the Grums, have way more money than he won in the lottery. And the Grums have been around since dirt. A heap of money plus power, connections, influence can get anything buried."

I said, "I think the technical medical term for that is politics."

"Not when it comes to murder and cover up. Then it's criminal."

"I know the Grums a little, mostly from Veronica and Edgar's wedding. I knew Edgar sort of."

Adlow snorted and banged the flat of his palm against his thigh. "That shit had been in and out of the sheriff's office since he was fifteen. We'd catch him for something, destruction of property, drunk driving, pissing on the rose bushes at the county court house."

"He kept his criminal activity confined to Harrison County?"

"I only know about the Harrison County stuff. I met with the parents once. They thanked me. They were a piece of work. Mrs. Grum carries a therapy dog."

"I've seen the dog."

"It's pathetic how she clutches it in her great big arms. The poor thing doesn't snarl and snap much. It just kind of looks like it's glad it hasn't smothered in her arms. You've met her so you know how huge they all are. I only met with them that once because all the calls went through the sheriff's office. He's been sheriff for a very long time. He and the Grums go back a long way."

"Why didn't you go to the Feds about the cover up of the reporter's murder?"

"Who knows how far the Grums' influence extends? I don't. You do your job for thirty-five years, and you see a lot, maybe too much."

I said, "I heard there was electronic cheating by the Mallon anti-recall campaign. Was that what the reporter was trying to investigate?"

"Frank Smith made these wild accusations about computers, electronics, programs, coding. He'd demand we investigate Flisterbiddle Von Struthers, the company that makes the computer program that's being used in the voting machines all across the state."

"Flisterbiddle Von Struthers sounds like a fake name."

"They exist. Their headquarters is in the next county west of here. I tried to look into them. I got nowhere. I went out there once. The buildings looked abandoned. They were locked and I couldn't get in. They may be a front company. I've had no reason to connect them with murder, but yes, I believe the Mallon people are capable of any kind of fucking around. It was after I reported Smith's accusations that the cooperation from the anti-recall campaign ended. When I first went there, people talked."

"Who'd the reporter work with?"

"He worked directly with Edgar Grum. They were doing a lot of electronic vote checking, who was registered, who had ever voted Republican, who had voted Republican in every election, that kind of stuff, trying to find anyone they could get to who was likely a Republican voter."

"How did the interview go with Edgar Grum when you interviewed him about the reporter's death?"

"He was a gregarious windbag, just a complete idiot. He blubbered on and on about how fabulous the campaign was, how great Zachary Ross the reporter was, how fabulous he, Edgar, was. He told me about all the fabulous plans he had and deals he could make. He wanted me to invest in some scheme."

"He did?"

By this time, Adlow was leaning forward in his chair emphasizing each sentence with a finger pointing at me. His rheumy old eyes met mine and rarely looked away.

"He wanted me to invest in gold futures. Gold was always going to go up. Except when it goes down. He talked politics. I knew who he was. I knew I had to be polite to him. For being Zachary's boss and working with him for six months, he actually knew very little about the kid. Edgar actually didn't seem to be doing a lot of work for the campaign, just kind of talking big.

The other people who worked with Ross liked him. Then Smith began interfering."

Adlow stretched his muscles and twisted his torso back and forth. He said, "Back hurts when I sit too long in one position especially in a chair without a back."

"What happened when Smith interfered?"

"The truth that the reporter was a spy came out and then nothing happened. Everyone stopped talking about the reporter. I went to talk to that Edgar Grum again. He looked scared."

"Of what?"

"His own shadow? I couldn't tell. It was as if someone had deflated a child's balloon. But it wasn't just him, they all shut up."

He gave me details about Ross then he said, "I went to talk to Ross's partner. I got nothing from him. He was suspicious of everybody, especially the police."

"What if I talked to him?"

"Well, I'd warn you about interfering in a police investigation, but there is no investigation as far as I know. I was taken off the case and nobody at headquarters claims to be working the case."

"So I could talk to him?"

"As far as I'm concerned, you can talk to whoever you want. It's a free country, at least it is for the millionaires who've got the money to spend on campaigns like this."

"They've got the kind of money to just stop the investigation?"

"No matter which 'they' you are referring to the answer is yes. If it's the Grums or the Ducharmés, the result is the same. All I know is that at this point in the department, it is best not to ask questions."

"You've met the Ducharmés?"

"A peon like me doesn't get to see royalty."

"Do you think someone from the Grum campaign killed the reporter?"

Adlow said, "If they didn't know he was a spy, why kill him? If they did know he was a spy, what had the spy done that was worth killing for?"

"If they really were cheating electronically, maybe he figured it out, uncovered the truth."

"But the knowledge of him being a spy came about because of Frank Smith's calls. I found no evidence that somebody knew before."

I said, "What was the time lapse between them being cooperative to them not being?"

"A matter of hours."

"Maybe they just shut up because politicians prefer to keep everything secret if they can. Maybe Edgar just blabbed because he didn't know better."

"And the others?"

"Who among the others was helpful? Who stopped?"

"They all were willing to help. Then they all stopped. They were scared. Then I got pulled off the investigation. Here's who I think you might be most likely to get stuff from in the campaign." He gave me names including that of the reporter's editor. "I can't follow up. You can."

"Someone will want to know where I got the names."

"You going to tell them?"

"I don't know anybody named Adlow."

The cop said, "Good answer."

I asked, "Why haven't the cops taken any of Edgar's computer stuff?"

"I don't know."

Scott appeared in the entrance to the shed. He had a tray with fast food choices from a nearby restaurant, plus glasses of orange juice and napkins.

He looked at me and said, "I thought you might be hungry."

He looked at the detective and said, "Hello. Would you care to join us?"

Adlow said, "You're the baseball player."

"Maybe someday again."

"Good luck with it." Scott set the food down on the workbench, and we three began to eat.

I explained to Scott what Adlow had said so far. Adlow didn't object to me telling him.

Scott spoke to the detective, "So you've gotten the shit end of the stick. Do you know what you've done wrong?"

"That's hard to know with the Grums. Maybe I haven't expressed enough enthusiasm or bowed and scraped enough or showed enough ambition or willingness to please them." He shrugged.

I said, "Someone doesn't want these murders investigated. Presumably that someone doesn't want the murderer found. Who has the power to stop an investigation? The Grums. Why would they want an investigation stopped? Because finding out who did it would reflect on them."

Adlow objected. "But that would mean they killed their own son, or caused it to happen. They are shits, but I don't think they are that big of shits."

Scott said, "The Ducharmés have power, supposedly more power than the Grums."

Adlow chewed his breakfast biscuit for a few minutes, drank some coffee. "I've never met any of the Ducharmés. They aren't from around here. You hear about them all the time. I suppose they've got the money and power to stop an investigation too."

"But why?" Scott asked.

I sipped some orange juice then said, "Because if the killer was found, it would reflect on them. And with at least two deaths surrounding this campaign, things could get very suspicious, especially if what you said is right that the reporter/spy worked directly under Edgar as a gofer and factotum. There has to be some kind of connection."

Scott said, "We should try and talk to the recall campaign that hired the spy. The people who worked with the reporter, his editor, his wife or partner if he had one."

Adlow said, "I gave your partner some names." Adlow munched for a moment, caught Scott's eyes, then mine. "What you really need to be worried about now is Edgar Grum's wife, your sister."

"Huh?"

"The higher ups in the police department or the Grums or the Ducharmés or some combination of them want to pin it on her."

"She was at home." I sounded more defensive than I should have.

"You can prove that?"

I snapped, "I know my sister."

Adlow said, "I haven't heard that defense work real well in a court of law recently."

I couldn't keep the sneer out of my tone. "Normally they need some kind of evidence and proof for an accusation or an arrest."

"This is Harrison County," Adlow said. "I've seen the power this crowd has."

"But you're helping us now," I said.

Adlow frowned into his coffee. "I wonder if bringing down the governor, this campaign, and the Ducharmés, and the Grums would save my pension. I can't finance a campaign. I can't risk my job, but I can do a little bit. I was told to let the whole thing go, which was told to me right after I mentioned going out to the computer company headquarters because of the computer connection with the reporter and the rumors that Edgar was shooting off his big mouth about winning the campaign any way possible. If he was on my side, I'd probably have tried to think of a way to shut him up."

The suspicion of a conspiracy against my sister angered me. I said, "I should call Enid Achtenberg and warn her about the danger Veronica is in."

Adlow said, "I'm not in charge of your cell phone, but you didn't hear it from me. If I'd ever eavesdrop on my idiot bosses in the department and I ever heard them talking I'd say they were thinking about making an arrest right after the funeral on Monday."

My mouth gaped.

Scott said, "Bullshit."

"Maybe so," Adlow responded. "If you know lawyers, and you seem to, you might want to give your cell phone a workout." He stood up, brushed crumbs off his clothes, downed the rest of his orange juice, and used a napkin to wipe his face and hands.

I asked, "Why put crime scene tape on the gun shed?"

"We have the gun that killed him, a Colt Mustang Pocketlight .380 Auto."

"What's that?" Scott asked.

"A small gun, fits in your hand."

I said, "He must have been shot up close."

"Yup."

"You've got the gun," I said. "Why close off this shed?"

He thought for several moments. "They've got me doing nonsensical shit work. I've got tons of paperwork to do back at headquarters. Somebody is getting away with murder. Why this? Why now? Beats the hell out of me. Maybe they want to plant the gun here. Maybe they want to see if it came from here."

"Plant the gun? That makes no sense. There have to be a zillion cops who know that the gun was found at the crime scene. They can get that many people to be silent? They can distort reality to that great of an extent?"

Adlow gave me a grim smile. "Welcome to my world."

"This is worse than Dorothy being dropped into Oz. I've

been dropped into Wonderland and Oz combined." I shook my head. "If they can do that, I am very frightened. Are you sure they want to plant it?"

"No, I'm not sure what the sheriff and the Grums are up to. I know I don't want any part of it. This is wrong."

We looked at each other in dismay and disbelief for several moments.

I broke the silence. I swept my arm around the room. "I didn't see an obvious empty spot where it may have been on display."

"It's a small gun that could have been concealed anywhere."

Could that have been what the Grums had all been looking for? But if the cops had the gun, what was the point?

Adlow continued, "There were no fingerprints on the gun that was used. Or maybe they just wanted to get me the hell out of the way."

He climbed up the stairs. At the top he turned around and said, "You, me, and your family should be very, very careful." He left.

I gaped at Scott. "They're going to frame her. Those mother-fucking asshole sons of bitches."

He said, "Incredible. Stunning. But I can believe they'd do something like that."

Achtenberg had given me her number Wednesday night before she left. I called and told her the news. She asked where I heard it from. I told her "a good source."

"What's going on?" she asked.

I said, "We're going to talk to some people who worked with Edgar."

"Don't get in the way of the police. Be careful. I think you should stay in the house."

"Good advice." Which I didn't plan to take. She promised to work her sources in the department and the courts to see if she could find out if anything was in the works concerning Veronica.

I asked, "Have the police made any progress on the investigation?"

"Not that I've been able to find out."

"Do you think I should tell Veronica about possibly being arrested?"

She paused for several moments. "Let me see what I can do. If they really are going to wait until after the funeral, we've got some time. She's dealing with a lot right now. I'll stop by. Maybe if I'm there when she's told, I'll be able to help minimize any fears she has."

"She'll be scared," I said. "Who wouldn't be?" She promised to check her sources and stop by later today.

While I talked, Scott crumpled our papers and empty cups and stuffed them back into the bags. I hung up and called our attorney. I trusted Achtenberg, but I wanted Todd Bristol in on everything, and I was very worried about a possible trumped up charge against Veronica.

I checked my watch. Nearly 8:30. Todd would be in the back of his Lincoln Town Car being driven to work by the house boy. I filled him in.

His first question was, "Did she kill him?"

"No." He was silent for several beats. I said, "She's my sister. I know she wouldn't."

Todd said, "You've described Edgar and his family as the kind of people who would be leading the cheering section as each person arrived in Dante's circles of hell, and Edgar as the kind of person who, if hell had a brass band, he would be the entire trumpet section. They sound like people who would cause a saint to contemplate murder."

"What can we do to avoid an unfounded accusation by the police?"

He had me go over what Adlow and then Achtenberg had said. He listened carefully then said, "It's Friday. I have a few appointments then I'll drive up. I'll make calls during the day.

Unfounded indictments are something I like to keep track of on the spot."

I didn't question his willingness to drive up. He offered, and Scott and I paid him a hefty retainer every year, and he'd bill us for any extra hours. If it took money to keep my sister away from Edgar's family's clutches, then I'd spend it. He said he'd be up late that afternoon or early evening.

I said, "What about this company that designed the computer program?"

"If I was a detective still on either case, I would pay a visit to their company."

"We're not doing anything right now."

Todd hesitated. "Be careful. Very, very careful."

Veronica had said she wanted me to find out who murdered her husband. Now I might have to take action to be proactive to keep her out of jail.

THIRTY-FIVE

Friday 8:48 A.M.

There was a crowd in the kitchen having breakfast. Mom was making omelets. Veronica was talking with Patricia. Dad and Gerald were discussing comic books. David was playing with a hand-held electronic device. Darryl and Lionel were discussing the Grums.

Veronica, Scott, and I stepped into the pantry. I told her what I learned except the part about their possibly trying to arrest her. Veronica said, "Good, I want you to get those goddamn Grums. I knew all the police couldn't be in their power."

"Do you need me here?"

"I think I'm not going to have so many people here today. It was nice these past couple days, but I need to take a rest."

I said, "We've got more boxes to go through but we're around half done. We'll finish before we leave. We'll stay as long as it takes."

Veronica stamped her foot. "Why haven't they found the killer? Why haven't they told us anything?" As per my discussion with Enid Achtenberg, I didn't say *because they're trying to pin it on you.*

I asked, "Do you know if Edgar owned a Colt Mustang Pocketlight .380 Auto?"

"What's that?"

After I described the gun to her, she shook her head. "I have no idea. He never showed me any of his guns. I never wanted to see any of his guns."

"Okay. As long as you don't need us here, we'll be able to spend the day asking questions."

"Good. You haven't found out anything yet?"

I didn't say, *we found out that your husband was a shit*, but then again I already knew that. I did say, "Nothing that says who did it."

She went back to the family.

We stood in the front room. Scott asked, "Are you sure you can trust this detective?"

"It's what we've got so far. I can't give him information about the murder because I don't have any. He hasn't asked me for information about Edgar because he knows him and his family far better than we do."

Scott said, "Would investigating this with you be on an equivalent level as me doing skateboard tricks yesterday afternoon, possibly dangerous, even career ending, kind of not too bright?"

"Well, yeah, sort of, maybe. I hope not."

I watched his eyes get their mischievous twinkle and his mouth form a bit of a grin. He said, "Well, then count me in."

We stopped in our room. I used the laptop to connect to the Internet to Google the names that Adlow had given me. That done, we left to try to stop the Grums from destroying Veronica's and our lives.

Thirty-six

Friday 9:17 A.M.

Two blocks past the gate to the subdivision, I was watching in the review mirror the black wrought-iron sides of the gate clang together when a black SUV came out of a side road. It hung back, but it made turns when I did and didn't close the distance. I made an abrupt turn and pulled up to a fast-food drive through and ordered some coffee. It was there again as we pulled away.

I said, "We are being followed."

Scott checked his mirrors. "I noticed him. Who would follow us and why?"

I abruptly cut into another fast food parking lot and got in a long line. The SUV kept going. I cut across the low curb that was meant to keep cars in line. The car bumped and scraped over the curbs. I took a back exit, doubled back the opposite way and parked behind a bank.

"What the hell is going on?" Scott asked.

"That's what I'd like to know. Adlow didn't mention any surveillance directed at us, but then I think he's completely cut out of the loop by now."

"Or we shouldn't trust him," Scott said.

"He gave us information. How much choice do we have?"

Thirty-seven

Friday 10:38 A.M.

I checked carefully as we drove away. For the moment at least, we had ditched the tail. Frank Smith, whose name Adlow had given us, had a home on Lake Michigan just south of Sheboygan. We drove up a circular, tree-lined drive to a rambling, red brick, ranch home. We'd called ahead and were expected.

A handsome young man answered the doorbell ring. He led us into a sunken living room that looked out over the gray lake. He asked if we wanted refreshments. We declined. He said he'd be back in a moment.

He came back leading Frank Smith - old and dumpy, sad jowls hanging, too much weight lost too quickly on a stooped frame, jeans too big, held up by a belt with holes cut in the strap by hand. A flannel shirt that had seen more washes than my underwear. He looked all of his ninety years as he leaned on a cane.

The young man lingered next to him with a hand out to help. The older man smiled at us. He ran his eyes up and down Scott's torso, stopped at the bulge at the front of his jeans then moved up to his eyes.

He staggered to Scott and touched his face the way a blind person would, lingering carefully on chin, lips, eyebrows. His mottled hand trembled as he lowered it to his side. Smith said, "Will your arm be okay?"

Scott said, "I hope so."

"I go to every game you pitch, no matter where it is in the country. When you're old and a fool and you win over a hundred million dollars in the lottery, you can do stupid things. I never thought I'd meet you. You are someone every gay person should be proud of."

Scott said, "You're very kind."

The old man half coughed, half cackled. "I'm a horny old fool."

The old man looked at me and swept his eyes over me from head to crotch, lingered at the bulge in the front of my jeans. He smiled and licked his lips. He switched his cane from right hand to left, then held out the right to me.

We shook.

With his cane, Smith nudged the younger man's leg. "This is my assistant, Brendan Bowers." The far younger man helped him to a seat. Bowers hovered as his meal ticket lowered himself into a chair. The young man wore faded, skinny-leg, blue jeans, black running shoes, a black T-shirt, covered by a black and gray letterman's jacket that he may actually have worn in high school not that many years ago.

Scott and I sat. I said, "We're here because my brother-in-law Edgar Grum was murdered. We're staying with my sister to help her. We think there might be something odd with the investigation. We were told you had an intimate knowledge of the campaign and might be able to give us some information about him and about Zachary Ross."

His eyes got teary. He coughed and hacked then leaned back in his chair. "Zachary was a dear, sweet boy, an angel."

I said, "We're sorry for your loss."

Smith coughed again, then sat up. "I can tell you everything about Zachary, about Edgar Grum, and that goddamn election. They stole it. I know they did. They stole it electronically. Absolutely, for sure, they did. I want you to get proof, and I want you to stop them. I can pay you. I won the lottery."

He pointed at his outfit. "I'm used to the clothes I've always worn, but I've got more millions than I can spend in my lifetime. It's hard to even find an escort who is willing to touch a saggy and fragile old man in his nineties. And I've got plenty to pay. Plenty. I've bankrolled the Jacob Nerz campaign. I gave a million to him in the primary. I gave a million to the general election. I gave a million to the party. I gave a million to the Unions."

We sat and listened. I had no idea of what, if anything, we'd find out from him about Edgar's death, but he was old and sad, and he might say something important to the subsequent investigation. Bowers kept his eyes on his boss.

What Smith said now mostly confirmed information I'd seen on the web before we left, but he was rambling and I was waiting.

He smirked. "I'm so glad I won the lottery. A hundred million, fifty after taxes. I got no family. I got no friends. I'm not very nice. But I've got causes. Lots of them. Liberal. Do-good. Gay causes. And I'm going to do what I can before I die. I gave a million to the Trevor Project. I gave a million to Lambda Legal. I'm going to make those straight people pay. If I can. I might not be as rich as those assholes trying to steal the election, but I can target my money specifically."

I wondered how many more times he'd mention winning all that money. No doubt his identity was caught up in it. He'd been a set designer for years at theaters throughout the Midwest and according to the Internet never earned enough to have more than a marginal existence. I wonder if the good fortune coming late in life ever caused him to be bitter.

Smith finally ran down. He let his eyes rove over the walls which were filled with paintings that looked to be Michael Breyette originals. Then his eyes rested on my crotch for a few moments. I spread my legs slightly. If it was giving the old guy a thrill to look between my legs, who was I to deny whatever thrill he got from it? I wasn't planning to ask him out on a date, and his looking cost me nothing. And he was in his nineties. What could it hurt?

He broke the silence. "Someone has to investigate the theft of the election. Someone has to prove it."

I said, "Aren't people filing law suits and going to court? We don't have that kind of expertise."

"But they don't know what I know. That Mary Mallon has got to be stopped at all cost. Do you know how rotten she is?" He didn't wait for an answer. "I'll tell you how rotten she is. You remember those incidents of cops pepper spraying peaceful protesters in California?"

I nodded.

Smith asked, "You know what she did?"

I shook my head.

"She made it her business to call them and offer them jobs as security guards on the state of Wisconsin payroll."

"Nobody's heard about this?" I asked. "Nobody's made a stink about it?"

"I tried. It was during this recall. The Grums have control of the media."

"Not the Internet."

"They've got their people hacking into every anti-Mallon site on the Internet. They go after every anti-Mallon posting, blog, Facebook page, and Tweet."

"I heard about that. Didn't they stop?"

"They got sneakier about it. Hired expert hackers instead of attacking directly. They learned from that idiot governor of Kansas when that eighteen-year-old attempted to express an opinion to sixty-five friends. That attack on an innocent kid backfired, but these guys here in Wisconsin," he shook his head, "this is money, real money. Hackers have been hired from all around the globe to fight anybody who opposes them."

"Hackers can stop the Internet?"

"They can do a lot of damage to our side. We've tried to fight back, but they've got money. Way more than my piddly millions. No, I'm just giving you examples of how they fought and are still fighting. Dirty, mean, and desperate."

Was he complaining that their side hadn't had the money to be as dirty and mean? Or that they wanted to but couldn't because of moral principles? Or that they had been beaten at the dirty-mean game?

"Are these hackers the ones who stole the election for them?"

"Maybe. I think the hacking has been very hush-hush, very low key. Few people really knew what was going on."

The best kind of conspiracy. Nobody really knows what's going on. The less people know, the more you can make up.

"You didn't hire hackers of your own?"

"We've hired counter-hackers. We couldn't afford both them and attack hackers. And we didn't want to win by out-hacking them. We wanted to win honestly."

"Why didn't you hire someone to investigate before the election?"

"I was foolish. I didn't think of it. I won money. I didn't win brains."

"You have proof they stole the election?"

"What election machines are being used in Wisconsin?" he asked.

I said, "I heard of a company, Flisterbiddle something."

"The machines are Firbutton 20's made by Flisterbiddle Von Struthers, Incorporated."

Adlow had told us a bit, but it turned out Smith knew more or claimed he did. Smith said, "Firbutton 20's were purchased with a no bid contract. They were built, designed, and programmed by minions of the republipigs. All of it was arranged and stage managed by the governor and the republipig party. That Mary Mallon is a threat to the existence of all that is decent. She's an idiot, an incompetent fool. She couldn't steal her own asshole."

What an odd concept, but the derogatory meaning kind of worked. I tried to picture the theft of this intimate part of your own anatomy, couldn't. I avoided looking at Scott and kept the smile off my face as Smith continued, "The actual people in charge of the republipig operation in Harrison County are a Mr. and Mrs. Grum. Your sister married into them, but how much do you know about them?"

"I know they're awful people, but I don't how they'd go about stealing an election."

Bowers looked bored. He'd yet to say a word. He was careful to act alert when his meal-ticket looked at him. I felt guilt about my disparaging of his caring for the old man. I'd been sneering at the Grums and now this simple thought about this poor kid who was probably trying his best to live his life made me feel guilty. I had to get a grip.

Smith said, "There's all kinds of history here, all kinds. Mrs. Grum has been in the news for election violations a number of times. A gay candidate for U.S. Congress ran in a district that included a slice of Harrison County. He lost because of the stunningly high turnout and lopsided vote in the Harrison County portion of the district." He thumped his cane on the ground next to his chair, waved a finger at me. "Accusations of fraud flew at the time. Investigations were held, lawyers fought, and six months later a squib at the bottom of page thirty-nine in the local paper said violations probably occurred, but no criminal charges were going to be filed. The item made the gay news websites, but the world doesn't often dance to the tune the gay media plays. Hell, I tried to buy space to advertise for the recall in the few nationwide gay magazines left. I never got my calls answered. No wonder so many of them folded."

I asked, "Do you know what the Grums did specifically this time?"

Smith continued, "Flisterbiddle Von Struthers is a fake company. The real owners are the Ducharmé brothers. You know them?"

I nodded.

"They are among the billionaire oligarchs determined to make sure laws are passed and tax breaks are given in local, state, and federal legislatures to make themselves and their cronies even more wealthy billionaire oligarchs. To win the election they are manipulating gasoline prices by using their money to drive up the cost of oil through mad speculation. There are those who doubt they would do such a thing. I don't. They want the economy to fail. That's treason. To the Ducharmés we are like toys in the hands of children. We are playthings for their amusement." He puffed hard, coughed and hacked. Bowers put a hand on his back and caressed him gently. Smith's spell subsided slowly.

"Are you okay?" I asked. "Do you want to stop?"

"I'm fine. I'm going to die." He waved a hand to stop my expressions of sympathy. "We're all going to die. I'm just nearer the head of the line than most." He drew several deep breaths. Bowers handed him what looked like a throat lozenge. Smith took it and sucked contentedly.

When he seemed better, I asked, "How did you find out about the company and the machines and their connection to them?"

He shifted in his seat. He glanced at Bowers.

"Some time ago one of their campaign workers came to me."

"They have a traitor in their midst?"

He said, "You can have a thousand campaign workers. One of them has to have a conscience, even if he's a republipig. One of them has got to be honest. However, this was the first I heard of it in my long life."

I didn't contradict him. There had to be at least one good Republican. I was fairly certain about that, maybe more than one, although I was less sure about that.

"What did the campaign worker say?"

"That she was suspicious. She's a lesbian. A closeted lesbian. A frightened, closeted lesbian. After I talked with her, I knew I needed a plan." He sighed. He clutched his cane with his right hand. His left began to twitch slightly. His left knee trembled. He continued, "Then I got too smart for my own good. I found a reporter for the *Milwaukee Gazette* who was hungry for a story. He had a suspicious editor as well. He got himself hired as one of the tech people on the campaign." He ran hands crinkled with arthritis over his eyes. He passed them over his sagging jowls. I saw tears in his eyes. He whispered, "And they killed him." Tears fell.

Bowers held out a tissue box for him.

Smith blotted his eyes and his nose, folded the tissue into a small wad, then continued while clutching the dampened wad of paper. "It's my fault he's dead. All my money, and I killed him. I wish I'd never won that money. All that money wasn't worth it. Not worth a beautiful, sweet young man's life." He drew deep breaths for several minutes.

Bowers put a hand on the man's shoulder. "You couldn't have known." His voice was gentle and soft. "You were doing what you hoped was best. You didn't know they were like that. You didn't know they'd kill to get what they wanted."

The old man nodded and sniffled. "I should have known. It was my own hubris, my own hubris that got someone killed. I thought that much money solved everything." He gulped, sniffled some more, wiped his nose. "Zachary Ross. He was a beautiful young man. Yes, physically, but most important, a kind, gentle soul, trying to do right, and he got in with those vipers, and they killed him. I will never forgive myself. But I'm old. I'll die soon anyway. He had wonderful years ahead of him." Bowers held out to him the trash can from the side of the desk. Smith threw in the tissue. He sat up straighter. "But I can avenge him. I can get even with these people. I can find out who killed him."

"We're not official investigators."

"You're here asking questions. Each time I create a new enemy for them, I'm taking a step in the right direction, and you're an in to the Grum family. We haven't had that before."

"I'm a brother-in-law."

"Who is staying at Edgar's house. It's a start and it's more than we had before you walked in the door."

True as far as it went, and I was there to help my sister. I didn't care much that Edgar was gone or who did it, but if finding that out would help Veronica, fine. If it would keep her from being arrested, perfect. As a bonus, if we discovered who and how either the Grums or the Ducharmés cheated on the election, even better.

Scott asked, "What exactly happened to the reporter?"

"The killers made it look like an accident. A week ago the

police found his body floating in the lake."

"How do you know it wasn't an accident?"

Bowers said, "How do you accidentally jump off a bridge?"

"It wasn't suicide?" Scott asked.

Bowers responded, "He would never kill himself, never."

"How do you know this?" I asked.

Bowers got a stubborn look. "I just know. I knew him. He was a friend."

Smith added, "And the police didn't say suicide. They said accident. It wasn't raining so it wasn't slippery. It was the Racine Avenue Bridge over the Milwaukee River. It's an old bridge that you have to climb several railings to be able to jump in. You can't just trip and fall off."

"It didn't make the news?" Scott asked.

"He was a minor reporter, little more than an intern. His position in the recall campaign was never mentioned. Even his death was hushed up. His editor is frightened. His editor has bosses. His editor has a publisher who takes a lot of advertising from Ducharmé-backed companies."

"How'd you get Zachary Ross the job in the first place?"

"He's a tech genius who decided not to get rich out in Silicon Valley. He was gay. He knew the good fight was going on right here. He wanted to be part of stopping them. Even six months ago we knew they'd try to pull something. If you don't win an election by a landslide, the republipigs will find a way to steal it. Florida. Ohio. Need I say more?"

"Who interviewed him for the job at the campaign?"

"I don't know a specific name. They were starting up the campaign, hiring all kinds of people. They started before we were done gathering signatures. Their budget was unlimited."

I asked, "Is the lesbian alive?"

"Yes, but even more frightened than she was."

"Will she talk to us?"

"I hope so."

"Maybe you could call her."

"I will."

Scott asked, "Why didn't they come after you? You were giving lots of money to the opposition."

"Yes, but see, they always had more money. They knew they couldn't be outspent. We had to outthink them, out plot them, out plan them, and I got somebody killed." His crabbed left hand clutched at Bower's sleeve, but he spoke to me. "You've got to do something. We've got to avenge his death."

I said, "If they killed once, what's to stop them from killing again?"

"You guys are famous. I just have money. They wouldn't kill someone with fame and money. You people can fight back."

"We don't have the resources of the Ducharmé brothers. If they have access to killers, we're in trouble. Even if I could, I'm not sure I want to summon killers."

Smith said, "They can't get away with this. You've got to investigate."

Bowers spoke up, "They broke into Frank's house last night."

Smith said, "We don't know who did it. I have many valuable things."

Bowers said, "We were planning to attend a protest in Madison about them stealing the election. We were going to stay overnight. We forgot one of Frank's medicines. We had to come back. We'd been gone maybe an hour. We saw a black SUV rush out of here just as we were pulling up the driveway. When we got inside, we saw that they tore up the house."

I said, "You were lucky not to be here." I looked around. "You cleaned up pretty fast."

"I stayed up late."

Frank said, "We don't know it was them."

Bowers said, "It had to be. I'm scared. What if they come back? What if they send an army of people?"

Frank said, "Does anybody have enough guns to defeat an army of the demented right wing? That's why we have laws and civilization."

"If they're enough," Bowers said.

Frank shook his head.

Scott said, "They came when you weren't here. They might or might not have had something to do with the campaign. Whatever they are looking for is the problem, not you."

They knew nothing more helpful. A few minutes later with Bowers' assistance, Smith tottered to his feet. He wiped a last tear from his face. "You'll be careful? I don't want another death on my conscience."

I said, "I make my own choices. You are not responsible for them."

Before we left, I got names and addresses of all the major characters he had mentioned. He agreed to set up meetings with those he had mentioned. Bowers said he would text us with possible times and venues.

Smith leaned heavily on Bowers arm as he tottered down the hall with us to the door. We watched him wave feebly as we walked down the driveway.

THIRTY-EIGHT

Friday 11:52 A.M.

We sat in the car in the winding driveway.

"That's very sad," Scott said.

"This is all sad and miserable. I can believe the Grums would be behind adding more sadness and misery to the world."

"You know what's frightening?" Scott asked.

"What?"

"That they don't think they're adding sadness and misery. They are completely oblivious. That brings it to the point of madness and tragedy."

My cell phone buzzed. It was a text from Bowers giving directions on where to meet the woman from the campaign. I put the car in gear and turned on the GPS in the car. We could have used either one of our phones for the same purpose. Gotta love modern technology.

As we turned onto the street, Scott said, "Somebody is looking for something."

"It would be logical to assume this break-in would be connected with the Grums trying to hunt through Edgar's stuff."

"What is it they're looking for?" Scott asked.

"It can't be something that only Edgar had, or they wouldn't have broken in here at Frank Smith's. What I can't figure out is what would Edgar Grum have and Frank Smith have that bad guys would want."

Scott said, "Depends on the bad guys and if it tells us who murdered Edgar or who stole the election electronically. If the election was for sure stolen."

"You don't think it was?"

"I think I want proof," Scott replied.

Kim Strobridge, the lesbian insider, wouldn't even meet us within the confines of Harrison County. Even Milwaukee County was too hot to hold her. She insisted on meeting at the Highway 20 exit in Racine County. At least she picked a place that had Kringle, the single greatest pastry the world has ever created. I had pecan.

I was into my second slice of Kringle when a woman fitting the description Smith had given us walked in. She looked the diners over and eased her way back toward us. Smith must have described us. I didn't think she'd see thirty again and might be pushing forty. The wrinkles around her eyes gave her away. She was a whole lot of ordinary: petite, edging toward anorexic, pale complexion, blond hair in a page boy haircut.

The frightened, closeted lesbian sat down, ordered coffee, and said, "They'll kill you next, both of you. I know you're famous. You'll still die. I think people have been following me. We should all be very frightened."

Not the conversation one normally has over a piece of Kringle.

I said, "Who is going to kill us?"

"Take your pick. You get your nose into it, the goons from the Grums, or the goons from the Ducharmés, doesn't matter which, we'll all still be dead. You stick your nose in. You will die."

"You're breathing."

The waitress brought coffee. Kim took hers black. When the waitress was out of ear shot she said, "I've managed to keep my nose clean."

"The Grums and Ducharmés have that much power they can kill with impunity?"

"Did you take extra naïve classes in college or does your doctor give you extra strength stupid pills?"

I chose not to respond to the insult. "If meeting with you and asking questions means we're going to die, why are you meeting with us?"

"I know Frank. I've known him for years. He's one of the few people who didn't berate me for my political leanings. He's a nice, sweet man."

"Why aren't you going to be killed?"

"I haven't been found out. I can just walk away."

"Why'd you get involved at all? Why work for them?"

"I hate unions. They sap the life out of this country. They make people lazy."

Scott said, "Someone in your family got hurt by a union once."

"Union thugs beat up my brother when he wouldn't become a teamster."

"All Union members are thugs?" I asked.

"Enough. My brother was crippled for life in the attack. They never caught who did it."

"But you're willing to help Frank."

"Yes, I also knew Zachary Ross. He was a good man."

"You knew who he was and didn't turn him in to your campaign?"

"That's right. The world of politics in Harrison County is a small world. He and I even talked. Early on I knew something was odd about the campaign. The whole thing just didn't make sense. Plus, I've got a conscience. Union thugs are one thing. Stealing this election electronically is another."

"You have proof?"

"No."

"Did Zachary Ross have proof?"

"Not that I know of."

Scott had limited himself to one piece of Kringle. I'd had several. He watches his diet religiously. I do huge amounts of extra exercise so I can have the extra sweets. He doesn't generally get into debates with people, but he asked, "Isn't Mallon virulently anti-gay? Why were you working with the anti-recall people?"

"I believe in limited government. I believe in working within the system to bring about the change."

He asked, "Why doesn't it work both ways?"

"Both ways what?" The sneer in her tone ripped past the offensive. Why was he debating this venom-drenched lesbian?

He said, "Why not work in the Democratic Party to change them from within? When they've been in power in the last three decades they've done more to cut taxes and limit government than the Republicans have."

"That's so not true."

I did not go nuts. The right-wing delusion disconnect from reality was more than I'd be able to cure with logic, reason, or common sense.

Scott asked, "Then why don't you work within the Democratic Party to change them?"

The sneer turned to a snarl. "I don't have to debate with you. I came here because a gay guy is dead. And I like Frank."

Scott leaned back and was silent. I said, "This whole thing is a mess. Maybe all of this is tied together, Edgar Grum's death, Zachary Ross's death, and the stealing of the election electronically."

She glared at me for an uncomfortable minute and then began without preliminary. "Frank Smith is a sweet, old, sad man. I'd like to help him but saving the world, or at least this election, I think is beyond any of us."

"Why were you so frightened to talk to us?"

"I'm not scared." She glanced furtively around the room. "I'm cautious. I don't know you. I don't know who to trust. Frank says you're good guys. I know about you, but I've never heard of you doing anything to help lesbian athletes."

Scott put his hand on my arm. I did not ask my next question, "What does that have to do with anything?" I took a breath, sipped coffee. I said, "What do you think happened with the election."

"I'm a computer expert. I should be able to get into the electronics for the election, at least to check them." She sipped her coffee. "I can't even get past the first level of passwords. The Ducharmé people have some of the best computer people in the world working on their side. If you were arrested for hacking any time in the past ten years, and you aren't in jail, you're probably working for them. I found those kinds of names, but I sure couldn't get into their system."

Without Scott having to place a calming hand on my arm, I did not say, maybe you're not as good a computer expert as you think you are.

I said, "Frank Smith said the campaign had electronic experts hacking into their stuff."

She laughed. "Our hackers are better than your hackers? Yeah. It was a joke. Their people were crap. We could shut down or counter any crap they put on the Net. They were good. We were better."

"How many of them were there?"

"Fifty or so."

"Is that a lot?"

"It was enough for us."

"All paid?"

"I was. Nobody talked about salary."

"Anyone among them you think I could talk to, who might tell me the truth?"

"I have no idea."

"Would you at least think about it?"

"I guess."

"What else can you tell me about the campaign?"

For the first time she took a bite of Kringle. She made a face.

Not a fan of Kringle? Something must be really wrong with her.

Strobridge said, "The Grums infested the place. One of them was always there. Mr. and Mrs. Grum were like a plague. Constantly asking people what they were doing. Were they working hard enough? Couldn't they stay longer? Asking people at the last minute to stay late or come in on their day off."

"Weren't these mostly volunteers?"

"There were tons of paid staff."

"They treated paid staff like this?"

"We didn't have a union." She didn't seem to recognize the irony in this statement. She took another sip of her coffee. She continued, "I never want to see another Grum. I had to work with their youngest son, Edgar. He was a piece of work. Sexist. Racist. Homophobic. Just a pig. Used the n-word in casual conversation. I finally said something to him about it. He stopped in a snarly teenage way."

"Was the rest of the family the same way?"

"Not overtly bigoted, at least not in front of me, but I don't know." She twisted her upper body as if she were warming up in an exercise class. Which also gave her a chance to scan the room without being obvious about it, or at least she thought she wasn't. "Mrs. Grum was the worst of the rest of them. I thought she'd maybe be nicer, her being a woman. Hah! She'd insult the workers, belittle them, demand they come in on short notice, work overtime. Didn't matter if you had plans."

"That can be rough."

"Both the volunteers and the paid staff got treated like dirt. A lot of the paid staff had been working with or associated with the Grums in Harrison County for a long time. The stuff they told was unbelievable. I heard and saw some of it up close a few times."

"Like what?"

"That Edgar, the n-word guy. He went hunting with a bunch of his buddies and got shot in the butt by his dog."

There'd been a rash of those dog-shooting-person reports on the Internet. I remembered vaguely hearing about Edgar and a hunting accident, but I never cared enough about hunting or Edgar to find out details.

"When was this?"

"Years ago, but they still laughed about it. Not to his face and that's simple stuff, small potatoes. That family did not get along. I've seen the Grum family members arguing and fighting with each other."

"What was the problem?"

"I was never sure, but they could go at it. They all always knew better than the others. Mr. and Mrs. Grum would go after each other viciously, right in front of people. They'd argue about campaign tactics, priorities, spending."

"I thought they had tons of money."

"That didn't mean they couldn't fight about it. They all thought they were in charge, but somehow they always seemed to dump on Edgar. Nobody supported him in any argument, yet, when dealing with us, he was always this cheerful buffoon. It never made a lot of sense. He'd brag that they were going to win no matter what."

"He was shot with a Colt Mustang Pocketlight .380 gun. Do you know anything about that?"

"That fool brought guns to work all the time. He loved the new concealed weapons law in this state. If he could have brought in a concealed tank, he would have. They say these gun people are over-compensating for a lack in the sexual department, well, Edgar needed to compensate a tank's worth."

"Can I talk to any of the other paid staff or volunteers?"

"It was a miracle you got me. Be glad you got that much."

"And you don't know what Zachary Ross knew?"

"No. Try his boyfriend and his mother. Sometimes he left stuff at both places. Zach was really organized and paranoid."

"Could anybody else have known he was a spy?"

"I don't know. That's what scares me. Someone could know I'm talking to you."

"How?"

"Who knows? If the Grums aren't all powerful, and they probably aren't, the Ducharmés probably are."

Thirty-nine

Friday 2:00 P.M.

Next on our list was the boyfriend of the reporter Zachary Ross. I contacted Frank Smith. Bowers answered and said we could meet the reporter's lover, Jordan Labrinski, at a Starbucks on the north side of Milwaukee near the University of Wisconsin campus.

The day had become overcast, cool, and humid. If it was winter, you'd know a snowstorm was coming. If it was summer, you'd know that strong storms would be in the forecast. For spring, it could be either, or just a placid calm atmosphere of waiting for the sun to warm the Earth into summer.

Labrinski sat at a table in a corner far from others who had their laptops open and coffee ready. I wondered sometimes what the ratio was between coffee spills and laptops destroyed in these shops. Labrinski's long legs encased in skinny jeans were spread wide. He had dark black hair cut short and wore black horn-rimmed glasses. He recognized Scott more than me. He stood and we shook hands. I said, "We're so sorry for your loss."

His eyes teared up. Scott offered to buy coffee for all of us. He got in line. I reached for some napkins from the condiments cart and handed them to Labrinski.

He muttered, "Thanks."

When we'd all been served, Labrinski said, "Frank Smith called. I know who you guys are. I never thought I'd meet Scott Carpenter. You're a hero."

Scott blushed, sipped coffee, and said, "Thanks."

I waited a beat then said, "We were hoping to find out about Zachary. Maybe it would help us figure this whole thing out."

"Frank said you wanted to find out who killed Edgar

Grum and Zachary, and expose the whole stealing the election electronically criminal stuff."

"It all seems to be tied together, but we thought you might know something about what Zachary knew."

He sighed, sipped some coffee, dabbed at his eyes. "Zachary was a saint." He didn't seem to mean this as a joke.

"How so?" Scott asked.

Labrinski leaned forward and said, "He always had to be political, always rushed off to the latest good cause. If a whale got stranded in Alaska, he was off to rescue it. If a dolphin got a cold in the Pacific, if an elephant had a hangnail in the middle of the jungle, whatever the cause, he had to be there. If a tree needed to be hugged, they called Zachary. You know what it's like being married to a saint?"

Scott was a good man, and I loved him, but neither he nor I would be up for sainthood any time soon.

Labrinski rushed on, "Don't get me wrong, I loved him. He was kind and considerate and thoughtful. He went out of his way for me. And I was into some of his causes. The gay rights ones anyway."

Scott asked, "How long had you been together?"

"Six years. We fell in love senior year of high school. We went to college here, me at Marquette, him at UW Milwaukee. We had an apartment together. I was a musician. He was a waiter at a bunch of different places." He waxed nostalgic for several minutes. The memories brought smiles to his lips and more tears to his eyes. He finished, "We graduated. He wanted to make a difference in the world, not get a job in some Silicon Valley cubicle. He got a job as a stringer for the paper out in Harrison County. And then he got involved in that damn campaign. I was all for it at first. I wanted to be part of bringing those goddamn homophobic pricks to their knees." He shook his head.

I asked, "What happened?"

"Over time Zachary got more and more tense. I'd never

seen him like that. His hands shook. He was paranoid, thought someone was following him."

"Did he tell you what was wrong?"

"I asked him about it. I think he was frightened. Turns out he was right. He should have been." Tears began to flow. "The police claimed it was an accident! An accident! You don't fall from a bridge and it be an accident. You either jump or you get pushed, and Zachary was not suicidal. He never said the word suicide in all the years we were together. We never discussed it. If he thought about it, he never brought it up, never, not once." More tears.

I got another supply of napkins from the dispenser. He blew his nose, got himself under control. I said, "We can stop if you want."

"No," he said. He was fierce and angry. "I want to know who did this. I want to find out what the hell's was going on. Someone killed him." He took great gasping breaths. Scott eased closer to him and put his hand on his arm.

"Are you sure this is okay?" Scott asked.

Jordan nodded but his tears still fell. The people in the Starbucks were beginning to notice. One of the baristas came over and asked if he could help. Jordan shook his head no. He said, "These guys are friends. I'll be all right."

It took a few minutes but Jordan pulled himself together. "Thank you," he whispered to Scott.

I stood up. "We should go."

"No, please, stay. I needed to do that. Thank you." He patted Scott's arm. "I want to try and get through this. I want to help."

I looked at Scott. He nodded. I sat back down.

Jordan blew his nose several times and tossed the used tissues in a small trash can next to the chair. He pulled in several deep breaths. He leaned against Scott as he spoke to me. "I have no proof that someone killed him. How is anyone going to get that kind of proof against the Ducharmés? Not against that kind of money. You can buy a lot of silence and a lot of death with that kind of cash."

I said, "Maybe if we start more simply."

Jordan looked at me.

"Did Zachary leave any clue about what he did every day in the recall campaign?"

"He was the assistant to Edgar Grum. He worked directly for him."

"Did he say what his job required?"

"He said he was kind of a babysitter. Edgar Grum was the idiot relative in that group, at least that's how Zachary described him."

"What idiot things did Edgar do?"

He gave us a convoluted list of Edgar bragging and being chastised by his mother, father, and oldest brother and other higher up campaign functionaries. "He would rail against them and threaten to get even with them. Right to their face, but as far as I know, he never did anything like that. At least Zachary never said so. He also was convinced that something really crooked was going on in the campaign. He never said what."

"No hint?" Scott asked. "Criminal mishandling of campaign contributions? Electronic computer stuff?"

"He just said he was suspicious about all of them, but he needed to get proof, but he must not have found it, or if he did he never said. He was suspicious of all of them, especially the Ducharmés. He said that kind of money was totally corrupting."

"Is there any way to know what he was doing that last night, why he was on that bridge?"

"He always kept a record. He always took notes. The answer might be in them."

"Can we see them?"

"I can't find them."

"Pardon?"

"He was very organized. Every day after work he'd go to a coffee shop a few blocks from the office and go over his notes, make additions and corrections. When he got home, he'd transcribe them first thing to make sure he hadn't missed anything. He kept them on his iPad. I can't find it."

"Why was he so meticulous?" Scott asked.

"He said a good reporter always checked his notes after every interview, after every event. It was good discipline."

"Maybe the killer stole the device or threw it off the bridge with him?"

Jordan sniffed and wiped at his eyes with a tissue. "He also e-mailed the notes to himself frequently while he was writing."

I knew writers who saved materials to their computers, to back up drives, made hard copies of it, and sent it to themselves as e-mails - at least four systems of backups, paranoid maybe, but you were unlikely to ever lose anything.

I said, "If he e-mailed it to himself, maybe we can retrieve that. Can you get into his e-mail account?"

"I don't know his password."

"Maybe we can try, or we can find a computer expert to give it a shot."

His place was two blocks away so we walked over.

At the first corner, Scott looked back over his right shoulder and stared.

"What?" I asked.

He shook his head. A chill wind had sprung up and the temperature had dropped. Jordan's apartment was half of the upstairs of an old home. At the door I saw that the wood around the doorknob had recently been replaced. I pointed to it, "You had a problem lately?"

"Somebody broke in a few days after Zachary died. They left a mess, but I didn't find anything missing."

It had a bathroom, living room/kitchen, and one bedroom.

The couch was a garage sale reject. The one easy chair sagged in the middle. There was no television. A few torn rock posters featuring bands I never heard of adorned the walls. No dirty dishes in the sink. Navy blue dish towels hung neatly. The floor was waxed.

A third of the bedroom had a desk with a computer where the three of us gathered. On the floor of the bedroom, I saw dirty socks, discarded underwear, waded up shirts and jeans, and several pairs of shoes. The bed was unmade.

We scrunched around the computer monitor. Jordan clicked over to Zachary's e-mail provider. The cursor blipped on the password box.

We tried as many variations we could think of: his birthday, 1,2,3,4,5, the most common sequence used as a password, his name backwards and forwards, his middle name both ways, his brothers and sisters names, birth date, Jordan's name and birth date in numerous combinations. And other statistically probable sequences. Nothing. And that was just to get into the e-mail in case there might have been anything in it.

"You know his dog's names when he was a kid?" I asked.

"I don't know if he had a dog."

"Who he worked with, friends, enemies?"

Jordan sat down on the bed. He looked from one to the other of us. "I don't have a clue, and this is kind of fruitless. Do you really think they might have killed him? For a campaign? For politics?"

"That's what we're trying to find out."

He gave us Zachary Ross's mother's address.

As we walked to the car, Scott said, "Another break in. They are certainly looking for something."

"You looked back at that first corner."

He shrugged. "For a minute I thought maybe we were being followed. I checked at each corner, but I didn't see anyone, but then we didn't walk far."

I looked out at the cool, cloudy day. "I haven't noticed anyone." I was tired so I gave him the keys. He started the car and turned the heater on.

He said, "I was probably wrong. I haven't seen anyone since that SUV this morning. I don't want to get as crazy paranoid as the rest of them."

"And they are crazy paranoid about something which fits the Grum family profile. I'm worried about the Ducharmés. They could afford an army of rotten people and lethal guns." I tapped the dashboard. "We'll have to keep more careful watch. We've got other questions. Why is Ross's iPad missing? Is that what people have been looking for? And if whoever 'they' is have it, are they now done looking?"

"The Grums have been trying to get into that office and the gun shed, and it's been over a week since the reporter died."

I shrugged. "Maybe the two events aren't connected."

Scott said, "I'm not so sure about going to see Zachary Ross's mom."

"Zachary might have left something there or told her something. Remember, we're up against the notion that the police and the Grums want to pin Edgar's murder on Veronica. Maybe they're just a fake fingerprint or two away from making an accusation." I found this a chilling and frightening thought. "We can at least ask her. If she wants us to go away, we can leave."

Scott acquiesced.

I got out my phone and keyed in the address for Zachary Ross's mom. She lived in a suburb at the south end of Harrison County.

Forty

Friday 3:41 P.M.

A blond woman in her mid-forties with hair pulled taut back from her face answered the door. Jordan had told us he had a good relationship with Zachary Ross's mother, and he would call ahead for us. We received a friendly albeit subdued greeting.

We sat in a living room. Two sandy-gold couches faced each other in the middle of a vast space of hardwood floor. The stone fireplace was immense, dead, and ashless. One wall had a painting about 24 by 36 inches. It showcased brushed right angle geometric objects.

She wore faded jeans, a heavy sweatshirt, and running shoes. She sat with her feet primly flat on the floor and her hands tightly clasped in her lap.

She offered coffee. We accepted. She left the room and returned with a tray of cups, served us, and resumed her posture.

I said, "We're sorry for your loss."

"Thank you. You are kind to stop by. I talk with Jordan almost every day. He made my son so happy. I was hoping some day they'd be able to have a wedding I could go to. Jordan is a good man. He said you were hoping to find out information that might lead to who murdered Zachary."

"You think it was murder?" I asked.

"Of course. Zachary would never have thrown himself off a bridge." She gave a brief sniff, dabbed at her eyes.

Scott said, "If this is a bad time, we can come back."

"No, now is best. The police don't return my calls. Nothing about this makes sense although I know what happened to him had to do with those evil people connected with that campaign."

"Which people?" I asked.

"The Grums and the Ducharmés. They are all evil incarnate."

"Evil?" As neutral a prompt as I could think of.

She said, "My son worked directly for Edgar Grum. If there is a hell, that man is in it. His parents, brothers, and sisters will join him. If hell has a band or an orchestra, that family will be the entire trumpet section, and Edgar Grum would be the conductor. If hell has a cheering section, he will be the head cheerleader. That whole family is evil."

I said, "I need to be honest. We probably should have said this earlier. We agree with you about Edgar, but he was married to my sister. I don't care about him, but I care about her."

"Everybody thinks she's this poor soul, intimidated by him. Oh really? She must have loved him. She must have found his piggish, obnoxious ways satisfying."

I avoided the attack on my sister, oblique as it might have been. I wanted information. "What was it he did that was piggish or obnoxious?"

"That family rules this county, and probably owns half the state. If you don't kowtow to them, you get frozen out. They have these barbecues every summer, July 4th weekend, and if you want to be in the elite in this county, you better damn well be there. Ha! The elite barn people! My husband and I went for the first few years. He worked for them, and we had to go. Then I put my foot down. My husband was a good man. He quit and found another job. He died of cancer five years ago."

"We're sorry," Scott said.

She gave us a thin lipped smile. "My husband had huge life insurance policies. I was lucky. With even more luck I'll be able to tell you something that brings those idiots down."

I asked, "What can you tell us that would bring them down?"

"One of the oddest things was that just before the people started eating at the barbeque, they'd gather everyone into a huge prayer circle. Imagine everyone out on the lawn on a hot, sweaty, Fourth of July bowing their heads in prayer before eating baked beans and hot dogs."

I kind of figured if people wanted to pray their hearts out night and day, that was their business. It was the Grum's home. Despite the societal pressure, the guests didn't really have to be there.

She shook her head. "That was slightly weird, but it's what they talked about constantly that was offensive."

"Oh?"

"Everything was a political discussion. You mention the heat, it was the Democrats who had the wrong policy on climate change. No matter how innocuous the subject, they had something bigoted and racist and irrational to say. That birther bull shit? They put money behind people to write things about it and to keep it going."

"That all sounds kind of rude for a party."

"Rude and stupid didn't bother those people. They have convoluted stupidity far beyond a dangerous, brainless idiocy." She sighed.

I gave her a sympathetic nod.

"I'm a Democrat. One of the few Democrats in Harrison County."

I took a guess. "You were working in the recall campaign?"

"Of course. Over the years I've worked, and I've marched, and I've protested, and now I've lost my son. They can all go to hell. All of them. I didn't use to hate politics, but I do now. I hate the Grums. I hate the Ducharmés. I hate them all."

Like Beulah Grum, she'd lost her son.

"Did you know what Zachary was doing at the campaign?"

"He told me he was investigating. I was afraid to ask him too much. I told him it was dangerous."

"You think they killed him."

"The Grums are capable of anything."

"But he didn't say anything specific?"

"No."

Scott asked, "Would Zachary have left notes or computer information here?"

"Not that I'm aware of."

"Who else knew he was a spy?"

"His editor, a good man, but a frightened man. He's got kids and a mortgage and a job. He called me and came to the wake and the funeral. I feel sorry for him."

"You think he'll talk to us?"

"You can try. I can give him a call."

She showed us Zachary's old room, but from the level of dust it was obvious nothing had been disturbed in a long time. There was a shelf with what looked like high school textbooks. A twin bed against one wall had a row of stuffed toy elephants lined up along the wall. Several more larger stuffed elephants sat in front of the dresser. One even sat on the desk chair.

Scott said, "He must have loved elephants."

"When they are little, some kids get into dinosaurs, but for some reason Zachary got into elephants. He wanted to go on a safari in the worst way. It was one of those "bucket list" things that now he'll never get to do."

She wiped at her eyes.

Scott said, "We're so sorry."

In the car I said, "Elephants."

"What elephants?" he asked.

"We didn't try it as a password."

He looked at me. "You think?"

"Can't hurt to try." Labrinski had shown us Zachary's e-mail provider and the e-mail address he used. We could try it when we got home.

Forty-one

Friday 4:48 P.M.

The wind was up. The afternoon had turned totally gray and misty. We'd followed up on Mrs. Ross's call to Zachary's editor, Jeremiah Gottlieb. Frank Smith, the aged gay millionaire, had done as we asked and called him as well. We met at another Starbucks. Thankfully there's always a Starbucks. The editor was in his fifties. Short and stout with a white beard, he had all the accoutrements of a Santa impersonator, including the rosy cheeks. He wasn't smiling, and after his first few words I knew he wasn't planning for any ho, ho, ho in his near future.

We huddled in a corner. Gottlieb stared out the window, glanced carefully at the other patrons, then leaned over his cup of coffee. His voice was low and quavery. "I caused that young man to die. It is my fault. I should have known better. I thought I was a good person. I thought I was a good editor. I was too smart for my own good."

I spoke just enough to be heard over the piped-in-music. "You must have been close to Zachary. We're sorry for your loss."

"I will never forgive myself. Never. No election is worth this. It just isn't. If anything I tell you can lead to finding out who murdered him, I'm glad, but it can't come back on me. It just can't." He mopped at his face with his hanky. "This is all so awful." He blew his nose, put the hanky away. "I'm not stupid. As soon as the campaign started, I worked with Frank Smith, and we set up a spy program on the campaign. I knew it would be too obvious late in the campaign. I sent that kid in. It got him killed. I've been in this business for years. I've seen some odd shit, some crazy shit, but I've never seen murder. Never been a part of it. And I'm scared."

He gave the other patrons another series of searching looks.

He examined each new person who walked in. "I'm afraid of everything and anything and anybody. You should be too. Anybody who gets too close to the Ducharmé brothers is in danger. Those boys get their way, and they play tough to get it. Nothing, nothing stands in their way."

Scott said, "This is America. They can get away with this shit?"

Gottlieb gave him a pitying look. "But they have. It doesn't have to be direct threats. Your reputation for viciousness can be enough and that which is unsaid can be just as powerful."

"You got threats?"

"Not personally. They didn't have to. My publisher called me in. Told me to stop running the story. I tried to ask questions. He became very angry and told me to drop it. I've got an ex-wife, plus a current wife, and kids with both. I don't want to lose this job." His sipped from his cup of coffee. He looked into it and murmured, "Although it may have cost me my soul."

"Should we try to talk to the publisher?"

"He can't know I talked to you. Nobody can. Listen, I liked Zachary. I mentored him. He trusted me. I feel such guilt, but I can't stick my neck out. I can't."

"Who in the Ducharmé company, family, any part of the organization, can we talk to? They've gotta have some weak link."

"We never found it, but then after Zachary died, we didn't look any further."

"Do you have his notes?"

"No. And if I did, I'd destroy them. If you find them, you better destroy them. I'm sure you're good and brave and tough and all that, but these guys stop at nothing. Nothing."

"They stole the election electronically?"

"Of course."

"How?"

"Frank Smith makes claims about those voting machines

being rigged. We checked their provenance. They are supposedly state of the art." He shrugged. "They could be state of the art cheating. Or state of the art unbuggable. Remember the Titanic was unsinkable. Until it sank. This whole election stinks."

"Did Zachary being gay have anything to do with his death?"

The editor looked thoughtful. "I never thought of that. I doubt it. Whatever happened on that bridge will never be known. And no, I don't know why he was there, or if he was supposed to be meeting someone."

"What did the police report say?"

"I tried one call to the cops about it. I got a final warning from my editor half an hour after the cop told me to go to hell."

"How did Zachary know Frank Smith?"

"Smith was paying the kid's way through graduate school. Zachary told me about it once. He met Smith at a coffee shop. Zach was at one of those low points in college. His loans weren't coming in. That day he paid for his coffee with pennies, nickels, and dimes. The old guy who saw this turned out to be Smith. Then he saw Zach asking for spare change on the street, and so the old guy helped him out. They knew each other three, maybe four, years. Frank won the lottery in his mid-to-late eighties. He must be over ninety now."

"What about a connection to the Grums?"

He snorted. "Them! They are too stupid to live. Them kill somebody? They aren't bright enough to plan a walk down the street."

I told him about our connection to the Grum family.

He frowned when I finished. "I feel sorry for your sister." He didn't say what I thought a lot of folks might, how bright could she be if she married into the family? I suppressed the thought.

Scott said, "They've been smart enough to rule the county."

Gottlieb sighed, sipped more coffee, hunched even closer to us. "This county is run like the KGB with spies and dirty tricks and death."

"Others have died?"

"I have no proof and trying to get proof on a simple damn election cost a life."

We paused and took hits from our drinks. Gottlieb said, "I've known the Grums for years. I grew up in the county. The *Harrison County Clarion* is the largest paper in the county. I've heard and seen them do incredible things."

"Like what?" Scott asked.

"They fight like an incestuous backwoods family on meth mixed with a group of siblings squabbling over billions."

"They have that much money?" Scott asked.

"They may or may not have over a billion, but it is a great deal. I've heard of screaming matches among them, accusations, physical fights."

"Between Mr. and Mrs. Grum?" Scott asked.

"Certainly between the brothers. Mrs. Grum is the one who rules that brood, but even she can't keep the peace. She and her husband hate each other."

"Why do they stay together?" Scott asked.

"Money? Power? I already said they're too stupid to live. The Grums have money, and Mrs. Grum married into it, but she comes from money as well. They'd do everything to preserve their position and their cash. The fights pale in comparison to the cash."

"Steal the election?" I asked.

"Oh my, yes. That would be among the smaller things they've done."

"How would they go about rigging voting machines?" Scott asked. "There must be some way to find out about them."

Gottlieb shrugged. "Zachary thought he had a lead on the cheating. I think that's where he was going that night, to see someone who could give him more information. I told him to call me immediately after the meeting. He never called."

I said, "There's something about those damn machines."

Gottlieb said, "I presume so."

"What can you tell us about them?"

"They've got offices in the next county west on Interstate 94. I'm not suggesting you go there or investigate. Why are you bothering?"

I said, "I think all these things are connected, Edgar Grum's death, Zachary's plummet off the bridge, and stealing the election."

He held my eyes. "The wife is always one of the main suspects. She's your sister. You're worried about her being accused."

"The police don't seem very trustable." I didn't tell him about my connection with Adlow.

He had no further insights and no knowledge of what Zachary might have done with his notes.

Forty-two

Friday 5:59 P.M.

It was just before six and the clouds had thickened and the drizzle had become a steady light rain all adding to the impending gloom of night.

I started the car, put the heater on low, and the windshield wipers on intermittent pulse. We joined the Friday evening traffic west on Interstate 94.

I said, "I feel sorry for Gottlieb. I hope I never have that much guilt or regret over a decision I make."

Scott said, "These people are all sad. They're all dealing with the horrific loss of a son, a husband, a friend, a coworker."

"Caused by some desperate conspiracy."

"What is it they gain?" Scott asked. "What possible good does this all do?"

We'd had this discussion numerous times. We hashed it out as we drove, the mad desire of humans to act irrationally and hurt deliberately or to act against their own or their loved ones self interest. We got no further than we usually did in figuring out why we humans did such awful things to each other.

As we crossed into Mendotta County, the first one west of Harrison County, I checked the review mirrors again. I'd been doing so since we started out."I haven't noticed anyone."

Scott said, "I've been checking too. I haven't seen anything odd."

"I'm eager to get into Zachary's e-mail and try "elephant" as the password, but we're out now and might as well finish what we started."

"We don't even know if it will work."

After several more miles the traffic had begun to thin out. Scott broke the silence. "Remind me, why are we going here?"

"To nose around. Because I think these deaths and this election and all this incredible paranoia are tied together."

Scott asked, "How can these people live in fear like this? Why don't they just get out?"

I said, "Maybe the boiled frog syndrome." This was an old conundrum. If you throw a frog into a pot of boiling water, it will jump out. If you put a frog into a pot of room temperature water and then turn heat on under it, the frog will not jump out as the water begins to boil. It simply stays inside and dies.

Scott asked, "And this world of Harrison County, their lives here were that great that they'd never want to leave?"

A semi-truck roared past us spraying us with his damp and dirty wake.

I said, "We've both gone through tough times at our jobs. Did it make us want to change or want to fight?"

"But these people aren't fighting. They're just giving in."

"And sometimes that's just easier. We can only do as much as we can when we're at work. Doing as much as we can right this minute includes going out to this place and hoping it gives us another clue to the mystery and helps us keep Veronica from being arrested by these creeps."

We got nowhere in our discussion of how an entire police department could be dedicated to preserving the Grums of Harrison County.

I drove to the exit Adlow had indicated. The GPS confirmed the turn off.

This exit had one BP gas station/convenience store. We filled the tank and stopped in the washroom. I didn't notice anyone who seemed suspicious or out of place. Then again, it was a reasonably busy exit at this time on Friday. We followed the GPS instructions off the Interstate two miles north past farms with fields tired from winter, resting before spring plowing and planting, isolated homes, two stories, wooden, built probably before 1930, most well kept. The light was failing fast so I slowed down considerably. No one that I could see followed us from the interstate. After another mile or so, we became the only car on the road. As we drove farther north, the lights of distant houses, the few signs of life, became more scattered.

The GPS indicated a turn onto a paved road to the right, east. I continued to check the review mirrors. Still, nobody was on the road with us.

I passed a warehouse that a sign said was for refrigerators and appliances. It had one car and one semi-truck in front.

After another mile, a left turn, north again, up a dirt road half a mile, even fewer houses, still no other cars. The light rain kept up and evening closed in.

I stopped in the middle of the road, rolled the window down. We listened to the silence of spring country, no bugs yet, the birds didn't seem interested, a slight breeze blew the ever increasing rain through the open window.

To the left I saw a line of old trees that began at the side of the road and trailed into the darkness. I saw the last shadows of lone trees, silos, and fences. A few unseen cows mooed.

I shifted around in my seat so I could take a 360° survey of my flat surroundings and saw no signs of pursuit.

We continued on. The GPS said we were still heading in the correct direction.

The road became rutted and pot-holed. I could hear the water splashing up onto the underside of the car. This was on the way to the headquarters of a multi-national corporation, or at least their local offices? And they were out here on a road that didn't get repaired?

In another half mile, I saw one fairly bright light in front of a larger set of buildings ahead of us on the right. The GPS said this was it, Flisterbiddle Von Struthers Wisconsin warehouse.

The gravel parking lot was empty. The windows showed no

lights on the inside, no curtains on the windows, no signs on the doors. I inched the car closer. The most suspicious thing at the moment was the lack of obvious security cameras. Nor did I see evidence of an alarm system.

Here in the middle of nowhere was a headquarters for a high tech firm, where someone could merrily break in and steal everything with not a soul as a witness? Remote was kind of believable but unsecured was not. We wouldn't find anything. Nobody as paranoid as the Grums would leave such a thing unguarded.

I did another 360° check of my surroundings. Nothing except the clumped-together buildings. I drove a full circuit around the them. Our headlights illumined what appeared to be three large corrugated, single level buildings in a railroad car formation.

Still no sigh of habitation.

I eased the car around to the back, parked next to the building, and turned out the lights.

"Now what?" Scott asked.

"We might as well get out and look around."

The darkness was now broken only by the dim lights on the dashboard. "Or we could leave. There's nothing here."

I turned off the car. "We came this far."

He took a flashlight out of the glove compartment. That's the thing about living with a neatnik, it also extends to preparations. In the car we had matches, flares, extra windshield wipers, umbrellas, blankets, dried food, and flashlights. We'd probably still carry a can of gasoline in the trunk if that hadn't been declared a hazard.

In the ever increasing rain, we walked the perimeter, looked in the windows, briefly shone the flashlight through them.

Empty, no boxes, desks, chairs, lights.

Should we break in? What was the point? Maybe we simply had the wrong address.

I used my phone to check the Internet. This was the address listed in Wisconsin on their web site. I called Frank Smith. Bowers answered. I got Smith on the line. I told him what we'd found.

He said, "Far as I know that's it. That's where the machines came from. Maybe it's empty because all the machines are in place."

I hung up. We huddled in a small recessed doorway in the back of the building ten steps from the car.

Scott said, "We could break in."

At the moment I couldn't catch his eyes. I said, "You think we should?" He was normally the cautious one. Then again, he'd been the one to rip on the governor.

His deep, sonorous voice bent the night in cautious whispers. "We've got proof the Grums were assholes. We really don't have anything else. What's to lose? We saw no sign of any kind of alarm system. If there's nothing inside, then we're no worse off than we are now." He took off his jacket, wadded it around his fist, broke the glass in the door, reached in, and unlocked the door.

No sirens rang, no lights blinked, nothing gave an indication that something was wrong.

We entered.

Scott turned on the flashlight and pointed it toward the ground to keep the circle of light to a minimum. We let our eyes adjust and then started a systematic walk through a very empty series of rooms. We stepped softly and carefully. Mostly we disturbed dust.

If we spoke, we kept our voices in whispers.

Scott said, "Nobody's been here in ages."

No footfalls sounded behind us. No lights appeared anywhere.

I asked, "Why aren't there emergency lights, exit lights? Why am I asking impossible questions?"

"You always do."

Each building was connected to each. Before we reached the connecting doors between them, Scott shut off the flashlight. We paused and gazed through the glass. The doors opened with a simple click of the push bars, the kind kids crashed through on their way outside of school at the end of the day. Using the exact opposite approach, I eased down on each one a fraction of an inch at a time. We opened the doors with equal care. We heard our own breathing and nothing more.

"This is odd," Scott said.

I agreed. "This isn't a headquarters of a going corporation or even a satellite headquarters."

"Maybe it was just storage."

We stood in the middle of the third building which was just like the other two, the size of a gymnasium with skinny iron pillars down the center holding up the roof.

It was the soft crunch of tires on gravel that alerted me that others were present. Scott turned off the flashlight. I peered carefully out one of the front windows. Three huge black SUVs slowly paraded into the parking lot and pulled up to the front of the building and parked. Their headlights spilled illumination into our gloom. They confirmed the nothing we'd seen so far.

Had we tripped a silent alarm? Had they seen the glow of our flashlight? Did they know there shouldn't be any light from inside?

The headlights turned off. Car doors opened. Two men started walking in opposite directions around the perimeter. If they circled the building, they'd find our car.

No cop lights flashing and rotating. I doubted if they were police. Their car windows were tinted. I had no idea how many people were here.

Abandon the car? No time to dither. We didn't want to be caught inside. We were trespassing in empty space that was not ours, a crime in any jurisdiction.

A few men we could see began walking to the front door,

which was in the middle building. The first one we entered was on the far end where the car was. We'd have to hope to get out and run back to the car faster than the guys walking around.

The damn door on the third building we tried to ease out of creaked like a horror movie portal on steroids.

We heard, "Halt!" and a gun shot.

We ran away from the buildings toward the nearest stand of trees. Once we got past the gravel, the ground was mushy from the persistent rain. I hoped the lack of light and the rain impaired their vision sufficiently not to get a good look at us or to be able to take aim and shoot.

Several bullets hit near us when we were ten feet from the trees. We flew toward cover.

We couldn't stand and fight. However few or many of them they were, we weren't armed. We rushed through the small stand of trees keeping the foliage between us and them. We got to the farther edge and then we ran some more. I was used to running five miles most mornings but the ground was uneven and wet.

I slowed and managed a look back. One of the SUVs had circled around the stand of trees and was trying to cross the open fields. The driver was going too fast. The vehicle bucked and swayed, sluiced to one side and then another. Another SUV was going back down the road, presumably to cut us off. Three men on foot were about fifty yards behind us to the left of the trees.

I surveyed the ground ahead. Uneven, tough to run through, tougher to drive through.

We stopped behind another stand of trees. I said, "We've got to get back to our car. They'll be able to trace it."

Scott said, "We can't fight them. We don't have any guns."

I said, "Let's wave the flashlight around then leave it pointing upward and then we'll run like hell perpendicular to that car and circle around the building."

He glanced at the car bobbing and sliding through the field around us. He observed the three men clumping through the mud toward us.

He flashed the light directly toward the men coming toward us on foot. He bellowed, "Halt, police. Don't move or we'll shoot." He set the flashlight in the crook of a tree.

We took off to the left.

Gun shots rang out. It took them only a few seconds to shoot out the light.

The mud and gunk sucked at our shoes. They couldn't be making much better progress. They didn't seem to have flashlights.

We'd started putting a little distance between us and them, when Scott fell. I turned and rushed back to him.

He struggled back up. "I'm fine." He said. I thought he might be bleeding from a cut on his face, but I couldn't be sure. We ran some more.

The darkness was our friend. The headlights from the car churning though the fields was actually a help. The lights weren't focused on us, but they gave some illumination.

Then the SUV plowing through the fields seemed to point almost directly up and then seconds later plunged nearly straight down and stayed put. They'd run themselves into a ditch. With luck the passengers had been injured enough that they couldn't follow.

With infinite care we circled back toward the rear of the building complex and our car. The car on the road was still heading in the direction of the Interstate. As far as I could see, the three men following us had gone toward where their buddies had crashed in the field.

When we were finally close enough, we rushed across the gravel parking lot to our car. We threw ourselves in. I started the car, didn't turn on the lights, and drove around the other side. We stopped at their SUV. Scott got out, opened the driver's side door, popped the hood, reached inside, and grabbed some wires.

After he threw himself back into the passenger seat, he said, "That might slow some of them down."

I eased the car out of the parking lot and headed down the road back to the Interstate. About five minutes later, I saw headlights coming toward us. They might have been a mile or so away.

"Turn off."

I took the first dirt road to the left and drove as fast as I could over the ruts. I slowed after we topped a rise. We looked back and saw the headlights continue back to the warehouse.

"Forward or back?" I asked.

He pulled out his phone and keyed in our position to the GPS. If we stayed on the current road, we'd come out in a few miles on a state road. Still with the lights off, I drove forward.

After a few minutes, I said, "What the hell was that?"

"An awful lot of gunfire and chasing around for protecting nothing."

"We were trespassing. They could have just been angry security guards."

"Three cars full?" he asked. "And how did they know we were there?"

"If they were after us. Maybe there was some kind of silent alarm system."

He said, "Or someone gave us away."

He pushed the button to lower his window and threw the wires he'd ripped from the SUV into the darkness. We drove on.

We had no answers to what the hell was going on.

FORTY-THREE

Friday 9:06 P.M.

We grabbed some burgers at a drive-through off the Interstate but parked in the lot to eat them. We didn't say much. We both just let the adrenaline rush ease off. I turned on the interior light and examined Scott. He was bleeding from a small cut on his left hand, his non-pitching hand, and he had a few scrapes on his face. I had teased him once about having everything in the car but the kitchen sink. Now he pulled out moist toilettes and hand towels. He grabbed some and used the rearview mirror to clean himself up.

We got to the gates at the Pleasant Valley subdivision just after 9:30. We drove up to the guard house and showed ID. We waited at the shut gates. Waiting five minutes seemed odd and then ten seemed strange.

"What the hell?" Scott asked.

I walked back to the guard shed and asked, "What's the problem?"

He said, "Get back in your car, now."

I took out my cell phone and called the house. My dad answered. I asked what the delay was.

"We weren't called about you. We'll send help."

He clicked off. Why didn't he just say they'd call the guard? I got back in the car and reported to Scott.

Moments later we saw rotating mars lights approaching the subdivision. In the street lights I counted at least six sheriffs' cars.

From the subdivision side I saw my parents' car and three others pelting down the road toward us.

The sheriff's cars left their lights on and turned on their spotlights. Guns were drawn. A booming voice came over a loud speaker, "Keep your hands on the steering wheel where we can see them. Don't move."

I didn't shout back but said to Scott, "Are we both supposed to put our hands on the steering wheel, and how do I or we do that without moving?"

Scott said, "We better look cooperative."

The gate began to swing open. I knew if you had a device like a garage door opener in your car, from the inside you could open the gates with it. Veronica would have that. The cars on the subdivision side began to disgorge passengers. Veronica, my mom and dad, Todd Bristol, and Enid Achtenberg rushed toward us. Three people I didn't know followed them.

Bristol and Achtenberg strode purposefully toward the car from which the cop had been practicing his voice-of-god imitation.

With all the car headlights from the various factions still on and the spotlights and streetlights, it was almost as bright as high noon. We got out of the car and faced the cops. Mom, dad, and Veronica rushed up to us. "Are you all right?" Mom asked. She noted the scrapes on Scott's face. "You're hurt."

Scott murmured, "I'm fine."

"What the hell is going on?" I asked.

"We don't know." Two of the strangers stood to each side of us. One was in his late fifties, the other in his early thirties. They stood silently. The third walked halfway between us and the cops and started taking pictures of the sheriff's posse.

The cop who was talking was Brendstin. Adlow stood a step behind him with his head down. Brendstin was saying, "These two are under arrest."

"On what charge?" Todd asked. He was at his most formal and most arch, and that's saying a lot for a prissy queen who specialized in both.

"We have them speeding and running from the police."

Todd gazed at the assembled police vehicles. He looked from

Brendstin to the cars and back again.

"What?" the detective snapped.

Todd said, "You sent all this for a speeding ticket?" He let the silence resume. I caught a fleeting smile on Adlow's tired features.

The cop said, "We think they were involved in something criminal."

"Where? When?"

A cop behind them spoke up with a time and highway designation.

Without turning Todd asked, "Tom Mason and Scott Carpenter were you on that road?"

Scott and I said, "No."

Todd asked, "You have video of them speeding or committing a crime?"

Brendstin broke several moments of confused silence with, "We want to take them down to headquarters and ask them questions."

Todd said, "No."

"We'll arrest all of you," the cop threatened.

The younger unknown guy next to me stirred. He took out ID and strolled toward the lawyer-cop group. The older guy took out ID and followed. The third person kept taking pictures. She was making a video record of all this.

Brendstin said, "We didn't say you could record this." He pointed to one of the minions behind him. "Get that camera."

Todd said, "No."

"And arrest this guy."

By this time mom, dad, Scott, and I had our cell phones out and were also recording the whole scene.

Brendstin said, "And get all those cameras."

Todd said, "No." Then turned to the older and younger men who now flanked him. "Let me introduce you."

The younger man held up ID and said, "I'm Douglas Kisco, head of the Southern District of the Wisconsin FBI office." The other guy said, "I'm Phil Webber, the US attorney for the eastern district of Wisconsin." Not from the offices of, or the head of the office, just plain, simple the US attorney. Todd knew how to pick cavalry.

A half hour later our side was ensconced in the living room in Veronica's house. Scott held a small pack of frozen gel ice to one side of his face. In the lights in the house, about a half dollar size spot close to his chin on the left looked pretty red, and mom had insisted he use the cold pack.

Todd sat in a corner of the largest couch. His legs were crossed, his suit coat buttoned. He sipped from a glass of white wine. I'd never seen Todd unbutton anything except an overcoat. Maybe he slept in his suit.

Todd explained, "This whole thing sounded very wrong to me. I made some calls and came right up." He nodded toward Kisco and Webber. "I thought we could use reinforcements." He pointed his glass at the third person, who was Janet Cristal from the *Chicago Sun-Times*. The police had refused to answer any of her questions. "Ms. Cristal is working off the record until we catch these sons of bitches."

The kids came in and Veronica hustled them out of the room. While she was gone, I said, "They're planning to arrest Veronica after the funeral."

My mother gasped. My dad frowned. Todd said, "I've told Kisco, Webber, and Cristal this."

"And why the hell were they trying to arrest us?" Scott asked.

My dad said, "To frighten and terrorize you and the rest of us. To frighten us into passivity and acquiescence."

Todd said, "Yes, that sums it up."

Webber said, "That's the way this county works. I've done what I can with my office, but we are limited."

"Can they arrest Veronica?" I asked.

Todd said, "We might not be able to stop them. If we can't find someone sane in the district attorney's office."

My mom asked, "What does this all mean?"

I said, "It means we were right. That the Grums and the Ducharmés are trying to steal the election and that they are responsible for at least two deaths. One of them is Edgar."

The US Attorney said, "When you get proof of that, come see us. Meanwhile, be careful with these people. I think you'll be safe for now, but these guys are out of control." The FBI guy nodded agreement. Todd walked them to the door.

"This is awful," my mom said.

My dad added, "We need to protect Veronica and the kids."

Enid said, "We'll do that. Todd and I will discuss this with Tom and Scott. They can fill you in later." I knew what we said to the lawyers would be confidential. Mom and dad could be questioned if they knew what we'd been up to. I didn't think we'd done anything wrong, but it was best to limit the circle of knowledge and protect them from possible coercion. Achtenberg explained that to them.

"Be careful," my mom said as she and dad left to go find Veronica. "Do you need something to eat?" mom asked from the doorway.

I said, "Thanks, we grabbed something on the way here."

Todd came back. We thanked him profusely. He, Enid, Scott, and I had a council of war. Scott and I explained all that we'd learned that day and what happened out at the warehouse.

Todd said, "None of this gives us proof of who did the killings or who ordered the killings or of who stole the election and how."

I said, "We'll find out."

Todd said, "You didn't hear?"

"What?"

"It seems they found twelve thousand ballots in Milwaukee

County that weren't in the initial count, a thousand more than they found in Harrison county. Governor Mallon seems to be losing, for the moment."

We all exchanged looks.

Scott said, "The Democrats have learned how to play the game."

Todd said, "I certainly hope so."

The real question of the moment was whether or not to tell Veronica about the word we had that they might be planning to arrest her.

Todd and Enid conferred. Enid came back and said, "I'm going to tell her. I'm her attorney. If she has something to say, Mr. Bristol and I agree that I should be the only one to hear it."

I said, "She didn't kill him."

"We know that," Enid said, "but investigations get complicated. I'm going to advise her not to talk to anyone."

"She already told me," I said.

Enid nodded. "That's fine. And she may tell you more. Your attorney can advise you of your status. I'm being formal here because we are in real danger."

Todd jumped in. "Enid is right. We've got to get this very formal and very correct."

When Veronica came back, Enid led her away. Todd waited for them to leave then spoke to us. "Whoever she talks to, remember if things get awful, you will be called to tell what she told you."

I said, "She hasn't told me anything about the murder because she doesn't know anything about the murder."

"Good." My lawyer stood up.

After my mom and dad went upstairs to bed, I asked, "Are Scott and I still investigating?"

"Would I be able to stop you?" Todd asked. We shook our heads.

"Be careful," he warned.

Scott asked, "Should we get Veronica out of Harrison County?"

Todd thought a minute. "This is her home. We're not going to be able to flee from jurisdiction to jurisdiction. I'll work on this with my connections."

I asked, "How did you have enough clout to call on these guys?"

Todd pulled out his cell phone and pressed a button. From somewhere deep in the house, his driver appeared with his Burberry overcoat. After Todd put it on, he said, "I've been an attorney for a very long time, a very good and very smart attorney. I happen to know some people who know people. Leave it at that."

Enid and Veronica appeared a few minutes after he left. Veronica looked like the next word she heard would drive her over the edge, but I agreed with telling her about her possible arrest. You don't keep that kind of news away from people to protect them.

We hugged each other for a very long time. When I looked up, Enid and Scott were gone.

"Find out who did this," she whispered in my ear. "I want you to destroy the Grums and everything they stand for."

I promised I would.

Forty-four

Friday 11:00 P.M.

Scott and I finally got to our room around eleven. He sat on the bed. "Hell of a day."

I hung up his jacket and mine. "Scared the hell out of me. Are you okay?" I sat next to him.

"Yeah, just scrapes and bruises. Who were those guys?"

"Which ones?"

"All of them." He lay back on the bed.

I sat next to his left side and put my hand on his chest. "The guys out at the empty warehouse, and the cops who came here, the whole crowd has to be connected to the Grums."

"Or the Ducharmés or both."

I said, "I think it's obvious that someone knows who killed Edgar, and they're trying to cover it up."

"That covers the information as we've speculated about it, but we have no facts."

"I know." I caressed his arm.

He said, "I felt bad for Jordan Labrinski. You're young and you're in love, and you've got your whole life ahead of you, and then your lover is gone."

I gave his chest a mild thump. "We should try getting into Zachary's e-mail account."

We pulled up chairs to the room's tiny desk. I fired up the laptop, got the wireless connection, and called up Zachary Ross's e-mail provider. When the provider's screen came up, I keyed in "elephant." A millisecond later the screen read "Invalid."

"That has to be it," I said. Thinking perhaps I mistyped it, I tried again. Nothing.

We sat in thought.

"Try the plural," Scott suggested.

I keyed in "elephants."

It opened.

There were twenty-seven unread e-mails. Twenty-four were porn junk and spam, two seemed to be personal e-mails, and one had just a date.

Down the left side of the screen were his list of folders. A few had titles or names but the vast majority were labeled by date beginning from six months ago and went in order up until the day before he died. The one still in his inbox was from the day he died.

I opened the last one. It contained four pages of detailed notes about everything he did that day up to about noon. It did not say why he was going to that bridge that night nor did it indicate if he was planning to meet someone.

I read a few paragraphs then switched to the folder dated six months ago and opened it. Pages and pages of more notes. Each day seemed to have two sets of notes. One he made for the morning, which I presumed had to have been done at around lunch time and the other before he left for the day or when he got home. This matched the methodology of the first page I'd opened.

Scott said, "Zachary Ross was very thorough."

"Is this what they've all been looking for?"

He shrugged. "If they even knew it existed."

"We're going to have to read all this."

I was tired from lack of sleep, the raw emotions of the day, and the physical exertion, but now that we had this key I was determined to read as much as I could before going to bed.

The first several of them were mostly tedious and filled with boring details, who was who in the campaign, what their functions were, their connections with each other. He included physical details, bits about people's personalities, and his speculations about who might have the ability, power, and knowledge to be able to steal the election. He had a lot of doubts that he'd be able to find anything.

As I finished each e-mail, I forwarded it to myself. I also created a Word document and downloaded them to my laptop, and also saved it to my zip drive. I then created a separate document and downloaded into it those items that revealed something of particular interest, especially those about the Grums.

Ross noted petty intrigues and vicious gossip, much of which surrounded desperate attempts to curry favor with various Grums. Upon seeing the Grum family gathered together for the first time, he compared them to rejected characters who had auditioned for a sinus infection commercial. With this third reference I was beginning to feel sorry for the animated characters in the ad. Other times he thought they reminded him of the "after" images of insects from a bug spray commercial. I wasn't sure I disagreed with either characterization.

Zachary was one of the first hires for the campaign. His boss seemed to appreciate him for his computer expertise and that he was willing to be flexible about taking a smaller office or a less desirable office placement, for example a cubicle far away from a window.

On his second day at work, a group of clergymen from a variety of denominations from around the county came in and performed a blessing for the office. One used an aspergillum to sprinkle water on them. Zachary didn't know until later that this was supposed to be holy water spread by the representative of the Roman Catholic denomination. All the employees attended this event. No one announced this as expected behavior on their part, it was presumed you would bow your head along with the rest of them.

Starting the first week, every day began with a prayer led by Mrs. Grum. After that, the prayer was electronically broadcast at 9:00 A.M. Zachary reported that none of the other employees and volunteers seemed to find this as odd as he did, or if they did, they certainly weren't confiding in him about it.

After the prayer every day, one of the Grums gave them a pep talk about the importance of their work. Mr. and Mrs. Grum rotated this duty with Barry. Neither Edgar, Dewey, or any of the legions of cousins, in-laws, aunts, or uncles performed this function.

In the early days Mrs. Grum would visit them personally with her dog in her arms to assign them tasks, to say cheerful words, to admonish them about working hard, or to tell them they were doing god's work, and that they needed to pray for guidance.

One day Zachary deliberately brought a bag of dog treats with him. He left one out on his desk. When the dog glommed onto the fact that there was food on the desk, it got excited. Mrs. Grum held the dog down to the treat so it could snap it up. Zachary took to leaving one out every day. This action seemed to endear him to Mrs. Grum.

The Grums were not tolerant of mistakes or what they perceived to be slow work. If an order was given and not carried out immediately and precisely to Mrs. Grum's specifications, the employee would be verbally flailed in front of whoever was nearby. The other Grums also indulged in this behavior. Public screaming did not seem to bother them, at employees or at each other.

I read through this tedium for an hour, afraid to start skimming in case something turned up. Not having someone at work to confide in, Zachary used his notes to record his observations.

Scott crawled into bed about one. I kept at it for another half hour.

I stopped where Zachary recorded that Edgar had come to work in the campaign. Ross had been assigned to be Edgar Grum's assistant. My eyes were beginning to close as I read, as if this were a novel about teenage vampires and the angst they shared with their human counterparts. I'd start again in the morning.

Forty-five

Saturday 2:00 A.M.

It must have been around two as I was snuggling up to Scott's lightly snoring torso and had dropped into a slight doze when I heard soft tapping at the door.

I threw on my jeans and padded to the door. I expected Veronica. It was Gerald, the middle kid. He wore green and gold sweat pants and a football jersey with Aaron Rodgers' name on it. His hair was tousled. He looked as if he might have been crying. A small bit of snot hung out of one nostril.

He said, "I'm scared."

"You want to come in?" I asked.

"Yeah."

I turned on the light next to the bed and sat on the edge. He sat next to me. I handed him a tissue from a box next to the bed. I suggested he wipe his nose. He did.

Scott turned over and opened his eyes and saw the two of us. He pulled the covers up to his chest.

Gerald said, "You guys sleep together like mommy and daddy."

I said, "Yes."

He nodded his head.

I asked, "Why are you scared?"

"I heard something in the house."

"What did you hear?" I asked.

"A cracking noise."

His bedroom was nearest the back stairs to the first floor.

I said, "Do you want us to investigate?"

He nodded.

I said, "You know you don't have to be scared because your mom is here, your grandma and grandpa, and me and Scott. We'll always protect you."

"I know."

I threw on a shirt. Scott said, "I'll be with you guys in a second." I ushered Gerald out the door so Scott could put some clothes on. Moments later he joined us in the hall.

Making as little noise as possible, the three of us crept through the second floor. We didn't listen at the bedroom doors, but kept our ears open. We eased down the back stairs and began on the wing of the first floor under our bedrooms but found nothing.

We crossed to the other wing. As we neared the office, I saw a faint light seeping under the door into the hall. Maybe Veronica checking the files or something sinister? Scott positioned himself in front of Gerald as I opened the door.

Light spilled from the closet. I heard a crash and a male voice swore.

I walked up to the opening and looked inside.

Dewey Grum, Edgar's next older brother, was hopping around, holding his right foot with his right hand, and reaching out with his left hand trying to support himself. His hand landed on a box on top of a stack to his left. The box lurched, fell, tumbled to the ground along with Dewey. His substantial butt landed on several of the boxes that had our finished files in them. He looked up. Several other boxes had become unbalanced. As they fell toward him, he tried to swat them away. The result was their contents added to the mess on the floor.

I said, "Hi, Dewey."

Dewey did dual shtick in the family. He was the photographer and the practical joker. Veronica told the story of him loudly and insistently moving the family into various combinations and poses at the Lincoln Memorial in Washington, D.C. One elderly tourist having finally had enough, asked him to tone it down.

Dewey had thrown a fit. Security had to intervene and ushered the Grum entourage away from the site.

He was most notorious for the photos and videos he'd made at Edgar and Veronica's wedding. Dewey was not the official photographer, otherwise Veronica would have been furious. He'd been quite proud of them. When enough time had passed, Veronica had gotten hold of the entire collection and turned it over to a friend of hers who could edit the whole thing together. Veronica called it *The Wedding Horror Show*. We'd had a viewing of the edited masterpiece at my parents a few years later. We'd laughed until our sides ached. Even better, the edited version was just as funny forward as backward. The photos that weren't blurry were at odd angles. They weren't artistic mood shots taking people unawares, but views of people scratching their butts or picking their noses or nodding off. Or maybe that's what Dewey meant to capture. The video portions included every awkward shuffle, trip, and twist. He even caught Mrs. Grum's little dog relieving himself against the head table.

The most disgusting practical jokes I knew about were his remote control fart machine and his liquid/spray ass smell. He found this amusing. Veronica had told me about his using them at various family functions. Veronica grimaced and made gagging noises as she told me, "The Grum brothers seemed to find them immensely amusing. It was disgusting."

Dewey scrambled to his feet. "What the hell are you doing here?" he demanded. Two cameras dangled from straps around his neck.

I said, "You don't live here. How did you get in?"

"Edgar gave us keys."

Note to self, have Veronica change the locks to the outer doors. The idea that the Grums could invade while we were sleeping creeped me out.

"You came to take pictures?"

He looked down and noticed the cameras that had thunked against the floor when he fell.

He said, "What pictures?"

"What are you looking for?"

Scott said, "This is the sound Gerald heard."

I turned back to him. In one hand he held a crowbar. He pointed it at the broken bits of wood around the door jamb. Gerald held Scott's other hand and was peering at his Uncle Dewey. Gerald said, "You look funny, Uncle Dewey."

I said, "Did Edgar give you keys and the crowbar to get into places in his house?"

Dewey snarled, "I don't answer to you."

"Get out." I spoke softly in deference to Gerald's presence. The child's proximity didn't seem to alter Dewey's performance as he shouted, "You two don't belong here. You're going to be very, very sorry. Wait until my mom and dad are through with you."

I'm afraid both Scott and I burst out laughing.

Dewey lunged for the crowbar. Scott moved himself in front of Gerald and held the implement over his head. Dewey was too short and too hefty to reach it. I stepped in between them and said, "There will be no physical assaults in this house, not while we are here. Now get out and stay out." We stepped aside so he had a path to leave through.

Dewey growled and grumbled in great Grum style and stalked out of the office. I followed him through the house to make sure he left while Scott stayed in the office with Gerald.

When Dewey was safely gone, I went back.

As I entered, I heard Scott saying to the child, "He was probably trying to help us."

Gerald said, "He made a mess."

"Your Uncle Tom and I will clean it up in the morning."

"You want me to help?" the kid asked.

"If you'd like," Scott said. "You know you were very brave and did the right thing to come get us when you were scared.

That was a smart decision."

Gerald smiled. I wasn't sure I'd ever seen him do that before. Then the kid yawned and said, "Will you let me stay with you?"

I looked at Scott and then squatted down so that I was on eye level with Gerald. I said, "Tell you what, I'll stay with you in your room until you fall asleep. You're safe now. No one is going to hurt you."

I took him to his room. He crawled into bed. Did an eight-year-old let adults tuck them in? He pulled up his covers, and I sat on the edge of the bed. In a tiny voice, he asked, "Will you sing me a song?"

I have a horrible singing voice. Did eight-year-olds get sung to sleep? Should I suggest reading a book as an alternative? His pale eyes looked at me in the soft light from the tiny bedside lamp. I began by humming "Puff the Magic Dragon" and even began what I remembered as the first verse. I sang softly in the hope that my horrendous lack of melodiousness would be less noticed. His eyes closed within half a minute. His breathing evened out.

I glanced around the room. Next to the bed were shelves with stuffed animals, not the dead critter type like in the office, but small, furry creatures. The top shelf had multiple sized figures of Pooh, Eeyore, Tigger, Kanga, and Roo. The next shelf were all forest and jungle creatures, miniature animals, giraffes, elephants. The bottom shelf were animals such as stuffed squirrels, small raccoons, and deer. It was a gentle, muted rendition of his father's shrine of death.

I shut the light and left the room. Usually Scott gets asked to do stuff by kids. I actually felt pretty good about this.

Back in our room, I eased into bed next to Scott.

"Is he asleep?"

"Yeah. He asked me to sing him a song."

Scott smiled.

"I did my best. He didn't wake back up and run out screaming. I figure that was a triumph."

He said, "If we had kids, you'd be a great dad."

I thanked him and snuggled close.

"What the hell is in that office?" Scott asked.

I said, "Maybe it was like you told Gerald. He was breaking in so he could help us sort the papers, kind of a middle-of-the-night spurt of altruism."

"From a Grum?"

"It could happen."

Scott said, "I hope whatever it is, is worth the effort. Presumably all the Grums know what it is they are looking for. We get a different one each time."

"None of the cousins, aunts, or uncles so far, but you're right. They've all got to be in on it. We just don't know what "it" is."

We had no answers. It took a while for me to drift off to sleep. Something in Harrison County was very wrong and the Grums were at the center of it. I just hoped no more dead bodies piled up. As I drifted off, I admitted to myself that I wouldn't mind if more Grum dead bodies accumulated. I might confess that to Scott, but it's the kind of thought you're not supposed to have.

Forty-six

Saturday 7:00 A.M.

I awoke much too early on Saturday morning. Scott was up doing his rehab exercises. I headed out for a morning run. The day was cool with a gorgeous orange, pink, and gray sunrise.

The house was quiet when I returned and hopped into the shower. Before going downstairs, I checked the Internet on my laptop. The local news was filled with election coverage, charges and counter charges, threats of lawsuits, and accusations of various levels and kinds of criminality. The governor and the Grums and the Ducharmés were prominently mentioned although none of the principals had agreed to be interviewed.

One rumor had it that Governor Mallon planned to barricade the capitol building. No one knew where the rumor started and no one knew why she would do so. Two of the local news stations had live pictures of the capitol building and the surrounding grounds. Nobody was trying to take it over. Did she think the teachers in the state had somehow overnight acquired a fleet of tanks and were prepared to overthrow her?

Scott and I set out breakfast things, munched on a few leftovers, and then got back to work in the dead animal den. The wake for Edgar was later today so we had hours this morning to keep working. We still had nearly half the boxes to go. I'd also brought my laptop and zip drive down with me.

Before starting work, I told Veronica about Dewey's break in. She didn't want to deal with the problem and agreed that I should call a locksmith. I offered a whole lot of money to get them to show up that morning. The locksmith arrived within the hour.

Gerald had come about nine to offer to help. Scott had given him the task of sorting campground brochures. After ten minutes Gerald left the brochures and was inspecting the animals. Poor kid was bored, but he wanted to help. Fortunately, Mom came in a few minutes later and took Gerald with her.

Scott got to work on the next box while I started reading more of Zachary Ross's dated e-mail folders.

After half an hour I realized that reading the e-mails was like slogging through a detailed nineteenth century Russian novel: lots of names, incredible details, and overwrought emotions.

It was after he became Edgar's assistant that he began to think he was on to something. On that very first day Edgar just blurted out about anything. Zachary said it was like listening to a continuous monologue from a fifteen-year-old who finally had someone who would listen to him.

In a very few days Zachary found out that Edgar invariably ate half a dozen Ding Dongs, a six ounce can of cashews, and drank a diet soda for lunch. He had snacks during the day of doughnuts from a variety of vendors.

According to Zachary, Edgar didn't seem to have a real job to do. He spent most of his time bloviating. His boss bragged about everything but mostly about guns. Zachary's observation on this emphasized the notion about the guns being Edgar's way of over compensating for lack of sexual prowess, low status in the family, or inability to articulate and relate to people in a meaningful way. Zachary finished that section that day with the comment, "The poor guy is more sad than anything. Of course, shooting things, and the need to bomb things, and invade other countries is probably all of a piece."

Zachary said it wasn't difficult to get Edgar to talk. Mostly Zachary just had to listen, nod, and occasionally say some version of, "My how interesting. Tell me more," and Edgar did.

Zachary recorded that Edgar brought a different gun to work each day. He'd talk about his collection of guns, hunting trips, and the animals he'd killed. Zachary made a note that he thought a lot of this was bullshit, but that he never mentioned this to Edgar. Zachary was also not comfortable when Edgar would show off his guns.

As I read on, Zachary noted that Edgar's favorite gun was a Colt Mustang Pocketlight .380 Auto, that he had several of them, and that he kept at least one of them in the office. The young reporter had asked Edgar why he kept a gun at the campaign headquarters. Edgar had simply said, "For protection."

"From what?" Zachary had asked.

"Union thugs, those stupid protesters. Who knows what they're going to do?"

Edgar never explained why he thought the opposition would invade. Zachary kept his feelings that this was nuts confined to his notes.

A week after Zachary started being his assistant, Edgar told the reporter about his secret room for building guns. So much for our big deal discovery about the hidden room which wasn't very. Zachary noted, "It can't be much of a secret if he's blabbing about it to me. He seems to talk to just about anybody. The workers around here are stuck listening to him. His family just blows him off. If he corners someone, he never stops talking. Sorry as I am for him, I get sick of it pretty quick, but he's just the kind to let something about the election slip." Zachary vowed to stick it out as Edgar's assistant.

After two hours, I needed a break. I turned to Scott and mentioned the Colt guns to him.

"He had several of them?"

"That's what Zachary says. Edgar claimed it was his favorite gun."

"We didn't find any. Is that important?"

I shrugged, leaned back from the computer and stretched my neck."What have you got this morning?"

"Camping brochures and US Savings Bonds. So far in this box I've found one bond stuffed into each brochure. He had at least fifty thousand dollars worth of them in here. They're all in the kids' names."

I moved over to the desk and looked, saw the stack of bonds, shrugged. The guy could save his money any way he wanted. I went back to work. I was into the last few days of Zach's notes. Edgar's brags and boasts had turned to a lot of paranoia connected with his family. There were numerous mentions of his desire to take revenge on one, some, or all of them. He claimed they were traitors. Other times Edgar declared he was going to get even with all of them and they'd be sorry. That he, Edgar, had information saved and stored that could destroy all of them if they didn't treat him right.

At one point Zachary asked Edgar, "Why do you all hate each other so much?"

Edgar had said, "We were brought up right."

Which indicated to me that Edgar either had more insight or a better sense of humor than I'd given him credit for. Or he meant it, which was ghastly sad.

Edgar had never told Zachary what he had or where it was stored. Zachary was convinced that Edgar knew about the plot to steal the election electronically. As far as I'd gotten, he had no proof.

Around noon we broke for lunch and to get ready to go to the wake which was to begin at the funeral home at 1:00 P.M.

As the time came to leave, I checked on Veronica. She and the kids looked as good as they could get in such awful circumstances. We left Darryl in the house to guard the place and headed to the funeral home.

Forty-seven

Saturday 1:00 P.M.

For much of the afternoon and evening I stood with Veronica and my mom and dad to the left of the closed casket.

My most vivid memory of the day, up until the last ugly incident, was Edgar's brother Dewey taking pictures. He was in the viewing room recording each flower arrangement, the casket, and the mourners. Most of the assembled mourners looked at him with distaste. Fortunately, he mostly avoided our family, but who takes pictures at a funeral? The simple, obvious answer here was Dewey Grum.

As the day went on Veronica clutched my arm less often. The Grum family was to the right of the casket. Neither side approached the other. Scott sat in the back observing both sides for quite some time. My family looked grieved and worried. The Grums looked variously dispirited, lost, or angry. Every hour or so Mrs. Grum had to sit down. It must have been hard for all of them to be standing there hours on end. I also noted that some of the people lined up to talk to the Grums didn't bother to stop and talk to Veronica. Were these politicians currying favor? Veronica's people tended to talk with her longer, hug more often. With the Grums it was handshakes, and an occasional hand to the elbow.

For a while Scott watched the kids. David, the oldest, got restless and bored. Gerald and Patricia sat solemnly with him for a while. Patricia fell asleep against his arm for half an hour. The family rotated duties taking care of them.

Often Scott took up a quiet spot down a hall at the opposite end from the entrance to the viewing room. Partly because he was bored, but I could still find him if he was needed.

The viewing room and hall toward the front door were fairly

crowded with people. Off to the side where Scott stood was mostly quiet.

Around five that afternoon, while Scott and I stood together in the hall, a very drunk man about Edgar's age staggered up to us. He slurred his words and his liquor-fueled breath reeked.

"Is this the way to the john?"

I pointed to a door a few feet away. He took a step in that direction and then peered closely at Scott. "Aren't you the baseball player?"

Scott said, "Derek Jeter, nice to meet you."

"Nah, you're not Jeter. I seen Jeter on Letterman. You ain't him. You're Verlander that Cleveland guy, no wait, Detroit guy. You're him. You're somebody. Why'd you say you're Jeter?"

Scott said, "I came for Edgar and his family. It's sad that he's dead."

"Ol' Edgar. I was his best buddy in college. I'm Bill Rabenaw." He thrust out his hand toward Scott who shook it. Scott said, "You knew him that long ago. You must have been good friends."

"The best of friends. The very best of friends. We went everywhere together. Couldn't keep us apart. Dated some of the same girls." He hiccupped and leaned toward Scott conspiratorially. "We even banged one chick together once. We didn't touch each other. We're not gay. It was hot her doing both of us at once. Each of us took a different end."

More information than I wanted.

Scott asked, "Had you seen much of him these past few years?"

"Hell, yes. Played poker with him. Me and his buddies, but I was his best buddy. Inseparable buddies."

"He usually win or lose at poker?"

"Lost. He was so great to play poker with. Could never pull off a bluff. Never."

"They say he was murdered."

"I heard that. I don't believe that. Who would want to murder him? He was harmless. Never hurt a fly. Always a good guy to be around."

"Did you work with him?"

"As kids we had jobs together at my dad's construction business. My dad fired him." He leaned close. "We couldn't go out and do carpentry work. God damn unions insisted we join. Wouldn't join no god damn union. Edgar and me, we hated unions. You in a Union?"

"Sort of one."

"That's right, Derek Jeter, the baseball player. You guys got a Union."

"So you worked in the office at the construction company?"

"Yeah." He leaned close to Scott again, but he was still loud enough to be heard halfway across the hall. "I like you cause you're a baseball player. I met some of the Milwaukee Brewers once or was it the Bucks? Anyway. Met them because my daddy's rich. I can tell you this stuff. Edgar got fired. By my dad. Edgar wouldn't say nothing. My dad just got rid of him. His dad and my dad are buddies. Good to have good buddies."

"But he fired him?"

"Well, that's what it amounted to. One day he was gone. I think my dad was missing some money and Edgar's dad, he paid up. I think it was a lot of money. Nobody wanted to involve lawyers or police or shit. Just friends, you know, but Edgar, he had to go." He burped spasmodically and said, "I think I'm gonna be sick." I steered him down the hall.

Around six my mom and dad took the kids to get something to eat and then promised to bring them home. I stayed up front with Veronica for a while.

The lines were still long as it neared 9:00 P.M. I stepped out in the hall to talk to Scott. We were in a far corner when Mrs. Grum tottered out of the viewing room. Two older women flanked her, one on each side. I thought they might be her sisters. Mrs.

Grum clutched her dog. She wore a nearly shapeless gray dress. With her free hand, she wiped her eyes. She wore black rimmed glasses. She must have been making her way to the washroom which was behind me and to the left.

We moved to make sure they had enough room. She only caught sight of us when we were within two feet of each other. She halted abruptly and staggered back. The dog wiggled, squirmed, and leapt free. On the ground the poor little dog yapped and shivered and then ran.

Mrs. Grum stooped toward it. She stumbled. Her companions grabbed for her, but Mrs. Grum's bulk propelled her forward. Scott reached out his hand to keep her from falling. Their flesh came in contact for an instant. She pulled herself back as if she'd been burned.

"Don't you touch me." Her voice was shrill, high, and loud.

I looked into the mad, unreasoning hatred in her eyes. She wagged a finger in Scott's face like Governor Brewer in the face of President Obama. She shrilled, "It's your fault my son is dead. You killed my son. I wish you were dead. I hope someday you suffer in the flames of hell."

Scott spoke very softly. "If it makes you feel better to belittle and berate me, it's okay. Your son is dead. I'm so sorry." I was standing right next to him. We turned to each other. I embraced him, held him close, and kissed him.

Mrs. Grum was sobbing. The two women led her away. A minion I didn't recognize ran after the dog.

Forty-eight

Sunday 12:10 A.M.

After the wake, back at Veronica's, we'd eaten with her in the kitchen and spent time with my brothers and mom and dad, talking in the living room. We went to bed just after midnight.

In the room I went to Scott and pulled him close. "I love you so much."

We held each other in a warm, safe embrace.

I said, "What you said to Mrs. Grum was the most kind and wonderful thing and in the face of such rage."

He murmured into my ear, "I don't think I started shaking until we got up here. I feel so sorry for her." He pulled back a few inches and looked me in the eye. "But I will hate her forever. What madness." He had tears in his eyes. We clinched again. I soothed and caressed him.

When we were calmer, he asked, "How are you after being up front with Veronica all day?"

"You do what you have to do. She liked having all those people just like Wednesday and Thursday. Good for her. I hope it helped."

We got undressed and ready for bed. We climbed in and held each other and said endearing things and finally I felt him relax into sleep.

Forty-nine

Sunday 4:00 A.M.

I woke about four. The house was silent. I often have a hard time sleeping when we aren't in our own bed. I got up and looked out the window. Nothing disturbed the quiet of the night. I watched Scott sleep for several minutes. I enjoy watching the man I love in quiet and repose.

I was tired but too keyed up to get back to sleep. I threw on jeans and a T-shirt and sat at the computer and called up Edgar's stuff that I'd saved to my zip drive that first morning. I worked very quietly so as not to disturb Scott. I started going through it again. Zachary Ross had written that Edgar was for sure hiding knowledge of the election being stolen.

I hunted through every document, clicked on every icon, and opened every folder. I checked recent items, pictures, applications, recent documents, recently downloaded items, and anything else that I could think of. There wasn't a nanobyte about the election.

Finally, I went back to the porn sites. Most of them I couldn't get on because I didn't have the password. Then I realized that there were some basic ways to pay for porn, some general processing sites that took credit card information. If I could get into his account there, I could retrieve his passwords. I didn't see much point in this, but I figured I might as well be totally thorough.

I eased out of the room and down the stairs to the dead animal den and got Edgar's credit card statements which contained his card number. Upstairs I eased shut the door and sat back down.

Scott stirred. I looked over and saw he was awake. He said, "It's five in the morning."

"Couldn't sleep."

He threw on tight black boxer briefs that had a special pouch in the front designed to hug the contours of the wearer's dick and balls. Then he walked over and stood next to me.

He asked, "What are you up to?"

"I thought I'd try these porn sites. I've looked at every single document in every folder I could find. None of them contain anything about the election. If I can get into the billing sites he used, I can probably retrieve his passwords."

"Is there a point to calling up all this porn?"

"It's the only thing on here I haven't been able to open."

"And you know about Internet pornographic billing sites how?"

"You really want to know?"

"Not particularly." He rubbed his brief covered crotch against my shoulder. I shut my eyes and leaned back into his warmth for a moment.

Fifty

Sunday 5:10 A.M.

With the credit card and e-mail address which I had from the mass of documents in the dead animal room closet, I was able to get into the billing site and retrieve his passwords. I began examining the porn sites.

Scott said, "How would information be on these sites?"

I shrugged. There was a slight chill in the room. He threw on pants and a shirt and brought me one to put on over my T-shirt.

I went to the bookmarked list and called each one up but got nothing. I went back to the desktop and its mass of icons listing pornographic pictures. I clicked on them to go to more sites. It was tedium upon tedium to open each one and examine pornographic images which I did not have the slightest interest in. It must have taken at least an hour. Edgar was a voracious consumer of porn.

When I got to Mona Moans for You, the one that had been opened when the computer came on the first time we'd tried it, I realized there were two for Mona.

"Why does she get two?" I asked.

Scott said, "She was his "go to" site when he wanted to get off?"

"How do you know about "go to" sites?"

"Do you really want to know?"

Touché.

I opened the first Mona and got pornographic pictures of a woman with gargantuan breasts. I opened the second. It looked the same to me.

I began to reach to click off them when Scott said, "Wait."

"What?"

"It's different. Your question was right. Why is it the only one that's a duplicate?"

I put the pictures next to each other on the screen. Like watching a tennis match back and forth, we compared the two. I listened to the two of us breathe. Finally, he reached out to the screen tapped the left breast of Mona on the left and the left breast of Mona on the right. He said, "The nipples are pointed in the opposite direction."

He was right.

He moved the cursor over her left nipple on the picture on the left and clicked. Nothing.

He tried the left nipple on the picture on the right.

I let out a breath. Data flooded the screen.

Before we even started to read, I saved it to my zip drive then e-mailed it to myself and to my attorney.

Then we started to read.

Fifty-one

Sunday 6:27 A.M.

We found charts with lists of rows and rows of voting machines by number on the machine, and the county and precinct they were assigned to.

But the bonanza came when we found hundreds and hundreds of notes written by Edgar. They were filled with anger and resentment about how his family didn't respect him or listen to him or want him around. That all they thought of him was that he was a fuck-up. That he was going to get even with them. That they were going to pay. He claimed he found out they were going to steal the election electronically. He claimed he had the goods on them.

Edgar's notes were far more scattered and less articulate than Zachary's, but they were no less clear in the insistent notion that criminality was afoot.

Then we found pages of dense code. Edgar's title for that section was Logarithmic Design. I scrolled to the end and found several paragraphs of summary. It said that the machines were geared to respond to a remote code from a cell phone to change vote totals.

"They were cheating," I said.

Edgar had outlined what he believed to be the whole convoluted scheme. Turns out the Grums hadn't trusted the Ducharmés and were not as enthralled to the brothers' billions as had been presumed. The Grums had hired people to infiltrate the Ducharmés' businesses so they would have their own information. They may have been patsies, but they were paranoid enough to want protection for themselves.

Mr. and Mrs. Grum had told Barry, their presumptive heir, all this information. They had wanted to be proactive and come up with a plan if the Ducharmés turned on them. Barry had told Dewey, who hadn't been able to keep his mouth shut and had blabbed to Edgar. Now we knew where Edgar had gotten his information.

Edgar in his notes was far more vicious than noble. He detailed who told lies to whom, who changed sides in familial disputes, who prayed hard enough. The family stuff included notes on alliances of brothers, parents, aunts, uncles, cousins, in-laws, even kids and grandkids. Many of the disputes seemed to be minor clashes over such things as the best directions to the summer reunion but rose to greater heights over things like who got to keep great grandmother Grum's souvenir plate from the 1912 Republican convention. Zachary had some items in notes about the family fights, but Edgar went into far more detail. To what effect, I had no idea except the election stuff. Edgar was hot about the election, stealing it, and how he could make what he found out work for him.

Armed with this knowledge about the election, he'd threatened to expose all of them. He had access to the campaign's passwords and managed to download all the information. This struck me as not too smart.

Edgar revealed in his notes that it was he who was going to meet with Zachary Ross that night on the bridge. Edgar's notes claimed Zachary never showed up. His last entry was written immediately after he found out Zachary was dead. It was ghastly reading it now. "They came for Zachary. They'll come for me." There were no further notes that I could find.

Had someone decided to take action to stop Edgar? Had Zachary and Edgar been working together and someone found out about it?

I turned back to the election results. I called up returns for the election by county.

I compared them to the data Edgar had. As far as I could understand the formula for the program, Edgar was right. Enough votes were to have been switched upon the machine's receipt of a command sent from a cell phone.

I compared columns of figures.

I pointed, "This isn't wrong."

"Huh?"

"According to what Edgar has here, if the vote was this close in this precinct the machine was supposed to change it by this many so that Governor Mallon would have more votes not less, but look at the official results. She actually wound up with less."

"Maybe they only changed certain precincts. They only had to change enough to win."

"But it wasn't enough to win."

We spent half an hour examining back and forth. I even took the zip drive down to the dead animal den, where there was a printer and hooked up my laptop to it so we could look at a hard copy instead of going back and forth on a computer screen.

We examined the numbers again. After another half hour, I announced, "Someone, the Grums or the Ducharmés, was trying to cheat. Presumably the Ducharmés since the machines were theirs, but the program didn't work. They had the machines rigged all right."

"All the machines failed?"

"All the machines counted correctly. The bug they put in the system didn't bug."

"Someone unbugged it?"

I tapped the screen. "These are the reported vote results by precinct for Harrison County." I pointed to a column of numbers on the printout. "Here's what the computer program was supposed to cheat by. It might have been sabotage. It might have just not worked. Whatever they planted didn't do what they wanted it to do."

"So the election results were honest?"

"Well, no. Fake. The Harrison County results still don't work mathematically. The skewed percents we talked about the other day are still skewed. I just can't believe nobody noticed all this.

Where the hell are newspapers and reporters?"

Scott said, "One person's fuzzy math is another person's truth. If the math is fixed, then obviously the election is won for their side."

I asked, "So who's got the power to fix the math?"

We looked at each other and answered simultaneously. "Beulah Grum."

We sat back in our chairs.

I said, "What I don't get is what Edgar was going to do. He was going to tell on them? On his family? Out them all as cheating crooks?"

"Maybe he was blackmailing them."

"He could have sold half of that crap in that stupid animal den. He had money coming in. Hell, I think the couch in that room is worth ten thousand dollars."

"Really?"

I said, "That's what it said in the *New York Times*."

"Edgar didn't talk about wrecking the Ducharmés or the election. He talked about wrecking his family."

"What would wreck his family?"

"Losing the recall election?"

"But the Ducharmés had the election successfully stolen. Or so they thought."

"Did they tell the Grums that?"

"We should ask."

"Edgar was out to wreck his family, not the Ducharmés. Did Edgar really care about the election?"

"He cared about getting even. He cared about getting something out of them. If the election results turned either way, did he care? If he got something from his family, maybe then he cared."

Scott asked, "Shouldn't the governor be questioned as well?

We seem to have two sets of cheating. I'm not ready to believe she didn't know about both, or at least one of them, and most likely had some part in it. Could she be that stupid, naïve, or despised?"

I said, "We've got no proof that any of this had something to do with murder."

"Was Edgar trying to blackmail the governor?"

"Edgar needed money?" I asked.

"According to his tax form last year, his income was over a million dollars."

I said, "Maybe he spent it all. We've still got a million of those damn boxes to go through."

"And is it his money or his family's? If the income we saw was from family Trust investments, does the money stop coming in at his death?"

"If it was reported on his tax form, it had to be his."

"If he had such shit jobs, how did he make so much money?"

"His investments paid well?" I asked.

I sat back in the chair. Dawn light streamed in the windows. I laced my fingers behind my head and leaned farther back. "So much of this doesn't make sense. Mr. and Mrs. Grum would let the police cover up who killed their son? Only if they did it."

"Maybe they don't know who did it."

"What about the Ducharmé brothers? They're the ones who stood to gain from all the lucrative contracts if the Republicans stayed in power. They're the ones who've been doing all the manipulating behind the scenes. They're the ones with power and motive."

"For more money? They've got enough to buy several third world countries. What the hell do they need more for?"

I said, "Reason not the need, said Lear to his daughters. But I actually had sympathy for Lear at that point. I have no sympathy for the Ducharmés."

Scott said, "As an English teacher, does getting a *King Lear* quote in earn you bonus points?"

"Only if it answers a question."

Scott grimaced. He said, "Let's start simple. Who knew about the electronic chicanery?"

"The Ducharmés. The person who programmed the computers, Mr. and Mrs. Grum, one, some, or all of their kids."

"Obviously Edgar."

"He was at campaign headquarters all the time according to Zachary, twelve to sixteen hours a day without much to do."

Scott said, "What it comes down to is, we ain't got proof, just a dead reporter and a dead Grum. We don't even have proof either one of them wrote all this. We believe they did, but even more we don't know who killed them both."

"Should we confront the Grums or the Ducharmés?"

"Would they even meet with us?"

"We just found all this shit out. Let's think about it, talk to legal people, and then make decisions."

Fifty-two

Sunday 7:27 A.M.

I was exhausted and exhilarated and depressed. We had tons of information and no proof. It was still early. I wasn't sure what to do with this knowledge. Who would believe us? What would it help? Presumably, we had proof of an election that wasn't stolen electronically. Call the press? Call the police? Kind of pointless.

After I got back from my run that Sunday morning, mom, dad, Veronica, and the kids were all dressed up. They were going to church for Easter Sunday. They said they'd be gone and that it was a family tradition to go to the Easter Sunday brunch at Schnitzel's in Milwaukee. Veronica wanted to keep up the tradition.

In our room Scott was finishing his shower. I joined him. Halfway through soaping his front after our climaxes soaked us both, my cell phone rang.

Dripping wet, I rushed out. It was Todd Bristol.

He began without preamble, "I have a meeting set up for you, with Albert Ducharmé for ten o'clock this morning."

I said, "He's not going to Easter Sunday service?"

"Do you care?"

"I guess not. Sorry." I explained what we found to which Todd said, "Hmmm."

"Is that your strict legal interpretation?"

"It explains why he might have been willing to agree to this meeting. I may think of myself as legally deft, but what you've got is better."

"Why am I meeting with him?"

"Because I am a wise and powerful lawyer who knows what

he is doing and sees a way out of this mess."

"He's the killer?"

"I have no idea."

"I'll get Scott…"

Todd interrupted, "No, you are to go yourself."

"Is it safe?"

"I certainly hope so."

"That's not as reassuring as I'd like it to be."

"It's as reassuring as I'm going to get." He paused a moment then resumed. "Think for a minute. This is a meeting I'm setting up. People know about it. I know about it. Enid Achtenberg is in the loop. Nobody is going to try and hurt you."

"Why not?"

He sighed. "Because he wants this whole thing to go away, and he thinks you're the key to that."

"What whole thing to go away?"

"Just go talk to him." He gave me an address.

"I'll leave Scott in the car."

"Fine."

Scott wasn't too happy with the arrangement, but if we were going to make progress, this was something we could do.

The meeting was to take place in a luxury penthouse condo on Lake Michigan south of Milwaukee.

We drove in silence. Speculation would be useless. Todd wouldn't have set it up if it wouldn't serve some kind of good purpose. We didn't leave a guard at the house. With the locks changed, we had less to fear from a Grum invasion. Plus, presumably, we had all the secret stuff and had begun disseminating it. We hadn't called the press or the cops, but that could certainly come. Now if we could just figure out who the killer was.

Fifty-three

Sunday 10:00 A.M.

The twenty-story building was chrome, glass, and steel. A guard in a blue blazer met me on the ground floor and escorted me into an elevator that took us up to the top floor suite. I stepped out of the elevator into a teak and oak realm that half a rain forest must have given its life to decorate, wood floors and wood paneled walls, on the walls lush 16th century paintings perfectly lit from ceiling spotlights.

Mr. Ducharmé entered the room. He wore white plastic frame glasses that covered washed-out blue eyes. His beige Italian-cut suit draped his slightly pudgy frame.

"Mr. Mason, would it be all right if you and I retired to the living room and discussed this unfortunate situation? I'd like to settle this. Wouldn't you?"

We entered a room which contained several intimate groupings. One area had a loveseat covered in beige velvet, linen and twill, plus a chaise outfitted with striped cotton ticking cushions, and a vintage coffee table with a slab of marble for the top. Another seating area had a brown leather couch that was big enough to use as a boat to head out onto the lake. Twentieth century art covered these walls. Embers glowed in a twelve foot fireplace which interrupted the march of Picassos on one wall. Matching armchairs flanked the gargantuan divan. The door shut softly behind us.

The view out the vast windows was of downtown Milwaukee and the lake.

"Drink?" he asked.

"No thanks."

He poured himself two fingers of an amber liquid into a beaded crystal glass. "Shall we be seated?"

I couldn't think of a reason to say no. I could try churlish and smart ass. I could try subservient and cringing. For now I'd go with curious.

We sat in the area with the brown leather furniture.

He crossed his legs, made a wide sweep with the hand that held the drink, and said, "Things are a mess."

"Yes."

"How did it come to this?" he asked.

"You tried to steal the election electronically. We've caught you. You're not going to be able to snap your all-powerful, very wealthy fingers and make all of this disappear."

"Really, I think this can be a civilized discussion. You can sneer at me if you wish. Maybe it will make you feel better when you tell the story later. Wouldn't you want to know what has really been going on?"

"And what you tell me will be the truth?"

"Why don't you let me tell you, and then you can decide, but if we're busy sneering at each other, neither one of us will make any progress toward our goal."

"What is your goal?"

"To get richer."

"And what will that gain you?" I quoted the lines from the movie *Chinatown* that Jack Gities says to Noah Cross, the rich evil character in the movie, "Why are you doing it? How much better can you eat? What could you buy that you can't already afford?"

"*Chinatown*, very good. And a few lines later, Mr. Cross says, "most people never have to face the fact that at the right time and the right place, they're capable of anything". Can you face that, Tom Mason?"

"I can live with my conscience."

He swirled the liquid in his glass. Took a sip. "As can I with mine. It's all a matter of perspective, isn't it?"

"What is it that you have to tell me?"

"My brother and I didn't steal the election."

I moved to rise.

"Please sit down, Mr. Mason. Let me finish. We did plan to steal the election." He shook his head. "The Firbutton 20's were set to shave or add enough votes in enough precincts to guarantee a win no matter what happened."

"You know Edgar Grum kept notes about you stealing the election, and now you admit it?"

"Oh, yes, because you see, it failed. It was brilliant. Flawless. Foolproof. Our people supplied the programming."

"How could you program each machine for each election?"

"Can your cell phone respond to remote commands, or give directives, turn things off and on, chat with you, cater to your every whim?"

"I know some can. Mine doesn't."

"Well, the best phones can. The most up-to-date have chips that can be synchronized and can be controlled from one location or multiple locations. You just have to put the right electronics into the machine in the first place. No one has to go from voting machine to voting machine in each precinct to rig or alter vote totals. One person in one location can activate the machines and give whatever commands that need to be given. It was perfect. The only problem was, it didn't work."

I didn't tell him we'd already figured a lot of this out.

He sipped from his drink. "No, the damn things didn't work. I was quite upset. Over a thousand people in various of our global facilities have lost their jobs already. We had it set so that no one person would know what was going on. You know how there can be glitches in electronics. Look at the space program or the military. All of them have the most advanced electronics on the globe and most of the time they work. And sometimes they don't. And sometimes there are glitches. And as you well know, humans screw up."

"What happened here?"

"A programmer in India created a flawed matrix that caused a worker in Silicon Valley to misinterpret a particular piece of code. The matrix was off by only the slightest, but that slight mistake was too much. We pressed "on," and the damn thing didn't turn on."

I was one of those who had discovered quite often getting "on" right when dealing with electronics could be hellish.

"So where did the extra votes come from in Harrison County?"

"I suggest, Mr. Mason, you look to Harrison County and those in charge of the operation."

"Don't the Grums work for you?"

"The Grums think they work for us, yes. Really, I hate to soil myself with those people, but they are useful. They think they're rich. I suppose in some minor way they are, but they are billions and billions behind my brother and I."

Being a kindly English teacher I didn't correct him and tell him that as an object of the preposition the correct form was my brother and me. And what was the point, but odd things flash though your mind at tense moments.

I asked, "Where is your brother?"

"He had to rush to Qatar for an emergency meeting."

"More people being fired?"

"A billion-dollar building complex deal with financing based in Mumbai, London, Hong Kong, and Sydney needed his immediate attention. You see, Mr. Mason, the election here was small time. Yes, we'd make a few more million in state contracts, but really it isn't like there are billions at stake here. The key, the reason I wanted to talk to you, is that you are causing us some trouble. I want that to go away."

"You could do that with the wave of a few millions."

"Yes, but that is messy, and you are not without resources. This could drag far beyond forever. We could easily launch a smear campaign against you and Mr. Carpenter to destroy each of you, and your parents, and your whole family. Your lawyer and his firm, however, while, again, not in the same league as our lawyers and our firms, are nevertheless rich enough, powerful enough, and smart enough to inconvenience us. This situation here is not worth the hassle. Mary Mallon and this governorship are most definitely not. She turned out to be far more stupid than even we imagined."

"What did the governor have to do with this?"

He grimaced. "She was a useful, mindless, buffoon."

"You're willing to foist that kind of person on the American people, just so you can make a few bucks?"

More smiling and chuckling and then he said, "Well, yes, obviously. Look at Sarah Palin as a candidate for vice-president. The mad desire to win triumphed over good sense, hence the Republican party."

"They're in power in a lot of places because they were backed by fools like you."

"Fools like me win most of the time. You know that. Now, can we get down to business?"

I got up and walked to the floor to ceiling windows. As I looked out, my anger swirled, I fantasized about smashing his head through the glass, tossing his body out, and watching it plummet to the ground. I shut my eyes for a moment then opened them back up to the bright blue sky and bright blue lake staring back at each other. I didn't believe in violence as a solution to problems, and I probably wasn't strong enough to break through the glass anyway, and this man wasn't worth going to jail for, and if it wasn't him, there would be some other rich guy to take his place.

Without looking at him, I asked, "Why did you try to kill us Friday at the Flisterbiddle von Struthers warehouse?"

"If I wanted to kill you, you would be dead."

I turned to look at him.

"But my brother and I are not killers. We wanted you

frightened."

"Why?"

"We didn't know what you'd find. We knew the Grums were going to pin the murder on your sister. We feared that would propel you to further action. We wanted to stop you from investigating."

"Why not just tell the Grums to stop the police from arresting my sister?"

"We are powerful. We are not all-powerful, much as I'd like to be. The Grums are out of control, and they do have a great deal to say about what happens in Harrison County."

"How'd you know we were at the warehouse?"

"You were using your GPS to find where you were. We were using it to track you."

"You can do that?"

"Of course. You've seen it done by police organizations in movies. It's not that expensive to replicate that kind of technology. Well, actually it can be purchased for relatively little. Comparatively. We find it handy to keep track of people we need to keep track of. We wanted you frightened. We didn't quite expect you to avail yourself of your own legal army."

"Did you send the cops Friday night?"

"I believe that was the Grums."

"Why was Frank Smith's house broken into?"

"I have no idea who that is."

"The guy who gave a lot of money to your opposition. He won the lottery."

"Oh, him. He wasn't important enough for us to notice."

"Did you use the tracking on Edgar Grum?"

"He was never someone important enough for us to track. I realize he was your brother-in-law, but I didn't care about him when he was alive. I certainly don't care about him now."

I turned my back on him again.

After a minute or so the silence was broken by Ducharmé, who said, "Please come back and sit down."

I swallowed my anger and sat. He refilled his drink and resumed, "No, my dear Mr. Mason. The key is, we didn't kill anyone. Isn't that the heart of your concern?"

"I think the election and the two murders are connected."

"Two?"

I explained about Zachary Ross.

He said, "I have no idea who that is either. Harrison County is where the vote changed. Who is in charge of Harrison County? This isn't rocket science, Mr. Mason. Look there for your killer."

"But if Edgar Grum or Zachary Ross died in part because of your schemes, you are in some way culpable."

"Morally perhaps you are right, but in the eyes of the law? That's a much more difficult proposition."

"And I'm just supposed to take your word for what you've told me?"

"You can do as you wish. You will bring no harm to me or my companies. You might even cost me a few million in legal fees. And what of those you know and love? You know the power of lies."

"And you're willing to tell such lies?"

"Manufacture them, use them. Look at the Republicans I use. They built their entire edifice on lies. The silly people serve me and mine nicely. They've learned to twist and squirm and turn and pivot as I wish. They so desperately want to be part of the one percent, they are quite willing to sell out the 99%. I don't pretend to understand it. I don't care if I ever understand it. I just want them to keep doing it."

He took another sip of his drink.

I wondered if the Grums knew with what scorn he regarded them. At least according to the man sitting in front of me, whatever the Grums felt made no difference to his existence.

And in some ways that was sad and in some ways that made me furious. All the Grums' mad rushing about to please this man was for what? Themselves? Certainly, he didn't care.

"You'd rather you and your partner and your lives go down in glorious flames in the hopes, the chance, that I might be harmed? Trust me, I will be on a private jet and gone in just a few hours."

"You must be very frightened of what we might find."

Even if all the condescending smiles of the Republicans fighting for the 2012 nomination were combined, they could not have matched the one he now gave me for sneering superiority. He topped off the smile with a chuckle and said, "Not really."

"Then why tell me this at all?"

"Because I truly want this to go away. I did not kill anyone nor did I order anyone killed. If underlings of mine went to excess, then I'd be quite happy to have them punished. We are not responsible for this. We are not responsible for anyone getting murdered."

"You're responsible for screwing a whole lot of things up. You may not have pulled any actual triggers on any actual guns, but your actions set in motion the events that led to this."

Ducharmé said, "Good luck with finding a prosecutor in this jurisdiction who will take legal action."

I said, "You must have violated any number of laws. You might not get some local politician in your pay to prosecute, but the federal authorities will go after you."

"You don't think I have influence there as well? You are naïve."

"You're so sure none of this will reflect on you?"

"Oh, my yes. I've got more lawyers on retainers than more than half the countries on the planet have in total."

"I'd prefer proof."

"You said you had the documentation from Edgar Grum's

home."

"I'd feel better if you showed me how it worked."

He frowned at me for a moment, downed the last of his drink, and said, "Okay."

He pressed a button on what looked like a remote control on steroids that sat on the coffee table next to him. A flat screen television to my left, his right, came to life. Using the same remote, he began to manipulate the icons on the screen. A program that looked like the one we found on Edgar's computer came up. He hunched forward on the couch and said, "This represents every Firbutton 20 voting machine in the state. Here are the vote totals. By manipulating the following formulas," he scrolled down and clicked, "the results should have changed in each machine in each precinct. They didn't. The command was sent. It never arrived. There should have been no need for Mrs. Grum's obvious mathematical chicanery." He took out his cell phone and manipulated the buttons on the front. The numbers on the screen didn't change. He said, "Go to the machines if you wish, or you can get a court order to do so. Take apart all that techno crap inside them. The program didn't work to change the votes, but it did work to erase itself. The self-destruct mechanism was set on a timer on all of the machines for forty-eight hours after the election. No paper trail. No electronic trail. None of the Grums were supposed to know about this. More people are going to be fired. I like firing people."

I thought for a minute. "We're not going to find proof."

"No, you aren't."

"So Mallon or the Grums stole the election?"

"The governor? You've met her. As I said, the woman doesn't have the brains that this table has. She has neither charm nor good looks. She happened to be in the right place at the right time for our purposes. No one thought she'd win the governorship in the first place. She did, and we were glad. She is certainly expendable."

"And the Grums?"

"Are also expendable. Whatever happened with the election, happened locally. For the cheating and the killing, look to them. Call off your people or have them search forever. You will get nothing on us."

"And if we get things on the people who worked for you?"

"As I said, nothing will redound to us."

I stood up. "I'll have to think about what I intend to do."

He rose as well. "Do that."

The man who accompanied me up did so as well on the reverse journey.

FIFTY-FOUR

Sunday 11:23 A.M.

When I got into the car, I asked Scott to drive along the lake. We got to the Wind Point Lighthouse in Racine and pulled into the deserted parking lot. All the good Christians were in church so we had the place to ourselves.

I'd told him the whole story as we drove. Now we walked along the lake. The sky had turned gray, the low clouds rushing in from the northeast, the wind off the lake snapping our clothes.

Scott asked, "Do we believe him?"

I said, "I don't, but I'm not sure what we believe makes much difference. It certainly doesn't to Ducharmé, but he certainly wants off the hook for the murders."

"He's afraid of something, or he wouldn't have met with you."

I agreed. Neither of us was sure precisely what he was afraid of, nor if we could ever find proof that would convict him in a courtroom of whatever crimes he may have committed.

I called Todd Bristol and filled him in. He promised to call Achtenberg and let her know the latest. I told him I wanted to confront the Grums immediately and to call the police to have them arrested.

He suggested we wait until after he had more time to confer with police and legal officials not connected with Harrison County.

Frustrated, I said, "They killed their own kid."

Todd was very patient. "Are you saying you know who pulled the trigger?"

"One of them did."

"You know we need evidence. You've got proof of internal

family hell. You don't have a smoking gun."

I knew he was right. I agreed to give him a chance to meet with legal people, possibly not easy on an Easter Sunday.

We picked up some pecan Kringle, a Seven Sisters, and coffee and drove back to Veronica's. Kringle is great, but if you've ever had a custard filled Seven Sisters from Racine, you'd know what true bliss is. Maybe I could drown my sorrow in the glorious confections we purchased.

After we were admitted to the subdivision without incident, we detoured and drove to the Grums'. I'd passed it on my morning runs. There were no cars parked outside their palatial mansion. Like good Christians they were in church where they belonged.

We drove to Veronica's and ate in the kitchen then headed back to the dead animal den, and got back to work on the mess in the closet.

Around one I found a box with disturbing news about Edgar's financial information. He'd had money coming in all right, but there were enormous investments over the years in schemes and deals and dreams, none of which worked out. I organized them by year and company. Often the paperwork included copies of legal briefs of people suing to get their money back. I found copies of court proceedings from some of them. The ones I found showed that the cases had been lost by Edgar. The bills I found for these legal issues were immense. Edgar's overseas money had rushed in each year and flooded out. Presumably if Veronica now stopped the idiot investment schemes, the family might be well off, unless Edgar's legal troubles came back to haunt them. Veronica would have to turn all this over to lawyers, more expense and frustration.

After I was done sorting the box of investment catastrophes and legal chaos, I went over the papers with Scott. As far as I could tell, there were at least three on-going legal cases and more than five that had already been settled. We set up separate files for each one, with court materials by date, letters from angry investors in a separate section, notes from Edgar's legal team. Half an hour into this, Scott said, "His brother Dewey is mentioned in a lot of these."

I looked where he pointed. "Dewey was involved in a lot of his money-losing schemes?"

"Seems so. The two of them were in these up to their eyeballs."

I said, "Why couldn't the killer be an angry investor?"

"I'm not sure that's a strong motive. I mean, so what if you kill Edgar? How does that get you your money back?"

The next box had even more court cases. We examined, separated, filed, read.

Scott held out another set of documents to me. He said, "Dewey lost a lot of cash on some of these," Scott said. "More than Edgar sometimes."

I examined the papers. "The two were losing money together?"

"The family that goes broke together sues each other together?"

When we were done with that box, Scott said, "This is so sad."

I held up a sheaf of legal papers from just one case. "His desperation for success, respect, and making it on his own combined with his lack of insight might yet bankrupt Veronica."

"And maybe his blindness got him killed."

We had maybe a quarter of the boxes yet to go. The very next one was another investment-legal nightmare. I started sorting.

Fifty-five

Sunday 3:00 P.M.

Veronica, the three kids, and my mom and dad didn't get back until nearly three.

Scott and I, Veronica and my mom and dad and my brother Darryl sat in her living room. Lionel was with the kids.

I told all of them everything. I had my laptop set up so I could simultaneously display the program on its monitor and on the large screen television. I showed them Edgar's and Ross's notes.

Veronica sat between mom and dad on the couch. Mostly she looked frozen and numb.

When Scott and I were done talking, her eyes scanned all the rest of us. We'd only summarized everything. If she wanted to, it would take her quite a while to finish reading all the details of what Edgar wrote.

Veronica said, "I'm not sure what to do."

I said, "You don't have to do anything."

Veronica said, "I'm too emotional to talk to the Grums. I don't want anything to do with them. I don't know how I'm going to get through the funeral tomorrow and the reception afterward."

Mom held her hand, "We'll be there with you, right next to you. Don't you worry about that."

I said, "We're waiting for Todd Bristol and probably Enid Achtenberg to come by. We can discuss what's to be done about the Grums with them."

"Am I going to be arrested?" Veronica asked.

My dad said, "We're not going to let that happen."

Veronica said, "I just want to get through tomorrow, then I want whoever killed Edgar to suffer. And if that poor reporter died because of it, I want them to spend the rest of their lives in prison for that too."

At 7:00 the lawyers appeared. We talked over everything. At 10:00 they left. We were to trust them, and they'd take care of everything.

Later in our bedroom I said, "I'm going to confront the Grums after the funeral. Those shits have got to pay."

"We've got a portrait of an idiot as a modern Republican."

"I thought you were the one who felt sorry for him."

"I do. That doesn't change the fact that he was one of the great assholes and morons in history."

Fifty-six

Monday 10:00 A.M.

The early morning was subdued. Mom was in the kitchen. The coffee was prepared. Scott and I made toast, got cereal and juice ready.

Veronica and Patricia came downstairs together. Veronica hugged my mom.

David appeared in a good suit. He held a tie in his hand. He went up to Scott and asked him to tie it for him. After Scott gave him a two-minute lesson, David smiled at himself in a mirror in the bathroom off the kitchen and said, "Thanks, Uncle Scott."

We drove to the funeral home. We left Darryl in charge of the caterers preparing for the after-funeral reception.

In the front parlor the great trollish Buddha that was Mrs. Grum sat by herself glaring straight ahead in silence, as disapproving as at the wedding. She wore a black velvet dress, draped in a black knock-off pashmina shawl, and a pill-box black hat with tiny feathers on one side. The hat had a veil attached. It was thrown back over her head. When she stood, she pulled the veil forward. It hung in front to the top of her breasts and in the back, halfway to her butt. As she walked out, I noted that the dress had a foot-long train. The dog was nowhere in evidence.

Dewey Grum took pictures of the casket leaving the funeral home, being moved into the hearse, of the people as they milled about. My family ignored him. At one point Patricia broke away and went over and tugged on his suit coat and asked, "Why are you taking dead pictures?" This did not stop Dewey, who marched quickly away from his niece.

We processed in our vehicles to the church.

Minutes later, the sound of Mrs. Grum's sobbing filled the sanctuary. She'd begun as her son's casket appeared at the far end of the center aisle of the Cathedral of Saints Majestic Church. Mr. Grum held her hand. A mother was weeping for her son. I felt rotten for all the bad things I'd thought about mother and son.

A misty rain fell throughout the entire ritual at the cemetery. This wasn't a problem, as an enormous tent had been erected around the gravesite. I was given to understand that it was a family plot.

I hoped maybe the rain would ruin Dewey's camera as he continued to record everything. I thought his behavior was vile, but I didn't have to live with him. Then again, maybe having pictures of this ceremony would give him or his family solace in such a difficult time. I couldn't see how, but I wasn't going to have to look at them.

At her son's graveside, Mrs. Grum wept, great sobbing gusts. And I felt sorry for her again. Perhaps she was seeing her child as a baby when she rocked him to sleep. I thought of Watson's comment in the *Hound of the Baskervilles* when the evil criminal Seldon has died and his sister weeps for him. Watson says, "Evil indeed is the man who has not one woman to mourn him."

And Edgar had more than one. I shoved the thought that this was better than he deserved deep into my subconscious.

Veronica had wept. His kids at various times showed their distress. I was being too harsh and too judgmental. Maybe this whole Republicans-are-totally-evil shtick was a little harsh. Or maybe I was just feeling guilt for recognizing my honest feelings about the asshole.

Around two back at the house in the living room, Scott and I took some bottled water and stood in a corner out of the way. People and caterers crowded the house. The dark suits were perfectly normal. The somber looks standard. Even wolfing down food seemed pretty usual. The liquor flowed. But a catered funeral? With waiters carrying canapés and drinks? Maybe I don't get to enough funerals.

Every politician of any note in the county was there. Half the chief Republicans in the state showed up.

All my family had been warned to keep an eye out for the appearance of Harrison County deputies or detectives with designs on arresting Veronica. None of them appeared.

Just after we arrived back at the house, I sought out Barry Grum and whispered in his ear, "I found what all of you have been so desperately looking for. I want to see all your family after we're done here today. Make sure it happens or I release it to the media and to as many police agencies not in this jurisdiction as I can find."

He glared daggers at me. "Don't fuck with me."

I just smiled at him and said, "I never bluff."

Fifty-seven

Monday 5:00 P.M.

The caterer had packed up and gone. All the other friends and relatives had oozed away. Scott, the rest of my family, and the Grums remained.

When I had the mystified and concerned-- my family-- and the angry and ill-disposed-- the Grums-- gathered together, I said, "I know who killed Edgar."

Mr. Grum said, "Don't be absurd."

I said, "Edgar kept detailed records of everything you and the Ducharmés were up to. You must have known he had something or why did you keep trying to get into various parts of this property to hunt for it?"

Mrs. Grum now had her dog with her. I set up my laptop as I had the day before so they could view what Edgar had written on the large television screen.

I sat the computer on a coffee table and adjusted the print on the screen so that it could be read easily.

I said, "First we have Edgar's notes." I began to show them.

After about three minutes, Mrs. Grum said, "We have no proof Edgar wrote this. If you know something, tell us."

Barry Grum said, "You claimed you know who killed him."

Veronica said, "Can't you people ever shut up?"

They all glared at her. Veronica sat between my mom and dad on a couch.

Slowly enough so that they could read and comprehend them, I continued to let the words scroll on the screen. They sat mostly in silence, mouths agape, as Edgar's version of the details of their lives emerged in front of them. Indeed, for a while at least, they were silent.

After ten minutes Veronica said, "Tom, please stop."

I said, "There's a great deal more to show you, but maybe I can summarize. Edgar knew about stealing the election. He was threatening you, or blackmailing you, maybe for money, maybe for respect, maybe for a lot of things. Zachary Ross's notes and e-mails confirm this."

Mr. Grum said, "If you know all this, why haven't you called the police. This is bullshit."

I said, "Dewey told Edgar about the Ducharmés' scheme to steal the election."

"I did not."

"Who told Dewey?" Mrs. Grum asked. Her gaze of baleful daggers landed on Barry.

Barry stood up. "Edgar came to me. He threatened all of us. He was going to destroy the family. He knew everything. Him and that reporter had figured it out. I didn't know Dewey had talked. Why the hell did you tell Edgar?"

Dewey said, "I did not."

I said, "We have the accusatory notes of two dead men."

Dewey was up and raging, "You've got nothing. I always get accused of things in this family. I didn't do anything." He pointed at Barry. "You were the one who always wanted to please the Ducharmés. You were the one that wanted to follow their marching orders. You were the one who fucked this all up."

Barry pointed his finger, "You're just as stupid as Edgar. I told you, and you couldn't keep your mouth shut."

Mrs. Grum's voice snapped and bit. "He should never have been told."

"Which he?" I asked. "Edgar, Dewey, or both."

The Grums ignored me.

Charles Dudley Grum stood up. "We should leave and discuss this at home."

I said, "No. It gets discussed now. Two people are dead. Your schemes for stealing the election have come crashing down. There will be arrests and indictments." I hoped that was more than a bluff.

Mr. Grum said, "There's nothing you can prove. You can't attempt to hold us here. That's kidnapping. That's unlawful restraint. It's you who will go to jail. Along with your faggot buddy."

Veronica arose from between my parents and rushed at him. She jabbed a finger onto his chest. "You will not speak to my brother that way. There are no words vile enough to call you. You killed the love of my life! And you don't care! He was your son! And you don't care!" She began pummeling, gouging, scratching, spitting, and screaming. He recoiled and stumbled backwards.

Scott, my Dad, and I rushed over. I held Veronica gently, and led her away from him. She wept. My dad said to my mother, "Maybe we should take Veronica away from here."

Veronica gulped and spoke in a savage whisper. "I'm staying for this."

Mr. Grum said, "I told you she was out of control. She killed…"

I interrupted him. "No, Veronica did not kill anyone. I wanted to get every one of you lying shit-for-brains in one spot. You are pigs who would lie, steal, cheat, and kill for any nonsensical gain your imaginations could conjure." I was nearly out of control. Scott stood next to me, but he did not stop me.

Gasps and protests from a few of them. Several stood up and turned to the door.

I got in their way. "Yes, kill." I was furious and on a roll. "My brother-in-law is dead. My sister is without a husband. Their children are without a father. And you shit-for-brains don't care who you kill or who you hurt. That poor reporter died."

Barry Grum said, "He was a spy for the opposition. So there's one more dead Democrat? So what?"

"So what," I thundered. "So fucking what? You moronic pig."

I realized my breathing was coming in great thunderous gasps. The Grums yelled and screamed back at us and at each other. The dog yapped continuously.

Chaos reigned.

When things began to settle and glaring at us all the while, several Grums tried moving toward the door. When Mrs. Grum attempted to heave her bulk off the couch, the dog became dislodged and scrambled into a corner.

Scott, Lionel, and Darryl placed themselves between the Grums and the exit. I waited for quiet from them and for myself to calm down.

Mr. Grum said, "How dare you?"

Scott's deep voice thrummed. "We're all going to sit down."

Slowly the Grums backed away from him and my brothers. Seats were taken.

When everyone was at rest, Scott stood in front of them. He said, "Murder has been done. One of you pulled the trigger. Edgar was a threat to all of you with his schemes and plots and plans. You cannot change reality. You will not deny reality."

Mr. Grum said, "Denying reality is not a crime."

Barry Grum said, "Whose reality? Yours or ours?"

Scott almost smiled. "You all have shown an innate inability to process reality."

Barry Grum said, "You're the weird one. You and your sick boyfriend. We always have to tiptoe around you."

I said, "It works both ways. I've had a whole lot of things I've wanted to say to all of you for years."

"Like what?" Barry demanded.

This was a mistake. I said, "I've got a list."

Scott said, "Tom, stop."

I looked at him. He came to me and took my hand. "There's

no point. They're the killers, and they're going to jail."

Barry Grum said, "We have powerful friends. You'll never get away with this."

Scott said, "The Ducharmés have abandoned you."

Barry took out his phone and pressed several buttons. He looked surprised as it continued to ring and ring.

I said, "They're not taking your calls. The Ducharmé brothers are out of the country. You're on your own."

Mrs. Grum thrust herself against the back of the couch in an attempt to rise. She made a move toward her dog, but it took off through the doorway into the kitchen. She said, "We've only ever needed our own family."

Scott said, "It's not enough, is it?"

I said, "You sold your soul for political gain. You sold your son to win an election."

A silence lengthened uncomfortably.

Scott and I stood together between them and the door. I said, "Who was Edgar's knowledge the biggest threat to? You, Mrs. Grum. Barry reported Edgar's threats to you. Edgar could destroy all you'd built up for your entire lifetime."

Mr. Grum said, "I didn't know anything about Edgar making any threats."

"No," I said. "Barry told Dewey. Dewey told Edgar. Edgar made his threats to Barry. Barry reported to you, Mrs. Grum. You decided something had to be done. Edgar must have mentioned Zachary Ross the reporter to you as part of his threats. You weren't sure what the reporter knew, you didn't even know he was a reporter or a spy at the time, but you decided to eliminate Zachary, a decent man."

Dewey got down on his knees in front of his mother. He said, "I only told Edgar. I didn't do anything wrong. I didn't do anything wrong."

Mrs. Grum turned her icy glare onto her son. Her voice hissed and snarled. "You fool. You stupid, stupid fool."

Dewey said, "I didn't kill anyone."

I said, "But you came to find Edgar's notes."

"They told me to."

"From things Edgar must have said, you had suspicions about Zachary. Your suspicion of him was enough to get him killed. But like Edgar, he made notes. You all desperately wanted to hunt through the office and the gun shed and Frank Smith's place and Ross's apartment because you didn't know who had what where. You knew Edgar had records because he said so. He did. We also have Ross's records. We've got everything. We can show the rest of it to you here and now. To be safe we've given copies of all of this to our attorneys. Edgar also had the goods on your electronic cheating, from both the machines the Ducharmés had set up to how you were going to rig those precincts in Harrison County."

Mrs. Grum blurted out, "Edgar didn't know about that."

Veronica wrenched herself from where she'd been in the background between my parents, marched to the couch, and stood in front of her mother-in-law. My sister put her hands on her hips and leaned toward the old harridan and snapped, "Pray now, you bitch."

Fifty-eight

Monday 7:00 P.M.

The Grums rushed to blame each other.

Scott and I and my brothers listened to the Grums deteriorate in grand style. Their behavior could have fueled a whole anger management industry.

It was Barry who had arranged the murder of Zachary Ross. Edgar had told him that Zachary was in his confidence. Barry didn't want another possible witness running around. He'd lured him to a meeting on the bridge promising to talk over the situation. The reporter had gone hoping to break the story completely.

Barry had also arranged all the break ins at Veronica's house, at the gun shed, at Frank Smith's house, and Ross's apartment. They'd been looking for the proof that Edgar had said he'd hidden. They also thought Zachary must have information as well, but they couldn't get to it.

Mr. Grum confessed that he ordered the cops to be sent on Friday to arrest us. They were meant to scare us away.

In the throes of their heated emotions, it was Mrs. Grum who was the most ghastly. In a gap in their screaming, she said, "All of you shut up." She rearranged her black dress around the folds of her fat and spoke. Her husband and sons gaped at her as she told the story that one, some, or all of them must have known. "I didn't mean to. That night Edgar was always so out of control. He wouldn't listen. He wouldn't shut up. I grabbed the gun. He was always waving around those stupid guns. For a while he even shoved it in my face. Me! His mother!" She paused to gasp for breath. "After he put it down, the gun was just sitting on the desk. He laughed and sneered and threatened to ruin me. What choice did I have?"

A moment of hideous truth was not the time to debate the choices we face in the universe. As the words tumbled out, she sat on the couch in Veronica's home and wept some more. At that moment I didn't have any sympathy for her tears.

She'd confessed to Barry who had helped her conceal her crime. Dewey and Charles Dudley Grum had gone along with all the cover up activity, if nothing else, out of the perverse Grum need for secretiveness.

Early on I summoned Todd Bristol and Enid Achtenberg. Later the police, the Grum's attorneys, and law enforcement personnel from a variety of jurisdictions showed up.

Fifty-nine

Monday 11:23 P.M.

That night while getting ready for bed, Scott said, "She killed him but she wept for her son."

"Maybe it was guilt, maybe it was loss. It was probably a lot of things, all horrible and terribly sad. Edgar had threatened her with exposure and disgrace. Her whole life was dedicated to politics and being prominent in Harrison County politics. He was going to destroy all of that."

"But what did he want?"

I said, "He needed money. Maybe he wanted control of the family Trust so he could bankrupt them too."

Scott said, "Whatever he wanted, she couldn't give enough of or didn't want to give it or was incapable of it whether it was love or money or respect or recognition."

EPILOGUE

The Grums' and the campaign's computers were all confiscated. It all came out. Including Governor Mallon's role in the election cheating. She was arrested along with several of her staff and the lieutenant governor. If the Ducharmés stepped foot in this country again, they would be in trouble. Maybe their money could get them out of it, maybe not.

§§§

Janet Cristal, the *Chicago Sun-Times* reporter from Friday night, and a host of national press had descended on the state. As arrests and the possibility of more indictments flew, it looked like the Grum reign of idiocy would come to an end as it was exposed to the harsh light of reality. The Ducharmés and their money were nowhere in evidence to attempt a right wing spin to the madness.

§§§

In the next few days we finished with the damn boxes. The upshot of Veronica's finances, after we finally had all the boxes emptied, the contents organized, categorized, filed, and explained to her was that Veronica and the kids would be okay. They had no savings, as Edgar had squandered everything on stupid investments, schemes, deals, and legal problems. But the income from the investments in his name would still come in. Veronica planned to sell the house and move out of state. She thought she might get a teaching job since her kids were all in school.

§§§

On our last morning I was a few steps from walking into Veronica's kitchen when I heard Scott talking to David. The thirteen-year-old was saying, "I miss my dad." I stopped in the hall and listened.

"It's tough to lose a parent at any age," Scott said, "but especially hard at thirteen."

"Was he a rotten guy like everybody is saying?"

Scott said, "The important thing to remember is that he loved you as best he could. That's all any of us can do."

A few moments of silence followed. I heard spoons clink against bowls.

David said, "I hate my grandmother."

Scott sighed. "She did something pretty awful."

"Is my mom going to be okay?"

"We're all going to help her and you and your brother and your sister as much as we can. We'll all be here for you. Your mom is a smart, tough woman, and she loves you very much."

"I'm glad you guys were here."

"You let me know if you need something. I'll be here to help."

§ § §

Before we left, I talked to Frank Bowers. He said, "Thank you for your help. Zachary will be avenged."

I said, "Doesn't look like you needed it. You had the extra votes you needed. Where'd you get the twelve thousand votes?"

"If Mayor Dailey in Chicago can learn, so can we."

I wasn't so sure I had much sympathy for him at this point. Learning to cheat was a good thing? If the bad guys lose and you cheated to win, haven't you become less? Then again, I knew reality and how ugly it could be, and there was nothing I could do about any of these people at all. Nor did I want to have much to do with any of them.

§ § §

Patricia got to keep the little dog. Gerald gave me one of his stuffed Eeyores to take with. David gave Scott his favorite skateboard.

§ § §

At home in bed a week later, Scott and I discussed the chaos. I thanked him over and over for helping me, Veronica, and the family.

I said, "I just don't get why all of this was so important to them."

He said, "No sane mind is able to penetrate the cobwebby maze those people had so steadily constructed."

"You put up with that grim, Grum gloom. You are wonderful."

"A saint, no doubt. Do you get more English teacher points for all that alliteration?"

"Accumulated ghastly, grim, Grum gloom. And no I can't say it fast three times. I'm having trouble getting it out once."

"For which I am grateful."

I said, "I do wonder about that whole prayer shit."

"What?"

"Did Mrs. Grum pray before she shot her son, while she was shooting him, or after she was done? Or all three."

"My guess is none, but there aren't enough prayers on the planet to make up for what she did."

I lay in his arms long after he'd fallen asleep that night wondering at the vicissitudes of the universe. I had no answer. I just had the man I loved. I hoped I could always give him the love he wanted and needed.

About the Author

Mark Zubro is the author of twenty-three mystery novels and five short stories. His book *A Simple Suburban Murder* won the Lambda Literary Award for Best Gay Men's mystery. He also wrote a thriller, *Foolproof*, with two other mystery writers, Jeanne Dams and Barb D'Amato. He taught eighth graders English and reading for thirty-four years. He was president of the teachers' union in his district from 1985 until 2006. He retired from teaching in 2006 and now spends his time reading, writing, napping, and eating chocolate. His newest book *Another Dead Republican*, is his thirteenth in the Tom and Scott series. One of the keys in Zubro's mysteries is you do not want to be a person who is racist, sexist, homophobic, or a school administrator. If you are any of those, it is likely you are the corpse, or, at the least, it can be fairly well guaranteed that bad things will happen to you by the end. And if in Zubro's books you happen to be a Republican and/or against workers' rights, it would be far better if you did not make a habit of broadcasting this. If you did, you're quite likely to be a suspect, or worse.

Rainbow Romance Writers

Raising the Bar for LGBT Romance

RRW offers support and advocacy to career-focused authors, expanding the horizons of romance. Changing minds, one heart at a time. www.rainbowromancewriters.com

The Trevor Project

The Trevor Project operates the only nationwide, around-the-clock crisis and suicide prevention helpline for lesbian, gay, bisexual, transgender and questioning youth. Every day, The Trevor Project saves lives though its free and confidential helpline, its website and its educational services. If you or a friend are feeling lost, alone, confused or in crisis, please call The Trevor Helpline. You'll be able to speak confidentially with a trained counselor 24/7.

The Trevor Helpline: 866-488-7386

On the Web: http://www.thetrevorproject.org/

The Gay Men's Domestic Violence Project

Founded in 1994, The Gay Men's Domestic Violence Project is a grassroots, non-profit organization founded by a gay male survivor of domestic violence and developed through the strength, contributions and participation of the community. The Gay Men's Domestic Violence Project supports victims and survivors through education, advocacy and direct services. Understanding that the serious public health issue of domestic violence is not gender specific, we serve men in relationships with men, regardless of how they identify, and stand ready to assist them in navigating through abusive relationships.

GMDVP Helpline: 800.832.1901

On the Web: http://gmdvp.org/

From J.P. Bowie ...

THE NICK FALLON INVESTIGATION SERIES

Print ISBN# 978-1-60820-142-6
Ebook ISBN# 978-1-60820-143-3

Print ISBN# 978-1-60820-144-0
Ebook ISBN# 978-1-60820-145-7

Print ISBN# 978-1-60820-119-8
Ebook ISBN# 978-1-60820-120-4

MLRPress.com

AVAILABLE ONLINE, AT LOCAL BOOKSTORES, THRU BOOKAZINE & INGRAM

CPSIA information can be obtained
at www.ICGtesting.com
Printed in the USA
LVOW12s1757311016
511029LV00001B/18/P

9 781608 207312